'Don't love me, Mira
stroked her body into
nothing in return, nothi

'You have given with
voice was fragmented ag the heat of his breath.

His hands stilled, then he raised them and cupped her face. He kissed her very gently on the lips, and his black boundless eyes were smudged with pain. 'You are young and fresh and untouched . . .'

'Only for you . . .'

A spark of anger shone in the black depths, 'And I am only human! However much you may think so, I am not made of stone!'

She sighed and slipped her arms round his neck, pulling his head down over hers until their lips met and kept meeting and he groaned in an agony of desire. 'I hate you for doing this to me,' he muttered against her ear, kissing it again and again. 'Before you came, Amarillo had one curse, that damned gold. And now it has two!'

Lynne Brooks spent much of her childhood in northern India. She now shares a rambling country cottage with her husband, an architect, several goats and a mynah bird. Her hobbies include continental cookery and dress-making, and she does most of her writing during the spring, on a houseboat in Kashmir. *Spaniard's Haven* is Lynne Brooks's third Masquerade Historical Romance. Her first two, set in India, are *Mistress of Koh-i-Noor* and *Master of Shalimar*.

SPANIARD'S HAVEN

LYNNE BROOKS

MILLS & BOON LIMITED
15–16 BROOK'S MEWS
LONDON W1A 1DR

All the characters in this book have no existence outside the imagination of the Author, and have no relation whatsoever to anyone bearing the same name or names. They are not even distantly inspired by any individual known or unknown to the Author, and all the incidents are pure invention.

The text of this publication or any part thereof may not be reproduced or transmitted in any form or by any means, electronic or mechanical, including photocopying, recording, storage in an information retrieval system, or otherwise, without the written permission of the publisher.

This book is sold subject to the condition that it shall not, by way of trade or otherwise, be lent, resold, hired out or otherwise circulated without the prior consent of the publisher in any form of binding or cover other than that in which it is published and without a similar condition including this condition being imposed on the subsequent purchaser.

*First published in Great Britain 1985
by Mills & Boon Limited*

© Lynne Brooks 1985

*Australian copyright 1985
Philippine copyright 1985
This edition 1985*

ISBN 0 263 75101 5

*Set in 10 on 11pt Linotron Times
04-0685-67,800*

*Photoset by Rowland Phototypesetting Ltd
Bury St Edmunds, Suffolk
Made and printed in Great Britain by
Cox & Wyman Ltd, Reading, Berks*

CHAPTER ONE

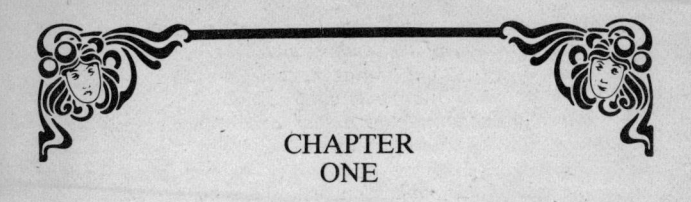

'Thar she blows!'

The voice of the lookout strapped to the mast high above the ship's deck sounded like a sudden thunderclap through the hot, still noontide. For a few seconds everyone went still; then, as the glad tidings penetrated through the men's minds dulled by tropical languor, all hell seemed to break loose on board the *Amiable Lady*. From his cabin, Captain Edward Chiltern stumbled up to the main deck trying to struggle hastily into his jacket; chief harpooner Dan Haggerty ran up the stairs with a litheness that belied his sixty-seven years, and the crew came pouring out from wherever they happened to be, immediately leaving whatever they happened to be doing.

Down below in her cabin, Miranda heard the shout from the lookout, and her heart leaped with joy. Hastily she put away the diary in which she had been scribbling and rose from the table. She paused a moment to look at the still figure lying on the other bunk.

'Are you asleep, Aunt Zoe?' she asked softly. There was no reply. Miranda tiptoed to the bed, gently felt her aunt's forehead. It was still very hot. With a sigh, she stepped back, opened the door of the cabin and ran up the stairs to the deck. *Please, God,* she murmured under her breath, *let Aunt Zoe be all right—and let it not be another false alarm from the lookout.*

She ran to the rails and stood beside Captain Chiltern and Dan, both peering through telescopes with their eyes crinkled.

'Can you see them?' asked Captain Chiltern, the telescope clamped tight against his eye.

Dan nodded slowly. 'They may be sealions again,' he murmured. 'We've had false signals before, God knows.'

'Does it look like sperm, Papa?' Miranda asked the Captain anxiously.

'Ay, lass, it does. And monsters too. Here,' he handed her the telescope, 'look for yourself.'

Excitedly Miranda focused on the spot to which he pointed. Across the vast blue expanse of the Pacific, out near the horizon, she saw a confused jumble of dark grey shapes playing hide and seek with the water. From this distance it was difficult to discern them clearly. But suddenly, as clear as daylight, she saw a fountain of water rise from one of the shapes and sparkle unmistakably in the dazzling sun.

'It's whales!' she cried exultantly. 'I just saw one spout.'

Gently she felt the telescope removed from her hands. 'Let me have a look, lass,' a voice at her elbow ordered.

'Oh, Peregrine . . .' she began in protest, but he took the telescope, regardless of her plea.

'This is man's work,' Peregrine Holmes said firmly, although his eyes looked at her with fondness. 'Little girls should be below deck when there's whaling to be done.'

'Below deck!' she exclaimed indignantly. 'At a time like this? Why, I wouldn't dream of such a thing.'

Edward Chiltern rubbed his hands together and a happy smile spread across his face. 'Yes, it's sperm all right. Come on, lads, on with the job!'

All over the ship, men were galvanised into action, each to his post with the confidence born of years of experience, for Captain Chiltern and his crew were among the finest whaling teams out of Nantucket. The air on deck was suddenly charged with excitement, and in every man's heart was the same prayer—let us have luck this time!

So far it had not been a particularly fruitful voyage for the *Amiable Lady* for, as everyone knew, whaling —like everything else in life—depended as much upon the goodwill of the Almighty as it did on skill. And this time it was obvious that the Almighty had chosen not to smile upon the *Amiable Lady* and her crew. They were already six months out of Martha's Vineyard on the east coast of America, during which time they had sailed down the coasts of North and South America, rounded Cape Horn, and were now in the midst of the vast South Pacific, with little to show for it. They had sighted few of the huge mammals out of whom they made their living, and those that had been sighted had, for one reason or another, not been successfully harpooned.

Whaling was at this time, in the mid-nineteenth century, one of the biggest and most important industries of North America. Nantucket, south of Cape Cod, where the Chilterns lived, was the centre of the trade. Many fortunes had been made out of whale products— oil for lamps across the western world, candles containing spermaceti, lubricating oil for machines in factories, soap and paints and a hundred other consumer articles. The delicate fragrance derived from ambergris, which came from the stomach of whales, anointed a million ladies of fashion, and where would be their trim figures without their stays of whalebone? The capacity of the *Amiable Lady* for carrying oil was three thousand barrels. Up to now they had not secured even a third of that. But, as the Captain often reminded his men, whalers were used to being in the Pacific for as long as three and four years; they still had a long time ahead of them.

This was not a prospect that caused Miranda any anxiety at all. She had waited all her life for this valued trip with her father, and nothing was going to spoil it for her. Her mother had died many years ago when she was only four, and the only real mother she had ever known was her beloved Aunt Zoe, Edward Chiltern's unmarried sister, who had taken charge of her bereaved brother and niece the day after her sister-in-law died, and had been with them ever since. Miranda missed her father dreadfully on his long voyages away from home, but while she was at school there was, of course, no question of being able to accompany him. Owners of whaling ships frowned upon the presence of women on board, knowing how rough and dangerous life could be on the Pacific.

Nurtured on gripping tales of the Pacific among the unbelievable dreamlike beauty of the south sea islands, Miranda had grown up with one single ambition in life—to experience, under the expert guidance of her sea-dog father, the untold pleasures that lay explored and unexplored in this ocean, the most mysterious, enticing ocean in the world. While other girls of her age dreamed of a smart, fun-filled city life, Miranda dreamed of coral atolls and beautiful Polynesian islanders, and spent her time re-living through books the adventures of such intrepid travellers as Captain James Cook, Will Mariner and Captain Bligh of the *Bounty*. She was particularly enchanted with accounts of the turbulent travels in the South Pacific on the Spanish lady adventurer, Doña Isabel de Mendaña, who had scoured the ocean in search of the gold said to exist on the islands of the legendary King Solomon. Nothing that she had seen so far had belied her expectations. They had touched many ports already and had headed westward into the Pacific after stopping briefly at Callao in Peru—the Marquesas, the Tuamotu group, the

Society Islands . . . What to others were mere collections of letters on a map were to Miranda the gateways to a dream.

The opportunity to accompany her father had not come her way until she was almost twenty-two. Neither Edward Chiltern nor his sister was in favour of this trip. First, these voyages could bring them face to face with many unknown hazards, and, second, both of them were very keen that Miranda should now settle down to wife- and motherhood with one of the many personable young men who already sought her hand, preferably young Peregrine Holmes, who was the engineer on the *Amiable Lady*. He came from good, solid, New England stock, was well educated and, in the eyes of everyone who knew him, a gentleman of high virtue.

Eventually, after much discussion, a compromise had been reached. Edward Chiltern would seek permission for Miranda to accompany him on a whaling trip, provided Aunt Zoe came as well and provided Miranda agreed to become engaged to Peregrine. Miranda agreed to the first condition without reservation, but the second required considerable thought. She knew that she was not in love with Peregrine Holmes but, on the other hand, she had known him all her life and he was kind and considerate. Finally, however, she decided to accept the second condition, too. The lure of the Pacific was too great to resist and it would not be laid to rest until she had experienced it at least once. The betrothal had taken place two days before the ship sailed. Miranda had every hope that, in time, she would learn to love Peregrine as he, obviously, loved her. It was decided that they would be married when the ship eventually reached Honolulu in the Hawaiian Islands.

The *Amiable Lady* was now close enough to the whales for them to be seen without the aid of telescopes.

There were, Miranda counted, about twenty of them, lounging and wallowing in the water and sending up fountains at least fifteen feet high—an absolute treasure of a find! But she knew that they would be lucky to get just one, so dangerous and uncertain was the whole business.

The small whaleboats had already been lowered and were creeping up on the unsuspecting beasts with the utmost caution. In the lead boat stood Dan, his harpoon ready. Beside her, Miranda could feel her father and Peregrine become taut with tension. Dan stood up slowly, trying to select a good spot to strike the dark grey hide. But, suddenly, the whale moved and the moment was lost. They began to look for another unsuspecting victim.

Edward Chiltern drew in his breath sharply and, to break the tension, asked, 'How is your Aunt Zoe?'

'The fever still rages,' said Miranda worriedly. 'I have given her another dose of the calomel, but it does not appear to be doing her much good.'

'Damn that man,' Captain Chiltern muttered angrily, and Miranda nodded in heartfelt agreement.

The doctor they had taken on board had deserted the ship among the Tuamotu, and disappeared without trace. They had been held up for two days while everyone searched for him, but he had not been found. Desertions among ships' crews travelling the Pacific were, of course, common. The temptations offered by the magical south sea islands were often too much for sailors to resist. Everyone knew that the islands brimmed not only with the bounties of Nature but also with the most luscious women in the world who lived and loved with easy morality. Which sailor in his right mind wanted to return home to a sour, nagging wife and seven hungry children, when he could so easily disappear for ever into the waiting arms of a delectable sixteen-year-old virgin willing to give him her all amid these lands of perpetual spring and plenty?

Nevertheless, it was a great shock to lose their doctor, for illnesses in the tropics were frequent. Now they would have to wait until they reached Honolulu to find a replacement, as it was doubtful whether another doctor would be available at Samoa, whither they were now heading. In the meantime it was becoming a matter of concern that Aunt Zoe's fever had not subsided in spite of Miranda's careful ministrations. Having taken a course in home nursing at school, she was reasonably adept in the treatment of minor illnesses—but what if Aunt Zoe's ailment happened not to be minor? What if it turned out to be the deadly malaria, for which, Miranda knew only too well, there was no cure? She shuddered at the thought and, closing her mind to the dreaded prospect, concentrated again on the hunt.

Dan had finally thrust his harpoon with tremendous force into an enormous grey-blue sperm whale, and the startled giant had leaped out of the water in surprised fury and then dived rapidly beneath the waves. Miranda could see the harpoon line flying out of the lead whaleboat as it uncoiled rapidly and followed the monster down into the deep. This was, she knew, a moment of great danger, for there was no knowing where the whale would surface again. So gigantic were these creatures that, if one came up too close to the ship, it could turn it over with ease or at least cause great damage.

Then, as they watched in painful suspense, a huge sigh of relief went up all over the ship. The giant head of the whale appeared ahead, well past the whaleboats, and they could see the harpoon still firmly fixed in its side. It had been a good strike, as was only to be expected from Dan, a master at his craft. The whale surged on at tremendous speed, angrily trying to shake the harpoon out of its back. But the harpoon remained secured. The fight was a spectacular one indeed: the death-throes of the whale lasted nearly three hours, but finally it tired and weakened. Two more harpoons had been launched into its thick hide, and then the fight was over. A great cheer went up on deck, and the happy, relieved smiles returned.

'Our fortunes have turned,' said Peregrine, giving Miranda a quick hug. 'We should get at least sixty barrels from this one.'

Now again there was much activity on board. Enormous stoves and wrought-iron cauldrons were made ready to receive the oil for boiling. The dead whale was towed near the ship and lashed to it, while a platform was lowered into the sea so that the men could get down to the business of cutting the blubber off the carcass. The head was cut off and hauled up on deck so that the precious spermaceti could be extracted. Dozens of vicious-looking sharks appeared from nowhere, smelling the possibility of a good feed, and had to be fought off continuously with axes.

It was very late that night when the men finally finished their exhausting work and every possible drop of oil had been extracted from the whale and the blubber was safely on the boil. Over a late dinner of fish stew and thick, crisp biscuits, Captain Chiltern was jubilant. 'If we continue to be as successful as we have been today we shall no doubt be able to fulfil our quota before we reach Honolulu.'

'I'm glad,' said Miranda tiredly, wrinkling her nose against the all-pervading stench of whale oil. 'I do look forward to Samoa. It will be pleasant to be on land again and wander around.'

'I do not much like the idea of you exploring these savage islands, Miranda,' said Peregrine categorically. 'They are not safe for women, their morals being what they are.'

'Oh, phooey!' exclaimed Miranda irritably. 'The islands are perfectly safe for women—indeed, much safer than New York, for instance. Aren't they, Papa?'

Edward Chiltern pretended to ponder the question, not willing to take sides. 'Well,' he said finally, 'some are, but some are still very hostile and primitive and, as you know, cannibalism does exist in a few places. But perhaps Samoa is reasonably safe, and if Peregrine will escort you ashore I have no objection to your going.'

Miranda frowned in displeasure. To be accompanied by Peregrine, with his rigid, old-fashioned ideas, would certainly ruin much of her pleasure. She would much rather take Dan who, like herself, was enamoured of the South Pacific and was, in addition, very learned about the entire region. But she refrained from comment, knowing that there was no point in arguing about it now. Samoa was still many, many, weeks ahead.

The Captain rose from the table and yawned tiredly. 'Time for bed, now,' he said. 'It's been a hard day for everyone and, with luck, tomorrow will be, too. We shall be fortunate tomorrow, I know. I feel it in my bones.'

But the morrow, when it came and finally went, proved that Edward Chiltern could not have been more wrong. Far from being lucky, the day was to be totally disastrous for the *Amiable Lady*.

In the morning, not long after dawn, the lookout reported another herd of sperm whale on the port horizon, and once again the crew sprang into action. But in trying to harpoon one whale, Dan had gravely injured another, which had dived, bleeding badly and in an utter fury. The creature did not appear again for quite a while. Then, suddenly, just as everyone was beginning to breathe again, it heaved itself against the ship, which shivered as if it would break apart. For a moment there was utter panic on board as coils of rope, tools, implements and utensils went flying. The stoves were, of course, carefully made fast so that there was no danger of the oil overspilling, but nevertheless some of the barrels slopped alarmingly, drenching the corridors and decks with a slippery swill. Fortunately, having landed his deadly blow, the whale finally sank beneath the waves, presumably to be able to die in peace on the ocean floor. Everyone heaved a sigh of relief.

However, as it happened, the wily whale had the last laugh after all. A few moments later, Peregrine rushed upon deck, his face pale and worried. 'We've got a gaping big hole in our hull, sir,' he informed Captain Chiltern. 'It's that last swing of the tail that did it.'

Immediately the ship's officers rushed below to examine the damage. It was considerable, and the water was pouring in to the hold with alarming rapidity.

'Get the pumps going,' the Captain ordered tersely. 'And put every man available on the job round the clock.'

A pall of gloom descended upon the *Amiable Lady*, all the jubilation of the previous two days evaporating like puffs of smoke. Barrels of the precious oil lay unattended, as the men were put on the pumps that would have to work day and night to keep the ship afloat.

Late in the evening, just as supper was over, Peregrine and Dan Haggerty came into the dining-room, their expressions extremely troubled. 'We have the pumps going full blast, sir.' Dan reported 'But if the hole gets any bigger, which it well might, we've had it.'

'We need to put in for repairs without much delay, sir,' Peregrine added, 'if we are to continue the journey at all.'

'Repairs?' the Captain asked worriedly. 'Repairs—

SPANIARD'S HAVEN 15

where? There isn't a repairing station within two thousand miles of Honolulu.'

'If we can put into any port—the nearest—we could do some patchwork repairs ourselves,' Peregrine pointed out.

Immediately charts were brought out and spread on the dining-tables. The ship was now somewhere between the Cook Islands and Tonga, with Samoa to the north-west. For some time the men were lost in discussions, and an air of sudden solemnity descended on the dining-room. Miranda listened silently, her heart thudding as she realised the dangerous situation they were now in.

Captain Chiltern stabbed the chart with his finger. 'We are here,' he said grimly, 'and there is not a port within a good five hundred miles of us. We could put in on one of these stray atolls, but most of them have no harbours one can use, and some of them have inhabitants who are known to be hostile to strangers.'

There was a moment's silence as each man pondered this truth. Then Dan, rubbing his chin thoughtfully, said, 'There is, of course, Amarillo, sir . . .' He left the sentence unfinished, and for a few moments the word seemed to hang in the air like a visible object. Nobody spoke.

Peregrine burst out into grim laughter. 'Amarillo? You must be mad, Dan! Why it might be safer to consign ourselves to the mercy of the sharks!'

Nobody appeared to disagree with the statement. Navigator Herbert Paulton scratched his head and nodded. 'It would be unthinkable to go to Amarillo,' he said very very definitely. 'Why he would lift us out of the ocean before we got past the reef. Everyone knows the man's mad.'

'What is Amarillo, and who is mad?' Miranda asked curiously.

But nobody volunteered an answer. Instead, the Captain folded the charts. 'That's decided, then. We cannot go to Amarillo. But, thank the Lord, we are not desperate yet. We'll make for Samoa, and put our trust in God.' Noticing Miranda's white face, he put his arm round her quickly.

'Don't look so worried, lass,' he said reassuringly. 'It hasn't happened yet and, who knows, it may never happen at all.'

Taking his cue from the Captain, Peregrine also smiled confidently, and the other men dutifully burst into forced smiles. 'These hazards are all in the day's work for sailors,' said Peregrine. 'We shall reach Samoa with ease. You'll see.'

But, as they had known only too well, both men were wrong. By the following morning, even with the pumps working without a moment's respite, the leak appeared to be getting the better of them and the level of water in the hold was rising. In addition, the morning air was dangerously still and to the south-west the sky was beginning to darken ominously. Ships built for the Pacific were generally sturdy, for the terrifying hurricanes and tornadoes—'devil winds' as they were called —were strong enough to tear ships from limb to limb. But the gaping hole in the side of the *Amiable Lady* had weakened her considerably, and although she had suffered and survived many storms, it was doubtful if she could survive one now. So far, they had been sailing well in front of the storm—but for how much longer?

As dusk gathered, all thoughts of whaling forgotten in the present dire crisis, the men again collected in the dining-room to discuss the situation. The room was tight with tension. Samoa was still more than a hundred miles away. It was doubtful if the ship could traverse even a quarter of that distance without certain disaster.

After completing her ministrations to Aunt Zoe

below, Miranda joined the men, but the grimness of their plight did not communicate itself to her immediately. She was now deeply worried about her aunt's condition, and a horrible certainty was forming in her mind. *Could* it be malaria? The pattern of the fever seemed to indicate it. It went up and down with regularity, but with no signs of abating completely. Miranda knew that all kinds of strange diseases, and malaria was one of them, raged in the tropics. She had been giving her aunt doses of calomel, but that too could be dangerous, for it did not suit certain people and could cause terrible complications. As it was, Aunt Zoe was continuously nauseous and complained of severe headaches.

Lost in her worrying thoughts, Miranda missed some of the conversation in which the men were heatedly engaged. With an effort she turned her mind to it.

'No!' Peregrine was saying emphatically. 'I do not agree!'

'As I see it,' said Dan warmly, 'we just do not have any choice in the matter now. We have to make for Amarillo . . .'

Miranda's ears perked up. There it was again—Amarillo! What on earth was it, and where? She rose and moved closer to the table, around which the argument was taking place.

'But sailing into Amarillo is the same as willingly going to the bottom of the Pacific,' said Peregrine, banging his fist on the table. 'I say we make for one of the atolls and take our chances with the natives. After all, we have muskets and cannon on board, and ample manpower . . .'

'No!' said the Captain sharply. 'I have never indulged in wanton killing, and I never shall. We are a peaceful ship of trade and we shall remain so, except when desperately threatened. If we fire, we fire only in self-defence. There has been enough killing in the Pacific already, and I will not be a party to any more.'

His voice was so stern that Peregrine immediately subsided into silence, although Miranda could see that he was far from satisfied with the answer. She observed his angry face in some surprise. How ugly it seemed all of a sudden, and how unlike the one she had been used to! Perhaps what men said was true after all—the Pacific was a witch that brought out the worst in humankind.

'It is not easy to get into Amarillo,' said Dan thoughtfully. 'I have heard that there is only one passage through the reef, and it is difficult to find.'

'But there is a passage, and we could reach it before dawn,' Bert Paulton persisted. 'And, surely, if we waved a white flag, he would not mow us down ruthlessly.'

'It is difficult to predict what he might do,' remarked Dan with an abrupt laugh. 'I know of only one ship that he has allowed within the reef, and that was a small single-master that carried no cannon. The ship had lost her rudder in a storm and the crew were half dead with disease and starvation. She foundered by the reef one night, and would have been smashed, had he not sent his men to rescue her. The men were kind to the crew and treated them until they were well. The ship was repaired and put on her way without any sort of harassment.'

'So,' said Captain Chiltern thoughtfully. 'He can be kind when he wishes. Perhaps we shall be lucky.'

Peregrine laughed unpleasantly. 'And what about all the others he has attacked without pity?'

'Only to warn them off,' reminded Dan sharply. 'He has never been known to kill for the sake of killing.'

'You sound almost as if you admired him,' sneered Peregrine. 'In my book he is nothing but a rogue and a scoundrel who wants Amarillo for himself for a reason we all know only too well.'

'He is a rascal, no doubt,' said Dan with an amused

laugh. 'But yes, there are things in him that some men admire.'

'*Who* are you talking about?' Miranda cried in exasperation, now consumed with curiosity. 'After all, I feel I too have a right to know—especially if we all stand a chance of being blown out of the sea into kingdom come!'

Her father did not answer her question but suddenly stood up as though he had come to a decision. The frown on his brow cleared. 'He will not blow us out of the sea, I am confident. In any case, it is a chance we shall have to take. So, Amarillo it is—and no more argument.'

The gloom in the dining-room seemed to lighten. At least they had decided on a definite plan of action. It was certainly better to chance the hazards of Amarillo, whatever they might be, than to do nothing and wait for the Pacific to swallow them up. Only Peregrine continued to glower, angry that his opinion had been over-ruled so categorically.

Miranda's now consuming curiosity was still far from satisfied. Later that night, when she knew Dan was on watch, she sought him out on the bridge.

'What is this place called Amarillo?' she asked, fixing him with a determined eye. 'And who is this man everyone keeps talking about?'

Dan shifted the wad of tobacco from one cheek to another, chewed silently for a moment, then spat it out into the sea below. 'Amarillo is an island,' he said slowly. 'Perhaps the most mysterious of them all in this ocean of a thousand mysteries.'

'And the man?'

A gleam came into his eyes. 'The man is—El Español.'

'El Español? But that just means "The Spaniard", doesn't it?'

Dan nodded. 'That is what he has ever been known

as. Where he comes from, with what name he was christened, nobody knows, although there are rumours by the hundred.'

Miranda digested the information in silence. Then she asked, much intrigued, 'But why should he want to kill us? We come in peace, seeking his help only because we are in trouble.'

'Because,' said Dan softly, 'we are strangers, and El Español hates all men from the outside world.'

'But *why*?' Miranda persisted. 'Surely he is an outsider himself? You said he was a Spaniard.'

'Ay. But he has turned his back on his own kind. He wants no part of them.'

'But why?' Miranda asked again. 'That is a very odd situation.'

'It is. But then, he is a very odd man, and one whom very few people know. Indeed, I do not know of a single sailor who has seen him in a decade.'

Miranda's eyes shone with interest. 'What about the crew of the vessel he is reputed to have saved? Did they not see him when they were on the island?'

Dan shook his head. 'They saw only his lieutenants, some of whom are Europeans too. Besides, they were confined to their quarters and not allowed to wander at will.'

There was not much more Dan could tell her. All that was known about the man was that fifteen or so years ago he had burst upon the south seas like a fiery meteor. His business? Piracy! Within the brief span of four years his ship, *El Condor,* became the most feared vessel in the Pacific, already rife with pirates and privateers. But El Español's methods seemed not only strange but unpredictable. He picked his victims with care, attacking ships for bullion only. Whatever else might be on board, neither he nor his men touched it. Even more strange, he killed only rarely but, when he did, it was with such ruthless cold-blooded fury that men trembled even at the thought. Often he would pick out only one man from a full ship's crew and murder him brutally before his mates; nobody knew why. There were other occasions when he would board a ship and, without touching either a hair on anyone's head or a crate of cargo, leave in peace. It was if he looked for something—or someone—special, but no one knew what or who. The mighty guns of *El Condor* were never the first to speak, but when they did they met their targets with deadly precision. El Español attacked always at night, he and his men not only kept their faces hidden but never spoke, therefore they had never been identified.

'And his ship,' said Dan, his eyes shining with excitement, 'was unlike any other in the two Pacifics. She was a clipper, sleek and smooth, such as used by opium-smugglers off the coast of China, and she was the fastest thing on water, outpacing all others with ease.'

'But where did he get such a ship?' Miranda was fascinated by Dan's tale.

'Well, according to rumour, he stole her from the British East India Company while she was returning from an opium run. They say he dumped the crew in their own longboats into the ocean near the Portuguese island of Macao, and they were picked up by a passing frigate.' Dan laughed gleefully. 'The British were hopping mad, of course, and immediately put a price on his head—not that they could ever find him!'

'But where did he go?'

'Well,' said Dan, 'it was being suspected now that El Español's hideout was probably the island of Amarillo. Until fifteen years ago, many ships called at Amarillo —or at least those that could find a passage through the coral reef that surrounded it almost entirely, and those that did not smash themselves on the reef in the effort.

But, with the emergence of El Español, Amarillo was suddenly closed to all. It became heavily fortified, with powerful cannon concealed in its mountainsides. Any ship that managed to enter the quiet lagoons surrounding it began to find herself pounded by volleys of cannon-balls aimed close enough to send her scuttling back hurriedly.

'Then, after four years of terrorising the Pacific, El Español and his ship suddenly disappeared from the face of the ocean—and had never been seen again in the Pacific. But his final escapade had been one that had chilled to the bone every man who heard of it. He had swooped down on a Portuguese whaler that carried not a single item of value in her cargo. And he had killed all but three of the men who sailed on her! Nobody knew the motive, least of all those who survived, but the ship had been totally wrecked. Every single item of equipment had been smashed and all the sails torn beyond repair. The unfortunate whaler drifted with her grisly load for weeks before she finally ran aground on the island of Tonga, the three survivors crazed with fear. Oddly enough, they had been supplied by El Español with sufficient food and water to see them safely through for two months, but their account of the carnage was fearful. It was as though El Español were waging a personal vendetta, but for what reason, nobody could tell.

'Since that last terrible act, the *Condor* has not sailed again,' said Dan. 'At least, nobody has reported having seen her on the high seas. But whether El Español is retired or merely resting, nobody knows.'

Miranda sat silent for a while, digesting this extraordinary story. Then she asked in a quavering voice, 'And that was ten years ago?'

'Ay. Near enough. The island is closed to all ships except those they themselves choose to let enter, such as copra boats or boats belonging to other islanders. But no boat belonging to white folk has passed through the reef in this past decade until that single-master was rescued. According to what little the crew were allowed to see, Amarillo is still heavily fortified and has its own natural harbour. The island, they said, seemed to be very beautiful and prosperous. Of the man himself they neither heard nor saw anything, but they knew that he was there.'

He relapsed again into silence, and Miranda became thoughtful. 'Why is it so important for ships to try to get to Amarillo?' she asked.

'Well, there are beautiful Polynesian women on it, and the islanders were reputed to be gentle people with no weapons and very hospitable—at least at one time. And sailors in the Pacific, away from home for years, are hungry for love.'

'But surely not hungry enough to risk being wrecked on the reef or being shot at ruthlessly! Every Pacific island has beauty and women in abundance—what is the special attraction of Amarillo?'

Dan eyed her ruminatively. 'Can you not guess, Miss Miranda? Does the name itself—Amarillo—not suggest anything to you?'

Miranda frowned and shook her head. 'No. Should it?'

Dan pulled in a sharp breath. 'Amarillo in Spanish means yellow.' His eyes twinkled with amusement. 'This island has something on it that every man in the world would sell his soul to the devil to possess.'

'Oh?' asked Miranda, bursting with curiosity. 'And what is that?'

Dan laughed. 'Gold, Miss Miranda. *Gold*!'

CHAPTER TWO

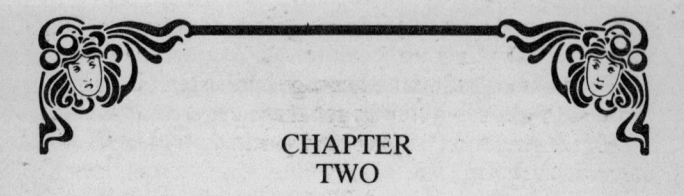

IT WAS a beautiful shell-pink dawn. The ocean, flickering blue and roseate, heaved around them in undulant swells, and the *Amiable Lady* swayed gently with the waves, her sails furled. In the hold, the pumps were still being worked feverishly and everyone looked tired and drawn.

Up on deck, the Captain and his men stood watching silently, their telescopes held tightly to their eyes. Not more than a mile away lay Amarillo, its indigo hills and green-gold beaches staring back at them in silent challenge. All round the island creamed the surf, as the ocean beat down again and again on the coral heads of the reef. From where they were looking, the barrier appeared unsurmountable, not a single break in the frothing seas indicating any passage. The noise of the surf was thunderous.

Standing next to her father, Miranda surveyed the scene with conflicting feelings. It was a panorama of exquisite tranquillity, for beyond the foaming line of surf spread out the lagoon of pale aquamarine as still as mirrors and as tempting as the devil himself. No more than a mile between them and safety!

'What now, Papa?' she asked.

'We shall wait here a while so that they have the chance to observe us well. It would be fatal for them to believe that we are uncaring marauders with evil intentions.'

'What if they start firing at us?' asked Peregrine tersely.

'We are well out of their range for the moment. But let us see what they do.'

'Even if we can find the passage,' persisted Peregrine, 'do you think he will let us get through?'

'He might,' the Captain said placidly. 'After all, we carry a white flag.'

'He might think it is a trick,' insisted Peregrine.

'Yes, possibly. Then we shall have to think of something else. Let us cross our bridges when we come to them.'

'I do think we should not remove our cannon,' said Peregrine stubbornly. 'If he does fire, we can at least give as good as we get.'

'Can we?' asked the Captain sharply. 'Look through your 'scope to see if there is a single target you can discern? What shall we fire at—mountain walls?'

'His cannon are well concealed, Mr Holmes,' Dan explained patiently. 'We shall not know where the balls come from until they fire.'

Miranda listened to the conversation avidly, and asked Dan, 'But are you sure that this is Amarillo?'

'It is Amarillo,' he replied curtly. 'The shape of the single mountain that rises from its centre is its mark of identity. It is shaped like a finger pointing heavenwards, and they say he calls it "El Dedo", which is the Spanish for finger.'

'But do you think he already knows that we are here?' Miranda asked. 'There seems not a sign of life on the island.'

'Yes,' said Dan softly. 'He knows.'

The *Amiable Lady* remained unmoving, sails securely furled, with a large white flag flying prominently from her mainmast, until the sun was directly overhead. In the south-west the bank of black clouds had grown and appeared to be spreading. How long would it be before the storm struck?

At noon Captain Chiltern ordered a longboat to be lowered from the midships gangway and, together with Dan, the navigator Marvin Salter and the oarsmen, clambered into it. Miranda watched them leave with her heart in her mouth, longing to be with them, but knowing that under no circumstances would her father allow it. In any case, there was no knowing how long the boat would be away searching for the passage in the reef, and Aunt Zoe needed constant attention.

On Amarillo itself, bathed now in brilliant sunshine, its green and purple appearance iridescent, there still was no sign of life or movement. The waters of the lagoon were now a deep turquoise and presented a sharp contrast to the seething white foam of the surf. The island presented a prospect of such beautiful serenity that Miranda found it difficult to visualise the menace that might lie beyond. Again and again her thoughts turned to the man who had made this his formidable kingdom, El Español. No man from the outside world had laid eyes on him for years. Would they be able to? The prospect, however remote, was suddenly unbearably exciting. It tasted of true adventure of the kind she had read in so many tales about the South Pacific.

The longboat did not return for two hours, and the news was cheerless. They had circled the island twice but had not found any trace of a passage.

'There has to be one somewhere,' said Dan doggedly. 'I know there is, for people have been through it.'

'We shall try again,' said Captain Chiltern tiredly, wiping the sweat from his forehead. 'But first, some food and drink. The heat is intolerable.'

After a rapid meal, they set out again in the longboat, and once again the long wait began for those left behind on the *Amiable Lady*. Miranda took care of Aunt Zoe's needs and administered another dose of calomel, then sought Peregrine out on the deck.

'Why is there no response at all from Amarillo?' she asked him worriedly. 'Surely they must know that we are in trouble?'

'*Of course* he knows we are in trouble and is hoping we shall go down quietly to the bottom of the sea to save his gunpowder!' Peregrine laughed unpleasantly. 'Or perhaps he is confident we shall not be able to find the passage. Who knows with this barbarian? I wouldn't be surprised if there are still cannibals on the island. In the Pacific the custom is widespread.'

Miranda blanched. 'But Papa is not even armed . . .'

Peregrine smiled grimly. 'If they do meet a canoe-load of cannibals carrying machetes, they will certainly wish they were!'

Suddenly, louder than the roar of the surf, came the distinct thunder of cannon-fire. Miranda screamed, and Peregrine and every other member of the crew—apart from those manning the pumps—rushed on deck. But around them there was nothing to be seen. The longboat was obviously on the other side of the island, and El Español was giving it his usual perverse form of welcome.

Immediately, Peregrine ordered another longboat to be lowered and grabbed his musket. In his belt he tucked a pistol and commanded four members of the crew to do the same. Miranda watched him, horrified. 'But what will you do, Peregrine? Two longboats can hardly form a defence against his diabolical cannon. Besides, Papa has expressly forbidden the use of arms . . .'

But he impatiently shook off her restraining hand. 'I cannot sit by and do nothing,' he said through clenched teeth. 'They may be in grave danger. At least we can put up some resistance.'

Helplessly, her heart beating like a hammer, Miranda watched the second longboat disappear into the swell. This time the wait was even longer. Determined not to let her nerves overcome her, she brought her diary up on deck and doggedly sat down to put into words all the events that she had not had time to record before. Aunt Zoe, mercifully, was sleeping soundly. She had eaten two spoonfuls of porridge for breakfast, but the fever still raged and she was terribly weak.

It was not until late into the afternoon that the longboats returned and Miranda heaved a massive sigh to see that all the men in them were safe. Wearily the men climbed the rope-ladder back on deck and the boats were raised. One look at her father's tense face was enough to tell Miranda all she wanted to know. Their mission had not been successful! For the rest of the story she had to wait until all the men had eaten, and she joined them in the dining-room.

They had eventually found the passage—but that had been the extent of their success. The moment the longboats had sailed into the lagoon, they had been welcomed by two cannon-balls which had landed close enough almost to capsize the boats. They had stopped rowing immediately and had waited quietly for something to happen, while the white flags fluttered significantly in the breeze. Within fifteen minutes, ten canoes laden with armed islanders had appeared from round the island. The lead canoe, however, carried in it three Europeans armed with muskets that pointed straight towards them. Fortunately, Peregrine's gun and those of the crew in his longboat were concealed, and so not observed by the men. They had not been aggressive, but their voices were cold and unaccommodating. Captain Chiltern had stated his case and requested permission to bring the ship into the lagoon so that they might start their repairs.

The Europeans had listened to their story patiently and then turned round and gone back to the island, obviously to consult their leader. Within the hour they had returned with his answer. Permission to enter the lagoon would not be given. El Español suggested that they try their luck on another island near by. Amarillo, he had sent word, was not open to strangers, peaceful or otherwise.

Silence reigned in the dining-room as Captain Chiltern related the brutal verdict. The men were stunned, now convinced that their ship, and they with her, was doomed. A thick pall of gloom descended as all the men sat quiet, lost in their own thoughts. Miranda felt a stab of fear run sharply through her. Was this, then, the end? Was there no hope left for them?

Captain Chiltern rose from his chair, the lines of fatigue and despair now deeply etched on his face. 'There is no point in talking about it endlessly tonight,' he said. 'We all need a good night's sleep. Perhaps the bright light of day tomorrow will bring forth a solution.' He kissed Miranda briefly on the cheek, inquired for a moment about his sister's health, and then left the room. As she watched him go, a knife turned slowly inside Miranda's heart. It was the figure of a man defeated.

Suddenly she felt a surge of blinding anger against the man who held all their lives in his hands and who had rejected their plea with such unthinking inhumanity. What kind of ogre was this with not a shred of compassion in his heart? How could his bitterness against his own race be so deep? Surely even animals were known to show consideration to each other when in trouble!

'You still have a place in your thoughts for admiration of this renegade?' Peregrine asked Dan after the Captain had withdrawn.

Dan met his eyes unflinchingly. 'Ay. He has been hurt by our world in some way,' he said quietly. 'Like a wounded animal, he turns upon anyone who crosses his path.'

'Rubbish, sir, *rubbish!*' retorted Peregrine. 'I watched those men in the lagoon today, and they were no better than ruffians of the first order. It was all I could do not to shoot out their guts with my musket.'

'It is just as well you didn't, Mr Holmes,' said Dan sharply. 'Had they known you had muskets with you, none of us would have returned to the ship in one piece.'

'*Hah!*' Peregrine stood up and kicked his chair so that it fell over. 'The Pacific has seen enough scoundrels, God knows, but without a doubt this damned rogue is the worst.' Without a backward glance, he stamped out of the room.

Watching Peregrine's show of temper, there was no doubt that Miranda tacitly agreed with him in every respect. There was no doubt now in her mind that this Spaniard was a man far from worthy of admiration, and she was becoming irritated by Dan's continual excuses for him. Whatever might be his reason for privacy, nothing could condone the merciless manner in which he was sending them all to their doom. Long after everyone else had gone to sleep, she paced the deck restlessly, her anger boiling. Were they just to sit here in the middle of nowhere and await certain death? She knew that there were few chances—if any—of their reaching another island in safety. Something had to be done. Some method had to be found to penetrate this reprehensible man's iron hide. But what? What, and *how*?

It was not until almost midnight that the faint stirrings of an idea in her mind formed itself into a definite plan. Impatiently, she waited until it was Dan's turn on watch, when they could talk without fear of being overheard. She sought him out on the bridge, where he was anxiously examining the sky.

'Dan,' she said, seating herself beside him on a coil of rope, 'I have a plan, for which I need your help.'

Dan looked at her in surprise. 'A plan, Miss Miranda? What kind of plan?'

'I want to go to meet El Español and I want you to come with me.'

For a moment Dan's face froze in an expression of such incredulity that Miranda almost laughed. In his shock, he nearly swallowed his wad of tobacco.

'*You* want to meet El Español, Miss Miranda?' he gasped.

'Yes,' she replied coolly. 'But I cannot do so unless you agree to come with me to take me through the passage.'

Dan recollected his wits and, annoyingly, his whole body shook with silent laughter. Lips pursed tight, Miranda allowed him his moment of merriment. When finally he stopped, he wiped his eyes with the back of his hand. 'To be sure, Miss Miranda,' he said, chuckling, 'you have a neat sense of humour.'

'I am not joking, Dan,' said Miranda grimly. 'I mean it. I refuse to take this man's word as some dictum from heaven and do nothing but sit back and await a watery grave. I know what he is like, but I feel very strongly that he will not harm me. And,' she added, her eyes twinkling slightly, 'women do have a way with them that has been denied to men, as you know.'

'But . . . But . . . your father would never permit it, Miss Miranda,' Dan pointed out, realising to his further astonishment that Miranda was not jesting. Indeed, it appeared that she had never been more serious in all her life.

'I do not intend that my father should know until after we have left.'

'I cannot deceive the Captain, Miss Miranda,' Dan said, horrified at such a suggestion. 'Why, he would hang and quarter me—which is only what I would deserve!'

Miranda sighed. 'Dan, listen! We have nothing to lose and everything to gain. Of course I may not be successful in getting to him, but I am more likely to do so than any of the men on the ship. Now, deny that if you can! We have a sick woman on board and I cannot let Aunt Zoe continue to suffer like this with no proper medication. We have no chance of reaching any island that will be able to accommodate us. There are no safe harbours within a thousand miles. The leak will give way at any moment, sending us to the bottom right here—and there is a storm brewing. Surely my plan is worth a try in a situation as desperate as this?'

Overwhelmed by her logic, Dan could think of nothing to say. Pressing home her advantage, Miranda persisted and persuaded until the old mariner rubbed his chin thoughtfully.

'Well . . .' he conceded, 'I can see your point, but . . .'

'Dan, you yourself said that there was good in this man. If you believe this, then can you see him opening fire on an unarmed woman and an old man?'

Dan thought about that for a moment then, much to Miranda's delight, began to smile. 'It might work, lass,' he mused slowly. 'It just might . . .'

Hastily, her heart bounding in excitement, Miranda ran below to her cabin and scribbled a hasty note to her father to tell him what she was planning, begging him to restrain himself and Peregrine from impulsive action. They would be livid with worry and fear for her. But, at the same time, in some strange, secret way, she also knew that, however many kinds of a monster El Español might be, he would not harm them.

The hour of pre-dawn was dark and cool when Dan silently lowered the smallest dinghy into the ocean. Despite its size, it was sturdy, and they knew that, however much they were buffeted by the waves, it would not capsize.

'How long will it take to reach the passage?' she asked, climbing in with him and tying her shawl around her head and shoulders.

'About an hour,' Dan gasped, using all his strength to row the boat.

'Will you be able to row through the passage?'

Dan nodded, and Miranda sat back in silence. Their only bearing at the moment was the shining line of white surf which indicated the location of the reef. There was no question of trying to row through before daybreak, by which time they hoped to be ready and waiting at the passage.

The sea was smooth. Mercifully, the gathering storm had blown itself out before reaching them, for last evening the black clouds had no longer been visible to the south-west. Miranda sat in the tiny boat with her hands demurely in her lap, and although her face was calm she trembled within at the momumental task she had undertaken, and without her father's knowledge. Was it insanity brought on by sheer desperation that had prompted this mad escapade? Suddenly she was appalled by the enormity of the mission that lay ahead.

The pale fingers of dawn were just beginning to push aside the night sky when the dinghy laboriously arrived at the spot where the passage into the lagoon began. As she saw the journey that now lay ahead of them, Miranda's face blanched. Only a very slight change in the pattern of foaming indicated the entrance. But the tide was low and some of the coral heads could be seen, their razor-sharp but incredibly beautiful shafts and bulbs peeping above the sea. The passage was fairly wide, but zigzagging. A chance breaker or an untimely blink of the eye could send them to kingdom come in smithereens.

Silently, his face expressionless, Dan turned the boat in the direction of the entrance and Miranda closed her eyes in cold trepidation. As they hit the surf, their boat spun alarmingly, and for a moment it was all Miranda could do to suppress a scream. Hastily she stuffed a handkerchief into her mouth and sat grim and rigid in silent prayer. An agonising eternity of suspense followed, and in those few seconds she must have died a thousand deaths. She had never been so frightened in all her life.

But then, miraculously, the dinghy was through the passage, and Dan swept into the lagoon with a last violent push. Everything became still and, cautiously, Miranda opened her eyes. They were safely enclosed in the still water!

Dan laid down his oars and rested for a while, wiping his forehead with a shaky hand. They were both drenched through and through with the spray. 'That, Miss Miranda,' he said in a thin voice, 'is the closest I hope you will ever come to meeting your Maker.'

Miranda laughed shakily, then stood up and wrung out her clothes. The sky had by now lightened considerably and the waters upon which they sat were as smooth as a sheet of glass. The lagoon was a very delicate green, almost translucent. Beneath them they could see hundreds of colourful fish dart about, and ahead, proud and dauntless, stood Amarillo, a bare two hundred yards away. Its hillsides were dense with greenery and clusters of flowering shrubs covered in wild blossoms. Occasionally the still of the early morning was shattered by the shriek of a parakeet or the twittering of other birds. It was a haven of such peace and loveliness that, for a moment, Miranda sat lost in absent thought.

Dan's voice brought her back to reality. 'What now, Miss Miranda? Shall we wait here until they come?'

'They will come?' she asked, frowning. She felt the pangs of nervousness returning.

'Oh ay, they will come,' Dan said flatly. 'This is roughly where we were yesterday when the cannon-ball came rushing at us.'

Miranda shivered and then gasped. Sure enough, from behind the island, two boats were approaching them rapidly. She swallowed hard. 'Now, you . . . you let me do the talking, Dan,' she breathed. 'I know what I am doing.'

'I sure hope so, Miss Miranda,' he said fervently. 'I sure hope so.'

The passengers in the two canoes became clearly visible. In the lead boat were two Europeans, both with muskets pointing at them, and two oarsmen. The second boat contained five or six islanders with machetes. The two Europeans wore only dark blue trousers, and in their belts glinted the shafts of daggers. Very deliberately, Miranda removed her shawl, and her fine golden hair came tumbling down on her shoulders. As the lead canoe came closer, she noticed with satisfaction the look of utter surprise on the faces of the two men. For a moment they stared at her without speaking; then the man closest to them swallowed and spoke. His voice was thick and guttural.

'Who are you, and what do you want?'

Miranda looked up at him haughtily. 'I am the daughter of Captain Chiltern of the *Amiable Lady*, and I wish to see El Español.'

Very slowly the men's jaws dropped, and opposite her Miranda heard a gurgle emerge from Dan's throat. The two men stiffened. 'El Español does not see anyone. Moreover you have already had his answer. Your ship will not be allowed to enter the lagoon.'

Miranda looked him squarely in the eye, and her jawline set determinedly. 'I do not believe you,' she said firmly. 'I would like to hear the refusal from his own lips.'

The nearest man flushed angrily. 'It is not a lie,' he said in a cold, hard voice. 'You will not be allowed to proceed.'

Miranda made a covert signal to Dan to start rowing. 'I intend to see your leader, and I do not think you can stop me!' The dinghy began to move forward.

'Stop!' the man roared. 'Or I shall shoot!'

'No, you won't,' Miranda called out calmly. 'Not without El Español's orders—and he has not ordered you to kill us, for he has not yet had the chance! Why don't you go and ask him whether you are to open fire or not?'

The dinghy kept moving forward and Miranda could see the sweat pouring down Dan's face as his lips moved in prayer. At any moment the trigger-happy ruffians could put a bullet through them with ease. But Miranda had called their bluff, and no bullets came their way. Instead, the lead European shouted something to the islanders in the second canoe and, before their dinghy could slide past, the men had stretched out their hands and grasped it firmly, forcing it to come to a halt.

'Very well, then,' said Miranda grimly, settling back comfortably. 'We shall sit here exactly like this for the rest of the day! I shall not leave until I have seen your leader, this Spaniard. Now you can go and tell him that.'

The face of the spokesman went dark with anger and for a moment he struggled to speak. Obviously it was a ludicrous situation. They could hardly remain on guard in the lagoon all day. And, equally obviously, he was flustered and no longer sure what to do.

'This is private property,' he finally burst out. 'You cannot remain here all day.'

'Oh, but I shall,' Miranda assured him, smiling, 'unless you take me to El Español.'

'I have already told you that El Español does not see anyone!' His voice was becoming exasperated and he was well aware that he was beginning to sound like a fool. Even the islanders, not understanding the language but understanding only too well the drift of the conversation, were beginning to smile and snigger.

'How do you know that he will not see me?' she challenged. 'You have not taken the trouble to ask him. And,' she added acidly, 'we are both unarmed, as you can see. You can put your muskets away. We shall not harm you!'

The man's face darkened to a dull red and, much too hastily, he put down his musket, as did the other European. They looked at each other frowning. In all their years with El Español they had never been in a situation such as this with a woman—and a white woman at that! Now, had it been a man, they would have known only too well how to deal with such impudence.

Taking advantage of their confusion, Miranda said, 'You will please go and inform El Español that I wish to see him on a matter of some urgency. Apart from our sinking ship, we have on board a desperately sick old lady who needs immediate treatment, for we carry no doctor. I have heard of occasions when El Español has shown compassion to many. I am certain that he will not want his conscience besmirched with the blood of innocent women. If nothing else, he can at least arrange for a doctor from the island to come aboard and examine the woman.'

For a moment the man hesitated, then consulted his companion for a while. He suddenly seemed to come to a decision. 'All right,' he said curtly. 'Wait here.'

The man sat down again in the canoe and it disappeared rapidly behind the island. The islanders in the second canoe, however, clung tenaciously to the dinghy, although they were now smiling openly and their eyes were filled with admiration. They murmured among themselves and Miranda found herself the focus of all eyes and, undoubtedly, the subject of much whispered comment.

At the opposite end of the dinghy she heard Dan's soft chuckle, which broke out into irrepressible laughter. He threw back his head and roared helplessly. Then he wiped his eyes and shook his head wonderingly. 'I would never have believed it, Miss Miranda, had I not seen it with my own eyes!'

Miranda's grim face relaxed into a smile, but her eyes remained troubled. 'Well, so far so good, but we are still no closer to meeting this wretched man.'

The canoe bearing the two Europeans returned within half an hour. Without undue preamble, the spokesman signalled to them from a distance. Astonishingly, the words he called out were, 'Follow me!'

Miranda gasped, and even Dan froze. Then, hastily recollecting himself, he picked up the oars and began rowing furiously.

Behind the canoe speeding on ahead, they rounded the curve of the island and before them the lagoon spread out even further. They kept going for a while and then, quite suddenly, the canoe took a sharp turn and seemed to disappear into the face of a rock. Wonderingly, they followed, and discovered that in the rock-face there was an opening which had not been visible until they were almost upon it. It was very wide and very high with sheer rock on either side. An overhang prevented all but the dimmest flicker of sunlight. Dan drew in his breath sharply.

'Well, strike me blind! No wonder the *Condor* could disappear so completely! Who would ever find her here?'

The channel took a dog's-leg turn and suddenly they were confronted with a most amazing sight. A perfect harbour set in a gigantic lagoon! On two sides the lagoon was protected by rocks, and on the third was a dense belt of coconuts, covering a low hill. From no angle could the harbour be seen from the open sea. On the far side of the lagoon was a strip of golden beach and clusters of grass huts. Groups of gaily-clad islanders stood round, watching them in open-mouthed curiosity. In the harbour itself were moored dozens of boats of all shapes and sizes from tiny canoes to larger single-masters. The normal sounds of everyday life filled the air as women shouted and children shrieked with laughter. Somewhere in the background was the sound of hammering, for it was obvious that the harbour also contained a busy shipyard.

Miranda and Dan stared about them dumbfounded, for it was a sight so unexpected that they could hardly believe their eyes. This could have been a port in any one of the dozens of Pacific islands, so natural was its atmosphere and so normal its activity.

Dominating the harbour was a ship, tall and huge, of such beauty that even Miranda gasped. She was incredibly sleek, and shining black with her fittings gleaming with spit and polish. From where they sat, she seemed like some enormous mythical sea-bird, her hull towering above their heads, and her three masts rising even higher. On her prow was perched a gigantic golden eagle with wings outstretched, obviously her mascot, and on the side of her prow was etched in golden letters *El Condor*.

'A thing of beauty,' Dan murmured in awe. 'A thing of beauty!'

At a signal from the lead canoe, Dan swung the dinghy to one side and beached it on a patch of sand. Several hands rushed forward to secure it to a stake with a thick rope. Dan rose out of the boat and stretched his legs, then held out a hand to help Miranda ashore. All around, work came to a standstill as a hundred pairs of eyes watched them. Among the crowd were some women, tall and lissom, clad in beautiful sarongs and with their breasts exposed, as was the custom in the south seas. Their hair, thick and glossy, hung loose over their backs, and they wore flowers behind one ear. They now stood and stared at Miranda in shock. Never in all their lives had they ever seen a white woman—and certainly never one with hair that looked like spun gold!

But Miranda was oblivious to all stares. Her eyes were glued to the jetty where, at the foot of a gangway leading to the deck of the *Condor,* stood three Europeans. Like the other two, they were bare-chested, and their bodies were the colour of tanned leather. Only their light eyes and sandy brown hair gave an indication of their race. Was one of them El Español?

Followed closely by Dan, Miranda walked up to them, as was obviously expected of her. She held herself perfectly erect, and her face belied all hints of agitation although the palms of her hands felt sticky and her throat was dry.

'Your message to El Español has been received,' said the tallest of the three men, his hair peppered with streaks of grey, as was his beard.

Miranda looked him squarely in the eye. 'Are you he?' she asked, knowing instinctively that he was not.

The man seemed taken aback, but only for a second. 'No. El Español does not see anyone. You may tell me whatever it is you wish to say.'

'I do not see the point,' retorted Miranda coldly, 'for you will only have to turn to him for advice.'

'These are the men who met us yesterday,' Dan whispered behind her. 'This one is a nasty specimen.'

'In that case, your visit is fruitless,' the man said tonelessly. 'He will not see you. And the decision about your ship remains firm. It will not be allowed to enter the lagoon.'

Miranda's heart sank. There was an air of authority

about this man that boded no good. Nevertheless, she met his gaze bravely. 'Then why has he troubled to have us brought here?'

'Because you say there is a sick woman on board. He is prepared to arrange for a doctor to go back with you to your ship. That is all.'

So, there was some cause to hope: the man did have a streak of humanity in him after all! But, having come so far, she was determined to exploit her advantage to the full. What good was medication if they were to die in the ocean anyway?

'We are a peaceful whaling vessel,' she said stubbornly, determined that she would at least have her full say. 'We have already dismantled our cannon. We are willing for your men to come on board and search the ship thoroughly for other arms you may suspect we are carrying. Our muskets are all laid out on the deck if you wish to confiscate them. We need only a few days' respite in which to repair the ship. We do not seek to disturb your privacy in any manner. Our ship will remain in the lagoon outside, and you are free to post as many guards on her as you like. What other possible guarantee can we give you of our good intentions?' In sheer desperation, her voice rang out loud and clear through the harbour.

The man listened in impassive silence, but it was obvious that her plea was falling upon deaf ears. 'El Español has given you his decision,' he said offhandedly. 'It will not be reversed. If you are still in need of a doctor, you may . . .'

She cut him off with an angry gesture, and suddenly, her temper exploded. 'Do you understand what I am trying to say?' she burst out furiously. 'We shall *die* if we cannot repair our ship! Has human life come to mean so little to your Spaniard that he brushes us off like flies? Has his hatred of the human race become so bitter that he is willing to wage war even against *petticoats*?' She was so angry that her eyes filled with hot tears and she brushed them aside quickly with the back of her hand, unwilling to let these abominable men see them.

For a moment after she had spoken, there was a hushed, shocked, silence. Even the hammering behind the ship stopped. Every man, woman and child stared at her in horror, aghast at her temerity.

Then, the spokesman for El Español recovered from his shock and his face became black with rage. His right hand settled on the hilt of the dagger in his belt. 'You will leave this place immediately!' he shouted. 'The offer of a doctor has been rescinded. You will tell your Captain that if he is not out of these waters by . . .'

'That will be all, Alvarez!'

The words, spoken in Spanish, were soft, but said with such precision that the spokesman stopped in midsentence. Everyone raised their eyes to look at the deck of the *Condor,* whence the voice came. It was neither angry nor strident. Yet, every word fell upon the jetty with the clarity of a stone going through water.

Behind her, Miranda heard Dan's swift intake of breath and a subdued whistle. Very slowly, she, too, looked up. On the deck of the clipper, standing on the midships gangway, she discerned a figure. From this distance she could not see the face clearly, but it was crowned by thick black hair. He wore a white shirt and his long legs were encased in black trousers that hugged them tightly. His shining black boots went up to his knees and, as he moved down the gangway, the sun caught their brass buckles, and they glinted.

The man called Alvarez, and the others with him, stared up at the figure incredulously, their mouths open. Miranda's heart lurched against her ribs and her throat went even dryer. She felt a hollow form in the pit of her stomach and a chill ran up and down her spine making it tingle. There was no need for anyone to tell her who the figure might be. It was El Español!

Slowly, and with a strange animal grace, the figure stalked down the gangway, placing each foot with care. Miranda could feel the indiscernible orbs containing his eyes bore into her without blinking. It was as if the gaze was something tangible, carrying with it a sharpness that cut into her flesh like a knife. Unable to bear its intensity, she lowered her eyes. At the last plank but one, he stopped. Dutifully, the men on the jetty sprang aside to make way for him to step down. But he remained standing where he was and his eyes did not leave hers for an instant.

Then he spoke. 'No. I do not wage war against petticoats. If I did, you would not be standing where you are.' His voice was very quiet and in it there was no hint of harshness. Miranda felt the heat rise from her neck and suffuse her face. She bit her lip, unable to raise her eyes to meet his. Had it not been for Dan's reassuring presence behind her, her knees would have turned to water and she would have stumbled. He spoke again, and this time the deep voice was a little sharper. 'For a woman as young as you, you have a tongue that is singularly unbridled.'

She swallowed hard, and forced herself to look at him. His eyes, impaling her from under thick eyebrows, were the blackest she had ever seen. But, to her surprise, they were not angry. Like his voice, they were quiet and unfathomable.

'It is unbridled,' she said, emboldened by his lack of anger, 'because our ship faces death and you hold our lives in your hand. It is a responsibility that no man is big enough to hold. It belongs to God alone.'

His eyes narrowed, but the expression on his face did not change. 'You came through the passage alone?'

She shook her head. 'Not alone. With our chief harpooner, Dan Haggerty.' She half-turned to identify him. Dan bowed.

The Spaniard barely looked at him, his eyes still fixed on her face. 'You were sent by your father to try to persuade me to change my mind?' he asked, and for the first time a note of mockery crept into the toneless voice.

'No,' she said sharply. 'My father has no idea that I have come. Had he known, he would have forbidden it.'

'But you felt that, as a woman, you would succeed in softening my heart with your helplessness and make me reverse my decision?'

'No,' she lied, and her head jerked up proudly. 'That would have been a futile hope, for it is rumoured that El Español has no heart!'

She had the satisfaction of noticing a very slight tightening of the hard, square jaw. 'Then why have you come at such peril to yourself?' The voice was becoming sharper.

'I came, out of curiosity,' she retorted with a daring that astonished even herself. 'Every man has the right to see the face of his executioner before he dies!'

The jawline tightened further, and this time a glint appeared somewhere in the depths of his bottomless black eyes. 'And now that you have seen it, will it make death easier for you?'

'No. Death is never easy. But since you have also seen ours, it may make life a little more difficult for *you*!' She felt sick with a sense of failure. It hardly mattered what she said now.

For a moment the cavernous eyes iced over and the air around them became cold. She shivered. Nobody moved: everyone waited with bated breath for all hell to break loose at this ultimate in impertinence. Behind her, Miranda felt Dan quiver as he put a hand fearfully on her arm.

But then, quite unexpectedly, the ice thawed. To everyone's amazement, El Español threw back his head and laughed. Miranda's eyes dilated and her mouth fell open with surprise.

'By heaven!' he exclaimed, still laughing. 'It is obviously true what they say—A fool will tread where angels dare not!'

'You find me a fool?' she asked, stung.

The laughter died out of his eyes and they again became sombre. 'No,' he said coldly. 'I find you very impudent.'

'It is easy to be impudent when one is faced with death,' she said, unable to keep the despondency out of her voice. 'One has nothing more to lose.'

For a long moment he remained silent, surveying her through half-closed eyes. Then he said very quietly, 'Very well. You may bring your ship in for repairs.'

He turned and said something in Spanish to the men on the jetty. Instantly they sprang to attention, barking out orders in a language that she did not understand. In any case, she hardly listened, paralysed into rigid immobility by the suddenness of the decision. She stared at him, stunned. He was speaking again, and she forced herself to listen, trying to still her whirling head.

'My conditions for the entry of your ship are many. There will be no bargaining.' Dumbly, she nodded. 'They will be given to your father by my men. But there is one condition that you have a right to know.'

She swallowed, her head still befuddled. 'Y-yes?'

'While your ship is under repairs in Amarillo, you yourself will remain in our custody as a hostage.'

Abruptly he turned on his heel and walked rapidly up the gangway. He did not look back.

CHAPTER THREE

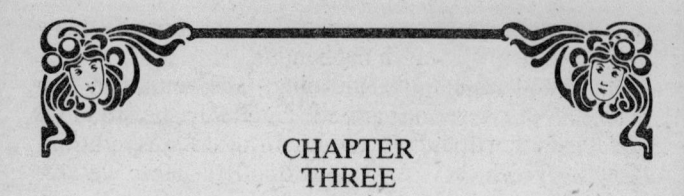

'A HOSTAGE?' Captain Chiltern's face was as black as thunder. 'You have agreed to become his hostage?'

Miranda sighed. 'You have to agree to all his conditions, Papa,' she explained patiently for the tenth time, 'and this is one of them.' His anger at her bold escapade was still fearsome.

'It is monstrous, unthinkable!' the Captain roared. 'I will not permit it!'

'It is neither monstrous nor unthinkable,' Miranda replied warmly, 'and I have already agreed to it.'

'It is not for you to agree or disagree,' Peregrine raged, thumping the table with his fist. 'And, apart from your father, *I* will not permit it!'

'You have no choice,' snapped Miranda, tired at the argument that had been going round in increasingly angry circles ever since Dan and she had returned to the ship. They had been escorted back by El Español's men in one of their own sturdy longboats. The men were now gathered on deck awaiting the Captain's decision as to the conditions imposed, which were many. 'Neither you nor Papa has the right to condemn us all to death—which is what you want to do—because of this one absurd, totally inconsequential, condition!'

Captain Chiltern slumped back in his chair dejectedly, his anger evaporating in the face of this indisputable truth. But Peregrine continued to pace the floor like an infuriated tiger, his fists clenched into tight balls. 'The man is a renegade and a scoundrel,' he fumed. 'How can you trust yourself in his hands?'

'I trusted myself this morning,' she reminded him acidly, 'and I was not harmed.' Suddenly she stood up and threw her hands in the air in utter exasperation. 'Oh, for goodness' sake,' she exploded. 'Here we are, on the threshold of death with our ship about to collapse, and all you can think about is my honour! Well, I can assure you my honour is not in the slightest danger. I shall keep Aunt Zoe with me and see to her treatment under their doctor's supervision. El Español has no interest whatever in laying a finger on me.'

Peregrine flushed, and Captain Chiltern buried his head in his hands and groaned. 'I do not trust him,' muttered Peregrine darkly, but it was obvious that the force was going out of his argument.

'Well, I do,' Miranda flung back defiantly. 'And since it is I he has demanded as a hostage, I have the right to make the decision. Papa,' she turned to her father, 'please let us not delay any more. Inform the men that you accept the conditions. *All* of them. I shall go and tell Aunt Zoe.' She flounced out.

The conditions laid down by El Español were stringent but, Miranda felt secretly, quite rational. Such precautions were only to be expected from a man so fiercely protective of his privacy. Indeed, she had been surprised that they had not been even lengthier and more severe. The *Amiable Lady* would be piloted through the passage by El Español's men, who were well used to taking the *Condor* in and out. Surprisingly, permission to repair the ship in the outside lagoon had not been granted; instead, the work would be done in the harbour under strict security. The crew of the *Amiable Lady* would be placed under semi-arrest, allowed only to their ship and back to their quarters. Under no circumstances were they to indulge in conversations with the islanders. Any man seen approaching any woman on the island would be summarily executed. El Español's men would re-check the dismantling of all cannon to ensure that none remained in firing order on board the whaler. Every firearm of any description would be confiscated from the crew and officers. These might or might not be returned after the repairs had been completed. It was a matter to be decided later. Any man caught wandering in a prohibited area would be shot. The whole of the island was to be out of bounds to the men of the *Amiable Lady,* except that part of the harbour where their ship was moored and the path leading from their quarters to it.

The last condition was the one over which tempers had frayed—that of keeping Miranda as a hostage during the period of repairs. The only two people on the *Amiable Lady* unworried by it were Miranda and Dan.

'He will not harm a single hair of your head,' said Dan jubilantly, but well out of earshot of his Captain, 'and Miss Zoe will be well looked after.'

'Yes, I know that,' said Miranda. She thought for a moment, then added, 'He is a strange man, is he not?'

'Ay, that he is. Do you realise, lass,' he said in hushed tones, 'that we two are the first white people to have gazed upon his face in this last decade?'

'I wonder why he decided to appear so suddenly before us?'

Dan's eyes twinkled. 'Like you said, lass, women have a way with them that men don't.'

Miranda coloured, and laughed to conceal her embarrassment. 'Oh, I don't think it had anything to do with that! I think he merely . . .' she paused and pondered, ' . . . he merely wanted to . . . *defend* himself in some strange way. Obviously, something I said struck a tender chord in the man . . .'

'Tender chord?' Dan chuckled. 'Why, you even denied him the possession of a heart!'

'I was very angry,' Miranda said with a toss of her head. 'But I am glad that I was wrong.'

'Ay, lass,' agreed Dan fervently, 'so am I, so am I! That shipyard of his,' his eyes shone in anticipation, 'is said to be the finest in the Pacific outside Honolulu, and his engineers are the best. Our little old lady will be more amiable than ever before by the time his men are through with her!'

By late afternoon the ship had been safely moored within the Amarillo harbour, and those of the crew not to remain on board comfortably housed in their quarters, a row of neatly whitewashed barracks not far from the waterfront. The damage to the ship, now considerable with the gaping hole even wider, had been inspected and the repairs would start in the morning.

As soon as the *Amiable Lady* had docked, a Spanish doctor called Fernando Gómez had been escorted aboard. His examination of Aunt Zoe was long and thorough. The disease he diagnosed was as Miranda had feared—malaria.

Her face went pale. 'But there is no cure for malaria . . .'

He smiled. 'There is no cure for malaria in your world. In the south seas and in the southern portion of America and, I hear, in some parts of south-east Asia, a remedy does exist.' Miranda's eyes sparkled with hope. 'It is the bark of a tree, known as cinchona, discovered in South America nearly two centuries ago and introduced into Europe, but sparingly. It is to be powdered and taken with water. In a day or so the fever will subside, I assure you, and she will regain her strength in no time after that.'

Miranda felt tears of gratitude welling up in her eyes.

'If she does, Dr Gómez,' she said feelingly, 'we shall be eternally grateful to you.'

'Not to me,' said the doctor mildly. 'I am acting under orders from El Español.'

It was dark by the time the doctor left, having presented Miranda with packets of the precious powder and precise instructions as to how each dose was to be given. Later, she fed her aunt a bowl of chicken broth and then a strong sleeping-draught, as the doctor had advised. Her father and most of the crew had already been taken off the ship and into their temporary quarters. The few who remained on the ship, under guard, were already asleep, worn out by the labours of the momentous day. Left alone, Miranda collapsed on to her bunk, exhausted. She closed her eyes and, for the first time since very early that morning, allowed her thoughts to run free. Unexpectedly, no move had been made so far to enforce the last condition laid down. Was she to remain a hostage on the ship? If not, where? Her father and Peregrine were deeply concerned as to her future whereabouts as a hostage, but their enquiries had elicited the curt reply, 'You will be told in good time.' Of El Español himself there was no sign.

El Español!

All her thoughts inevitably centred on the one man who was, at the moment, the pivotal point of their lives. That she had actually stood face to face with this man, who had become a legend in the Pacific, was something she still found difficult to believe. What did he look like? Closing her eyes, Miranda tried to conjure up a vision of his face—and failed. That morning, her mind had been far too befuddled, too confused, to be able to observe his features well. All she could remember was an extraordinarily tall figure, with heavy, broad shoulders tapering into a narrow waist, and unusually long legs. There was also a lingering impression of a darkly bronzed face weatherbeaten by a hundred storms, a hard, square jaw and thickly luxuriant, ruffled hair. And then the eyes. It was the eyes that she remembered most of all. They were eyes that forced attention, locking themselves with hers in a gaze that was riveting, a gaze that travelled deep into the soul. She could imagine men trembling before their relentless attack but, very surprisingly indeed, she herself felt no fear of them. As she reconstructed them in her memory, she recalled something she had noticed in them, but so fleetingly that she had forgotten. As she remembered what it was, she sat up with a jolt. It was a deep, disturbing, touch of sadness.

With a sense of shock she lay back again, pondering this startling discovery. *He has been hurt by our world . . .* Dan's words came back to her. Who could have dared to hurt so powerful a man as El Español? How? When and why? A thousand questions tumbled through Miranda's mind, but they had no answer. To the world at large, the figure of El Español remained shrouded in mystery. But it was a mystery that she now longed to explore. Would she ever see him again? She did not know. But what she did know, all of a sudden, was that never to see him again was a prospect that was somehow disappointing.

She was roused out of a sound, peaceful sleep very early the next morning by her aunt's voice calling out to her. She sprang out of bed in alarm and felt her forehead. It was still warm, but the fever seemed definitely to have subsided.

'Thank God,' she breathed, kissing her aunt on the cheek. 'You are in good hands now, Aunt Zoe. They will have you well in no time.'

Her aunt frowned and pursed her lips. 'And about time too!' she muttered crossly. 'I have been lying here for days with no one telling me anything about what is going on. Who was that man who came last night?'

'Dr Gómez. It is his medicine that has made you feel better.'

'I do not feel better at all,' said her aunt severely. 'My head still has a hundred hammers inside it!'

Miranda laughed, delighted to hear the familiar exasperation again. 'When Zoe does not give you a good argument,' her father always said, 'then you know she is not well.' There was no doubt about it now. Aunt Zoe was definitely getting well, judging by the sharpness of her tones.

'Where are we and why have we stopped?' she asked querulously. 'I did not understand a word of what you jabbered on about yesterday.'

'We are in Amarillo and we have stopped for repairs,' was all Miranda decided to tell her for the moment. The rest of the story could wait until later.

'Amarillo?' her aunt exclaimed with a frown. 'Isn't that where that rascal lives? Edward was telling me something about pirates and cannon, but it all sounded like his usual nonsense to me!'

Miranda laughed. 'Yes, it is just that—nonsense. We are in safe hands and nobody is going to harm us. He will see to that.'

'Who?'

'El Español. Amarillo is his island.'

'El Español!' her aunt clucked in annoyance. 'Why he can't have a decent name like regular folk, I don't know!'

'I suppose he has,' said Miranda patiently, 'but nobody knows what it is.'

Muttering darkly, Aunt Zoe laid down again, exhausted by the effort of her discussion. 'Well, am I going to get some breakfast, or do you expect me to starve all day?'

It was as they were finishing their meal, with Aunt

Zoe devouring everything within sight, much to Miranda's joy, that there was a knock on the cabin door. A member of the crew stood there holding an enormous basket of fruit.

'One of the men from the island has just brought this,' he said, his face reflecting his bewilderment. 'He says it is for the sick lady.'

Miranda blinked her eyes and took charge of the basket laden with luscious-looking pineapples, papayas, mangoes and three different kinds of bananas. 'P-please thank him kindly,' she stammered. 'It is most thoughtful of . . . of whoever is responsible.' A warm glow bathed her face; she did not need to be told the name of the sender.

'The bearer of the basket would like to see you,' said the crewman.

'Oh.' Miranda's heart lurched. This, then, was the hour for them to be taken off the ship to goodness knew where. She felt a pang of nervousness but, smiling bravely, followed the crewman up to the deck. Waiting for her was the man she had talked to so angrily on the jetty the morning before and who had so nearly sent them packing: the man called Alvarez. With him, much to her surprise, was a plump, elderly Polynesian woman clad in a brilliant orange sarong with a red hibiscus tucked behind her ear. She smiled broadly at Miranda —quite unlike Alvarez who, obviously still very resentful of their presence, continued to glower.

'You are to come with me,' he said curtly in his thick, guttural English.

'Where am I to be taken?'

'That is no concern of yours. It is all arranged.'

'And the sick lady? I refuse to leave without her!'

'She will stay with you,' he said nastily. 'You will be looked after by Lori.' He pointed to the woman beside him. It was clear from his expression that he considered all this fuss unnecessary. If I had had my way, he seemed to say, things would have been very different indeed! Walking to the rails, he yelled out something to the people below. Within a few moments six strapping young islanders scrambled on to the deck, bearing with them a woven bamboo litter. They stopped and looked towards Alvarez for further orders. He turned to Miranda.

'You will please prepare yourself and the sick lady to leave,' he said, and went off down the gangway.

It did not take long to put together their belongings and get their trunks up on the deck. Miranda then supervised the transfer of Aunt Zoe, complaining incessantly, from the bunk to the litter, instructing the men by gestures to carry her with caution. As she turned to have a last look, Miranda's heart sank a little. She had no idea where they were going or for how long, and the little cabin had been home to them for so many months.

Boats waited to take them across the lagoon. The harbour hummed with activity and she could see some of the men from the *Amiable Lady*, including Dan, standing on the jetty. They waved to her, and she waved back, and she could see that Dan's expression was slightly troubled for her. Involuntarily, her eyes stole up towards the deck of the *Condor*. Several figures moved about, but not the one her eyes sought. Where was he, she wondered? She knew it would be useless to ask, for she would be given no answer.

An open cart and pony and several mules waited for them on the other side of the lagoon, and while Aunt Zoe was laid down in the cart with care, Lori supervised the loading of their baggage on to the mules. She seemed a bright, cheerful woman with a perpetual smile, and Miranda felt sorry that they would not be able to communicate with her, since she could speak neither English nor Spanish. As they were getting ready to leave, Miranda was delighted to see a small boat beach on the sand, containing her father and Peregrine. With them was Alvarez, his fingers settled lovingly on his musket.

Miranda flung herself into her father's arms. 'Oh, Papa, I am happy to see you!'

Captain Chiltern kissed her fondly, much relieved at finding her in such good spirits. 'And how is Zoe this morning?' he asked, taking his sister's hand in his. 'Are you well enough to give me a good argument yet? We've all been missing your very remarkable voice on deck!'

'I'll give you a better argument than you've ever had before,' she snapped. 'Loading me on to this tumbril like a bundle of hay to be fed to the cows!'

'I see you are almost back to normal,' he said, delighted. 'Well, the argument will have to wait a while until we set sail again. I don't know if . . . we will be able to see you before then.' He looked uncertainly at Alvarez, who disdained an answer and turned away.

'How long will the repairs take, Papa?'

'We do not know. The damage is being inspected now, and it appears to be extensive.'

'They insist on doing the repairs themselves,' said Peregrine with a touch of petulance. Lowering his voice so that Alvarez could not hear him, he added, 'There is something very fishy in that.'

Miranda looked at him sharply. 'It is good of them to take the trouble. Why should there be anything fishy in a generous gesture?'

Peregrine fell silent and looked at her strangely. 'This man,' he said finally and very sarcastically, 'this Spaniard, appears to have made quite an impression on you, I note.'

Miranda flushed and frowned in annoyance. 'He has made no impression on me,' she retorted, 'except of a man who has offered us his help. In your dislike for him you should not, perhaps, forget the alternative.'

Before Peregrine could reply, Alvarez sauntered up. 'It is time to go,' he said sourly. 'I can't stand about all day waiting for you. I have work to do. Here, you . . .' He pointed insolently towards Peregrine. 'You can come with us, if you like, but the Captain stays here.'

'Will I be . . . allowed to see my daughter and sister?' Edward Chiltern asked hesitantly.

Alvarez shrugged. 'It is not up to me. You'll find out sooner or later. Now come on, let's go.'

The cavalcade started up the hill. Peregrine and Miranda sat in the cart beside Aunt Zoe, while Alvarez rode alongside on his horse. Lori had perched herself on top of one of the mules that followed with their baggage.

The road was no more than a track, but it was wide and well flattened. All around them were fields of sugar-cane, with fruit trees clustered in between. The track began to climb, and they passed through a gentle valley with groups of grass huts, outside which black-haired islanders went about their daily work. There seemed to be an easy, comfortable air about the people and, as they passed, they stopped to stare and smile, exchanging comments with Lori. From what they could see, it was obvious that Amarillo was indeed blessed by Nature in every possible way. As they crested a hill, beneath them lay the azure expanse of the Pacific, winking and sparkling in the midday sun. There was a faint fragrance in the air, but Miranda could not identify it. Perhaps it came from some tropical wild flowers that she was not familiar with.

The gentle rocking of the cart had sent Aunt Zoe off to sleep, and Peregrine sat opposite Miranda, absorbed in his own thoughts.

'What are you thinking?' she asked him curiously, so serious was his expression.

For a moment he did not reply, then he laughed. 'What does anyone think of on Amarillo?' he said enigmatically. Noticing her puzzled expression, he laughed again and, with a quick glance sideways at Alvarez, lowered his voice to a whisper. '*Gold!*' There was a strange gleam in his eye that made her very uneasy.

'It is nothing to do with us,' she reminded him sharply.

'No, of course not,' he agreed quickly. 'It was just an idle thought. You can forget I ever said it.'

But Miranda continued to stare at him with some apprehension. She knew how impulsive Peregrine was on occasion—surely he was not thinking of anything stupid?

Ahead of them they could now see the tall, proud mountain they called 'El Dedo', its peak pointing upwards towards the sky, as blue as a kingfisher's wing. The track was now curving round the hill, and they had left the main road to make a turn down a narrow path just barely wide enough for the cart to pass. Around them was a beautiful forest, cool and fluttering with winged life, and the trees were festooned with lovely wild orchids such as Miranda had never seen before.

They stopped, and her eyes widened with pleasure. Before them was a small whitewashed villa perched on top of a hillock. It was built in the Spanish style with rounded archways and a flagged stone courtyard outside, in the centre of which stood a single hibiscus tree covered in red flowers. On the other side, overlooking the ocean, the house was covered with all kinds of strange tropical creepers that stood out sharply against the white walls. It was quite beautiful.

'Is this where we are to be?' Miranda asked, as Alvarez dismounted. He nodded briefly, giving instructions to the men to unload the mules. Lori slid to the ground heavily and called out something in a loud, shrill voice. Instantly two young girls came running out of the house, smiling and chattering without a pause. They stared at them all, then turned to Peregrine. They were both bare-breasted, and as fresh and innocent as the first rose of summer. Immediately, with an oath, Alvarez strode towards them, waving his hands and throwing telling glances at Peregrine. He appeared to be quite angry. The girls instantly fell silent and, looking over their shoulders towards Peregrine, slunk back into the house. Without understanding a word of what had been said, it was quite obvious what the gist of the conversation had been.

Peregrine turned a dark red, not so much with embarrassment as with anger. 'You don't have to worry about your precious women,' he snapped. 'I am not a barbarian like you—I know how to behave with them!'

'*Bastante!*' Alvarez roared, raising his musket. 'You forget you are here on sufferance, and your impudence will not be tolerated!'

Before Peregrine could unclench his balled-up fists and use them on the Spaniard, Aunt Zoe sat up in the cart abruptly. 'Can't a soul have a decent sleep on this island?' she demanded. 'What is all this infernal racket about?'

Hastily Miranda ran to her side and pacified her. 'It's all right, Aunt Zoe, it's all right. They were just . . . just having a . . . a discussion . . .' Quickly, glowering at Peregrine, she signalled to the men to unload the litter and hastily followed Lori into the house.

The villa was as lovely inside as out. It had four rooms, all opening out on to the sea on the far side, and a small but well-tended garden behind it, spilling over with flowers. The view to the ocean was uninterrupted, but on either side the garden was shaded by enormous trees full of leaf and blossom. The air around was now more strongly scented than ever. What was it, she wondered, as she surveyed her temporary home with frank pleasure. She would have to try and ask Lori about it, she decided, but first things first.

The rooms were not very large, but airy and bright and furnished with the utmost simplicity. There were colourful rugs on the stone floors, and the furniture, what little there was of it, was of unpainted wood. Miranda decided that the larger of the two bedrooms should be Aunt Zoe's and set about making the arrangements accordingly.

Sitting up in her new bed, Aunt Zoe gazed out of the large windows to the garden and the ocean beyond. It said much for the view that not even she could find a single fault to complain about. Instead, she stared for a moment in silence, for once speechless. Then she took a deep breath, and nodded. 'Yes,' she said. 'Yes. I think it will do.' And, from Aunt Zoe, Miranda knew, that was high praise indeed!

Even Peregrine could find nothing to warrant criticism. He strolled round the house looking into every nook and cranny, loath to admit just how surprised he was.

'Did you think I would be cast inside a dungeon?' Miranda could not resist asking, her eyes dancing with merriment.

'Well . . .' he admitted slowly. 'It certainly isn't what I had expected, but,' he looked at her severely, 'you be careful of all these louts hovering about. I would not trust them further than I could throw them!'

On the veranda outside, Alvarez leaned insolently against one of the arches. 'Time to go back to the harbour,' he informed Peregrine abruptly. 'I have work to do, even if you haven't.'

'Will you be able to come again?' asked Miranda anxiously, laying a hand on Peregrine's arm.

He shrugged. 'I don't know, but there will be hell to

pay if I'm not! In any case, the Captain may be allowed to visit you this evening.'

'Oh, I do hope so! Papa is so worried about me that I would like him to see just how well looked after we are. Will you tell him that we are all right?'

Peregrine nodded, then turned his eyes towards the mountain that dominated the island. For a moment he stayed silent then, with a quick smile, went nimbly down the steps.

'Get back into the cart,' ordered Alvarez.

'I think not,' retorted Peregrine lightly. 'I think I shall walk down.' He strode out purposefully towards the forest track. With an oath, Alvarez mounted his horse and set off after him. Miranda listened anxiously to see if there would be any sounds of a fight, but there was none. Alvarez, it seemed, had allowed Peregrine to have his way this time.

There was much to be done around the house, and it took Miranda all the afternoon to get properly settled in. As soon as Peregrine had left, the two young girls had reappeared and there was great activity in the kitchen where a meal was being prepared for them. They ate outside in the garden because Aunt Zoe insisted she was well enough to do so, and indeed she had revived marvellously. The enormous basket of fruit that had been sent to them by El Español—who else? —was already much diminished, but Miranda knew that on this lush island there was more where that had come from. Indeed, in their own garden, banana and papaya trees grew, and not far from the villa she had noticed a field of pineapples ripening golden yellow in the sun.

Sitting in the garden after having eaten well, Miranda's thoughts again turned towards the inevitable. Where, in all this, was El Español? Did he rule his island from afar or did he mingle freely with the people?

Would he come to see them, at least to inquire after their well-being? Her pulse quickened at the prospect of meeting him again. There was something about him that fascinated her alarmingly. She had never met any man like him. Even from a distance, invisible to her eyes, he seemed to be weaving some strange spell around her. She could not tolerate the thought that she might not see him again, that the ship would be repaired before long and they would sail away, never to return —and that she would have no opportunity to discover what lay behind the shroud that hid El Español from the world's eyes.

It was as dusk was falling and the western sky was still up in flames that Lori rushed out into the garden and said with much excitement, 'Malamma . . . *Malamma* . . . !'

Miranda looked at her, puzzled. 'Malamma?'

But before Lori could make any further comment, the answer appeared in person. Miranda could not help the inadvertent gasp that came to her throat. Confronting her was, perhaps, the most beautiful woman she had ever seen. She was Polynesian, tall for an islander, and very slim. Indeed her body seemed to float, rather than walk, as she strolled gracefully down towards her. The usual sarong covered her body but, even with the garment, Miranda could see just how perfectly formed her figure was. The large, pointed breasts were firm underneath the cloth, the hips full and seductive. She had curiously light hazel eyes fringed with long black lashes that curled upwards in sensual sweeps. Her complexion was fairer than that of the other islanders Miranda had seen, and it glowed as if lit from within. Her mouth was provocative and her lips wet and a shade of delicate pink.

For a moment Miranda could do nothing but stare, taken by surprise at this unexpected apparition of loveliness. The girl tossed her head slightly and brushed back her glossy waist-length hair.

'El Español wishes to know if you are comfortable. He inquires after the condition of the sick lady.' Even more surprising, she spoke in English in a husky voice.

Miranda recovered from her shock, and smiled. 'I . . . Yes, we are both very comfortable, thank you. My aunt is much better, thanks to the ministrations of Dr Gómez.'

The girl looked around silently, then made a signal with her hand to the two young girls standing to one side, watching her with obvious awe. Immediately they ran inside. Miranda observed the visitor, her face flushed with sudden pleasure that he had remembered them. The girls returned bearing two green coconuts on a woven grass platter, and offered them to their visitor. She took one, then motioned the other towards Miranda. Taking the coconut to her lips, she drank deeply, then, with a casual gesture, tossed the empty shell over the side of the hill. Slowly, Miranda took the other coconut from the platter and took a sip. It was cool, sweet and delicious.

While she sipped, she noticed a sudden tension in the air, but she did not know why. The girl was surveying her very carefully. Then she spoke. 'Your hair is very beautiful,' she said softly, and in her hazel eyes gleamed a spark of envy.

Miranda smiled self-consciously at the unexpected compliment. 'You are . . . Malamma?'

The girl nodded briefly.

'You speak very good English,' Miranda said. 'Where did you learn?'

'In Honolulu.' The girl was obviously pleased at the remark.

Miranda stared in surprise. 'You are Hawaiian?'

'Yes.' Her head rose high with pride and her eyes

shone with a light of supreme arrogance. 'I was brought to Amarillo by El Español.'

As the significance of the words sank in, Miranda felt herself go a little cold. This was El Español's woman! Of course—that accounted for the arrogance of her bearing, and the awe with which the Polynesian women had received her. Naturally, as the mistress of El Español, she would command much respect. Undoubtedly it was a position which all the young girls of Amarillo must regard with admiration and envy. Unaccountably, Miranda's heart filled with disappointment, though why, she could not say. Abruptly she turned and walked towards the edge of the garden, keeping her back towards Malamma.

She had read enough about the south sea islands to know that among the islanders prevailed a system of free love. They looked upon physical love, not as a sin in the eyes of God, but as a blessing from heaven to be enjoyed to the full without guilt or censure. El Español was undoubtedly a full-blooded man, aggressively virile, with all the natural appetites of a normal male. The temptations offered by the luscious women of the south seas, uninhibited, gloriously passionate and willing, were such that few white men had been able to resist them. Why should El Español, with his fiery temperament, be any different?

Malamma was still talking to Lori and the young girls, giving orders with imperious gestures of her long, tapering hands. She walked up to where Miranda stood. 'El Español would like to be informed if there is anything you lack,' she said dispassionately making it only too clear that this was not a concern that she shared. 'Dr Gómez will visit the sick lady again later this evening.'

Miranda forced herself to smile. 'Please thank him for . . . for everything he is doing for us,' she said with an effort. 'We are very grateful.'

The girl looked at her shrewdly through half-closed eyes. 'It is the first time in years that he has allowed an alien ship into Amarillo,' she said softly. 'Everyone on the island is curious to know why.'

Under her incisive gaze, Miranda suddenly felt hot. It was obvious that there was much more to the remark than she could understand. Nevertheless, she replied evenly, 'Perhaps it is because it is not easy to condemn a shipload of innocent, harmless people to death—and, somewhere within him, El Español still has a breath of compassion for humanity.'

The girl laughed, an unexpectedly harsh sound. 'You know nothing about El Español,' she said fiercely. *'Nothing!'* Without another word, she turned on her bare heel and walked out of the garden, her head held arrogantly high. Miranda stood stock still, gazing sightlessly after the vanishing figure. It was not a visit that she had enjoyed. Indeed, it had left her cold and unaccountably dismal.

By the time Dr Gómez called, bright and cheerful, Miranda had recovered her composure sufficiently to be able to converse with him quite normally. He examined the patient, pronounced himself satisfied with the progress, exchanged banter with Aunt Zoe and, after having given instructions to the three women about the diet required for the sick lady, left. It was as Miranda was preparing for bed and wondering if her father would be allowed to visit, that Captain Chiltern suddenly arrived.

Miranda was delighted, and even her aunt decided to commemorate the occasion by smiling constantly. Proudly, Miranda showed him round the house and wondered why the two young girls were not in evidence. But Captain Chiltern only smiled.

'I am not surprised at the attitude they have taken,' he said, referring to El Español's men. 'There has been much abuse of innocent island women at the hands of white sailors, and I am in favour of keeping temptation out of everyone's way.'

'That was not how Peregrine looked upon the matter,' Miranda explained to him, relating the events of the previous day.

Captain Chiltern frowned. 'I am worried about young Peregrine,' he said slowly. 'He appears to be going out of his way to provoke these men as far as possible. He seems quite unlike himself and I fear for him.'

Wisely, Miranda refrained from informing her father about his sudden and very dangerous interest in Amarillo's gold. There was no point in adding to the Captain's troubles. Maybe Peregrine was merely indulging in idle daydreams. For an hour they sat and chatted in the garden enjoying the wonderful beauty of a Pacific sky heavy with stars and diffused with the light of a half-moon. Miranda was anxious to learn about all their experiences in the harbour.

'The repairs will start tomorrow,' her father said. 'There is no doubt that these men know what they are doing. Since they have taken over the work, it leaves my crew free to concentrate on preparing the crude oil in the barrels.'

'Are there many white men on the island?' Miranda asked.

'About twenty, I would say, although we do not know if we have seen them all.'

'And are they all Spaniards?'

'No. They seem to be a very mixed bunch—Dutch, French, German, and even two men from America.'

'Oh? And have they all been with El Español since his piracy days?'

Her father shrugged. 'We don't know. We are not allowed to converse with them about anything except matters that concern the repairs. But they appear to be decent enough.'

'And are you being well looked after? Are your quarters comfortable?'

He nodded. 'Quite. The food is good, and there seems to be plenty of it, although,' he teased, 'we are obviously not as well off as you are!'

Miranda laughed. 'There is something to be said for being a hostage then, isn't there?' she teased back. 'It is hardly as grim as you had envisaged.'

'True,' he admitted, then added worriedly, 'but you will be careful, won't you, Miranda? So far, we have landed on our feet, thanks to your courage—and I am big enough to admit that now. But there is still something to this business that I cannot understand. Why should he suddenly allow us in, the first white ship he has favoured in ten years? Peregrine feels he may even now change colour and hold the ship to ransom. It is no secret that our company is rich. Faced with the loss of so many lives and a valuable ship, our principals would probably pay up—if not happily, certainly without much argument.'

'He will not deceive us,' said Miranda, aware of the sudden sharpness in her tones. 'He is a man of his word.'

Captain Chiltern looked at her curiously, as if trying to read her thoughts. He seemed on the verge of saying something, but then changed his mind and instead rose to his feet.

'I have been allowed one hour here,' he said. 'Has Zoe gone to sleep?'

'Yes. She is still weak and can stomach no more than soft foods. Dr Gómez is pleased with her progress and is confident she will be up and about within a couple of days.'

'Good. I admit we do have much to be thankful for. So far, he has behaved like a gentleman.'

Outside the house, two armed white men waited with horses to escort the Captain back to the harbour. He smiled ruefully, noticing Miranda's anxious expression. 'We are not allowed to go anywhere on the island except under armed guard. But they are not offensive, so there is nothing to worry about. I shall see you again tomorrow, if I am permitted.' He kissed her on the cheek and mounted his horse. In the pale light of the moon, Miranda watched them until they were swallowed up by the darkness of the forest.

Slowly, she walked back through the house into the garden. In spite of her aunt's continuing progress, her father's visit and the beautiful surroundings, she felt unaccountably depressed. She could think of no reason why she should be so except perhaps—Malamma. In her mind she conjured up again and again a vision of that lovely, sensual face and the seductive figure. In her imagination she saw those sinuous arms wound around his neck, those hungry lips showering kisses upon his face. And she saw him responding, his lithe, taut body welded with hers as he caressed her with those big brown hands.

It was a vision that appeared to create havoc inside her and send her stomach churning. She shook herself angrily, annoyed at the unacceptable fantasies of her mind. This man, whose face even she could not remember, was beginning to haunt her thoughts more than she was willing to admit. She was becoming increasingly fascinated by him. It was a situation that was fraught with dangers.

But, when she finally slept, there was no respite from him even in her dreams. He continued to dominate her slumber with as much tenacity as he did her every waking moment.

CHAPTER FOUR

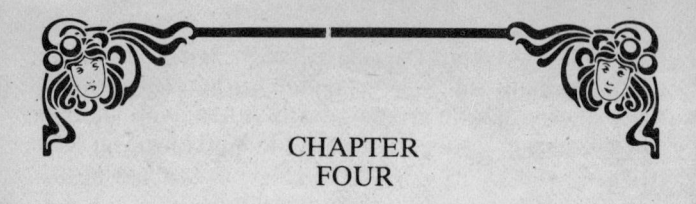

WITHIN THE next few days, their lives settled down into a pleasant and comfortable routine. Aunt Zoe was now fit enough to walk about and spent long hours in the garden overlooking the Pacific, reading a book, or dozing or involved in her tapestry work. There was no doubt that she was recovering her strength rapidly, encouraged by the nourishing and succulent meals that Lori was cooking for them. The food, lightly spiced and flavoured with aromatic herbs and spices, consisted mostly of pork, chicken, fish and cereals, with copious quantities of fresh fruit and vegetables.

'Why is he doing all this for us?' she asked, one day. 'They say he is a heartless man.'

'Perhaps they are mistaken,' Miranda said lightly.

'Edward said that he does not allow ships to enter Amarillo. Why, then, has he allowed ours?'

Miranda bit her lip. It was clearly time for Aunt Zoe to know the whole story, and she related it in detail. When she had finished, she sat back and waited apprehensively for her aunt's caustic comments. But when her aunt did, finally, speak, it was to ask a very strange question and her eyes surveyed her shrewdly. 'Tell me about this man,' she ordered, watching her closely. 'What is he like? Young?'

Miranda's eyes were cool. 'I am not sure. I was not in a mood to observe details, as you can well imagine.'

'Hmph!' her aunt grunted. 'So we are hostages, are we?'

'So I believe.'

'Well,' said Aunt Zoe unexpectedly, 'I cannot see the harm in that—unless he has some further design up his sleeve of which we are not aware.' Then, with another rapid change of subject, she asked, 'And have you seen this Spaniard since?'

'No.'

'Good!' remarked her aunt grimly. 'Nor should you. I would not approve of you meeting him again, and certainly not alone.'

Miranda laughed at the ferocity in her aunt's voice. 'You don't need to worry, Aunt Zoe,' she said dolefully, 'He does not like to meet strangers.' If her aunt noticed the note of dismay in her niece's voice, she did not remark on it, but her thoughts were troubled.

Miranda was spending many hours filling her diary. She had also got into the habit of making sketches of the many new things she saw, and her drawing-book bulged with pictures of flora and fauna. She had sketched Lori and the two girls and was longing for the chance to record some of the handsome young Polynesian men she had seen briefly on their way to the villa. Now, with plenty of time available, she began to go for long walks through the lush forests surrounding the house. Dr Gómez, who had already called twice, helped her to name some of the flowers she had sketched and was a fount of knowledge about the island. Her father had not called since that first evening, and neither had Peregrine. Miranda worried about Peregrine incessantly, wondering where his thoughts lay at present. Were they still with the gold? It was very disquieting to think that they might be, and there was no way in which she could contact him and find out.

There were no further visits from Malamma, for which Miranda was grateful. She did not like the woman: there was something about her that was sly and unpleasant. Neither had there been any more messages from El Español. It was obvious that he had no intention of furthering their meagre acquaintance, such as it had been. It was a thought that depressed her terribly, for the strange, shadowy man continued to haunt her persistently.

And then, one day, she saw him again!

Wandering through the marvellously tranquil forest one morning, she came upon a low valley in the middle of which, in the far distance, she noticed a movement and a splash of colour. Of the two figures on horseback, she recognised one, and her heart flew into her mouth. It was he! He wore a yellow shirt and the customary black trousers and he sat on his horse gazing out over the rolling slopes before him. The other man, obviously an islander, Miranda did not recognise. Her eyes remained focused on the figure in yellow and black.

He sat very tall in his saddle and held his back rigid and straight. Her heart was thudding madly against her ribs as she observed every detail of the figure—the arrogant profile, the thick tangle of black hair blowing wildly in the wind, the firm broadness of his shoulders. He pointed to something in the distance and lowered his head to talk to his companion. For a moment they remained engaged in discussion. His face, at this distance, was not at all clear, but there was something about his bearing that she could not resist. She hastily pulled out her sketch-pad and sat down to depict the scene as rapidly as she could. She was a skilled artist, and with a few swift strokes she managed to bring out the striking power of his personality, which was evident even at this distance.

All of a sudden he turned his head and, for a moment or two, appeared to be looking straight at her. She shrank within the trees instinctively, although she knew not why. His head remained motionless for a while;

then it turned away. She saw the quick movement of his legs as he dug his spurs into his horse and galloped away. Until he disappeared from her sight behind a clump of trees, she could not tear her eyes away. And when he had vanished, she felt that she was trembling. Slowly she sank on to a fallen tree-trunk and clasped her shaking hands together in an effort to still them. What was it about this man that disturbed her so much? Even at such a distance she could feel the irresistible magnetism of his personality—and she could not even remember his face!

It was not until the afternoon, when they had finished luncheon and her aunt had retired for her siesta, that Miranda opened her sketchbook again. She stared at the drawing she had made that morning and decided to try to fill in the face from memory. Putting her materials and her diary into her basket, she walked back through the forest, looking for a pleasant place to settle in. Below the path that she followed was a grassy shelf, strewn with boulders, which overlooked the ocean. It was a wonderful, balmy afternoon and the shade of the surrounding trees provided shelter from the sun. She proceeded to lay out her pencils and other materials on one of the boulders, making herself as comfortable as she could.

Miranda studied her sketch again, and set to work filling in the outlines of the figure and the contours of the splendid horse on which he sat. She worked with concentration, letting her thoughts wander into vague but delightful fantasies. With fine and strong strokes she drew in his thick, unruly hair, and was well pleased with the result. But, much to her irritation, she could conjure up no memory of his face, feature by feature. It was amazing, she thought to herself in frustration, how she could stand before a man for so long and yet be unable to recall what he looked like. Indeed, it was absurd! Determinedly, she closed her eyes tight and forced herself into even deeper concentration.

Suddenly she had the strange and alarming sensation that she was being watched very closely. With a start she looked around, but she seemed to be alone. Just as she was about to close her eyes again in renewed concentration, an arm snaked down over her shoulder and picked up the sketchbook. With a tiny scream of fear, she scrambled to her feet, clutching her throat with a hand.

Behind her, quietly studying the book, was El Español!

For an eternity she stared at him, motionless. He seemed unaware of her, his eyes glued on the drawing, with his forehead creased in a frown. Miranda remained transfixed, careful not even to breathe in case he vanished. She studied his features apprehensively, but absorbed nothing, her heart fluttering and her hands cold.

She thought he would never look up, but when he did his eyes were bland. 'Why have you left out the face?'

She swallowed hard and willed herself to look at him. With a shock she remembered just how black his eyes were. He awaited her answer, the sketchbook still in his hand.

'I could not remember it,' she said, her voice holding only the shadow of a tremor. How foolish she sounded!

He raised an eyebrow, taken back by her reply. 'Indeed!' He replaced the book on the boulder casually and allowed himself the faint apology of a smile. 'I admit it may not be a face that could launch a thousand ships, but I had not realised that it was so eminently forgettable!' He walked to the end of the shelf and stood watching the sea below.

Miranda's pallor deepened as she sat down again on

the boulder, and she forced a tiny laugh to cover her confusion at being so suddenly confronted by him. How had he arrived so unexpectedly? Was this his private preserve she was poaching on? 'It is sometimes difficult to recall a face in retrospect, feature by feature,' she said, anxious to make some polite explanation, 'and I was not in my full senses that . . . that morning . . .'

He turned round quickly. 'Weren't you?' There was no smile on his face. 'I would have thought the contrary. There was not a single trick you seemed to miss.' The voice was very dry.

She looked at him, frowning. 'You believe I used trickery?' Her eyes locked with his and seemed engulfed in his blackness.

'No,' he said coldly. 'Trickery is not something I am usually susceptible to—especially from women.'

She flushed at the contempt in his voice. 'But you regret having changed your decision . . .' The dismay in her voice was audible.

'I do not believe in regrets,' he said arrogantly. 'At least . . . not yet.' He paced up and down the shelf, looking down at the grass. 'It was a change that surprised me, perhaps, even more than it did you!' He laughed under his breath, but it was a sound without humour. In fact, he looked annoyed.

She breathed in deeply. 'Then why did you make it?' she asked, wondering if she was going too far with this overwhelming, unpredictable man.

'I don't think the reason need concern you,' he said sharply. 'Just be thankful that I did.' He dismissed the matter, and asked suddenly, 'Fernando tells me that your aunt is better?'

'Yes,' said Miranda feelingly, 'she is. We are indeed grateful to you for . . . for . . .' She fumbled in confusion.

He cut her off with an impatient gesture. 'Do you

have everything you need at the villa? I am informed tha you are well settled.'

Who by, she wondered briefly—Malamma? 'Yes, thank you.' The image of Malamma's beautiful face produced in her a flash of perversity. 'Do you always treat your . . . hostages as well as this?'

His eyes narrowed. 'No, not always. Only when they are as impertinent as you are.'

She coloured uncomfortably. 'I did not intend to be . . .'

'Didn't you?'

She looked at him defiantly. 'We were desperate . . .'

'Indeed, you must have been,' he retorted drily. 'I cannot imagine a tongue as incisive as yours under other circumstances.' The traces of annoyance in his voice were more pronounced. He made as if to leave. Quickly, before her courage failed her, she asked breathlessly, loath to see him go, 'Would you allow me now to fill in the blank face?'

She hung in suspense for his answer. It was a long moment in coming. 'Why?'

'Only . . . only as a remembrance . . .' She bit her lip and stopped.

'Of an . . . executioner?' he asked crisply, his eyes blacker than ever.

'No,' she cried. 'As a . . . a saviour!'

Again a shadow of a smile flickered across his face. 'And, without the picture, are you likely to forget me?'

A strange emotion surged through her as she looked at him without flinching. 'No,' she breathed, 'I shall not forget you . . .'

For an instant he seemed about to refuse. Then, wordlessly, he walked back and without hurry settled himself on the grass with his long legs stretched out before him. He leaned back against the boulder and crossed his arms on his chest. For the first time there was an expression of some amusement on his granite face.

It was an action of tacit approval and, hastily, before he changed his mercurial mind again, Miranda turned to a fresh sheet of paper and picked up a pencil. A silence fell between them, but it was not a silence of peacefulness. Even when he sat still, there seemed to be a restlessness within him, an inner fire, that exuded a tension that was disturbing. Mercifully, he no longer looked at her and his eyes stared into the far distance. For this Miranda was grateful; pierced by those disquieting eyes, she would not have been able to make a single stroke. As it was, her heart raced madly at his uncomfortable nearness and it was all she could do to stop her hands from shaking and ruining the picture.

As she drew his face, she noticed now all the fine details she had missed earlier. He wore his hair long, and part of it curled over the nape of his neck. The nose was sharp and aquiline, and the mouth, set and unbending, showed full lips that held a latent sensuality. She thought suddenly of Malamma, but cast out the annoying vision immediately. It was the here and the now that was important . . .

The soft scratchings of her pencil halted. He still did not stir, and his eyes were closed. 'Why have you stopped?' he asked.

'Because I cannot see your eyes,' she reminded him hesitantly.

'Oh.' He opened them and changed his position slightly to suit her purpose better. 'I wonder, sometimes,' he asked with faint irritation, 'why it is that I am not able to refuse any of your preposterous requests?'

She did not look at him, but her heart somersaulted rapidly. 'Perhaps,' she said lightly, again busying herself with her sketch, 'because they are not so preposterous after all!'

'And why is it,' he asked with a definite frown, 'that you must have the last word on everything?'

For a moment she wondered if she should let that go unanswered, then decided she could not allow it to pass without retaliation. 'Because it is one of the many curses of our sex,' she said smiling. 'I'm told it started with the apple in the garden of Eden.'

The corners of his mouth suddenly relaxed and he smiled. It was a smile of such genuine amusement that it seemed to light up his entire face. 'You have a way with words that is quite . . . disconcerting.'

'I cannot imagine,' she ventured coolly without taking her eyes off the paper, 'that anything could disconcert El Español!'

'Well, *you* do,' he said calmly, but there was no harshness in his voice.

Her heart skipped several beats. 'Why?' She still did not lift her eyes, but she knew that, suddenly, her face glowed and there was a warmth pervading her body that was unbearably satisfying.

He did not answer her question, but countered with another. 'What is your name?'

'Miranda.' She was surprised that he should want to know, and the warmth became more pronounced.

His eyes widened fractionally. 'Miranda!' he exclaimed. Then, for the first time, he laughed. 'I might have guessed it. "The mistress which I serve quickens what's dead and makes my labours pleasures."' He said it almost under his breath, and laughed again at her look of bewilderment. 'Ferdinand about Miranda in *The Tempest*.'

'You read Shakespeare?' she asked, astonished, her pencil poised in mid-air.

'Why—is it forbidden?'

She was covered in confusion. 'No, I . . . I didn't mean . . . I meant . . . you hardly seem the kind of man who . . .' She stopped, appalled at how clumsy she sounded.

'I don't spend *all* my time pillaging,' he remarked very caustically. 'There is some left for reading now and then. What do you know about the kind of man I am?' The voice was again frigid.

'A man everybody . . . fears,' she dared.

The line of his jaw tightened. 'But *you* obviously don't!'

She willed herself to keep her eyes unblinking and her face calm as she felt his overwhelming power reach out to her. 'No,' she said quietly, 'I do not fear you.'

The answer did not please him at all. 'Why not?' he asked with biting sarcasm. 'Since I am a man of such monstrous reputation?'

'Reputations are often removed from the truth.'

'And you think that mine is?' She could see that he was now getting angry. 'Why?'

She filled her lungs with a very deep breath. 'Because that morning . . .' she gave him a quick glance, but his face was impassive. Only the eyes swirled dangerously, black and deep. 'That morning I saw something in your eyes that I cannot forget. It is the only thing I remembered about your face . . .'

Instantly the shutters descended, and his eyes became remote and secret again. 'And that is?' What was it she heard in his voice—a hint of alarm?

Without a word she handed him the completed sketch. He took it and stared at it for a while, his face darkening. Then, abruptly, he rose and brushed the stray blades of grass and dead leaves off his black trousers. He towered above her, glowering angrily.

'You are more impertinent than I had thought,' he said acidly. He picked up her book and, very deliberately, ripped out the sketch. Then, without looking at her, he tore the sheet into tiny fragments and tossed them over the side. He stood with his back towards her and watched the scraps float and swirl on the air until they disappeared from view. Then he turned and subjected her to a stare that sent a ripple of icy chills up and down her spine. His anger was cold, but it was monumental. Wordlessly, with his usual leonine grace, he leaped on to the path that led to the forest. Miranda watched him in dismay, filled with biting remorse. She had angered him, and now he was going away! Perhaps she would not see him again.

'Wait . . .'

He stopped abruptly and glanced back. 'Yes?'

'There is something I want of you,' she asked, the words tumbling out breathlessly.

'*Another* preposterous request?' he asked in exasperated astonishment.

'Your island is very beautiful,' she said quickly. 'I would like your permission to see it more thoroughly.'

A look of surprise came over his face. Then he pursed his lips. 'With or without my permission you seem to be doing very well in your wanderings!'

'Had you not wanted me to, you would have posted guards at our gate. There is none.'

'There are not many places you can escape to without being found within the hour,' he assured her.

'In that case,' she said boldly, 'you will not object to my request. I would like a horse. I shall not go down to the harbour, or to any other place you specify, and willingly accept a guard to accompany me.'

As he considered the matter, she was certain he would refuse, so unrelenting were the lines of his mouth. Then his head nodded once, briefly.

'Very well. You shall have it.' He was gone.

Miranda stared after him for a while, and then, with a hefty sigh, she sank back on the boulder. The strange encounter, so unexpected but so exhilarating, had left her weak and quivering like a leaf. Inside her heart, something stirred and began to sing softly. She closed her eyes and immediately his face sprang into clear focus, every detail bold and memorable. She saw again the sweep of the high forehead upon which stray locks occasionally ventured; the fringe of dark lashes around those incredibly forceful eyes; the slight tilt of the mouth as he sat in abstract thought; and that slow, wondrous smile that had lighted up his face beyond recognition.

The quotation from Shakespeare came back to her, and a warm glow bathed her cheeks—'*The mistress which I serve quickens what's dead and makes my labours pleasures* . . . ' What was it that was dead inside him—and what had she quickened? He was not completely uncaring of her, then; he had thought of her on occasion. It was a realisation that filled her with such unreasoning happiness that she could hardly keep from smiling.

She would draw the face again, sorry now that she had shown him the sketch at all. And she was certain she would be able to do it from memory, so firmly was his face etched in her mind this time. How old was he? She had no way of telling, even now. He seemed to carry on his shoulders a thousand years, yet his tall, muscular body was lithe and firm. He must be young, she concluded, perhaps in his early thirties.

Her mind turned again to the sketch, and she knew exactly what it was that had incensed him so much. The face that she had drawn was that of a man deeply troubled. The skill of her fingers had not betrayed her intention. She had portrayed him not as he appeared to others, and certainly not as he wished to appear to himself. She had shown him as she saw him—a man with grief in his heart. It was not an image that gave him any pleasure.

The colours of the sky were beginning to change to tangerine and claret red, and the great bundles of white clouds flamed with colour. Slowly, hugging her thoughts to her heart, Miranda wended her way back up the path and through the forest. There was a lightness in her step that lent wings to her feet, but she did not hurry. It was as if, by being alone, she would continue to savour the lingering fragrances of his presence. The spell with which he had ensnared her wove itself round her in an even finer mesh. The prospect of having to wait a long time before she saw him again was now intolerable . . .

She was taken aback to find Peregrine waiting for her at the villa.

'Where have you been?' he asked impatiently, as she stepped into the garden where he was sitting with Aunt Zoe.

'I went for a walk,' she said calmly, but her face flooded with guilty colour.

'All alone?' he demanded, observing her closely.

'Of course all alone! I . . . I am making some . . . sketches of the flora on this island,' she explained, taking out her sketchbook. She had almost handed it to him when she suddenly remembered the drawing she had made that morning of El Español on the remote hill across the valley. Quickly she replaced the book in her basket and turned to go in. 'I shall be with you after a wash,' she called out over her shoulder. In her room, after another long look at the sketch, she hid the book underneath a pile of clothes. Just looking at it made her pulses race again, and she felt resentful that Peregrine had chosen this moment to intrude into the memories of the day that she longed to re-live in solitude. Then, remorseful at her lack of charity, she quickly washed and returned to the garden, her face shining with a smile of welcome.

They sat and chatted over the cool, fresh coconut water that Lori served them. The repairs to the ship were going well, he admitted reluctantly, adding,

'Thank goodness. We can be away from this infernal place as soon as possible.'

Miranda's heart sank, but she said nothing. Instead, Aunt Zoe asked, 'Why? Don't you like this holiday that we are all having in such heavenly surroundings?'

Peregrine shrugged. 'It could be worse,' he said ungraciously. 'It's just that I cannot abide all these shifty foreigners around.'

'Hark at him!' Aunt Zoe exclaimed in exasperation. 'Shifty foreigners, indeed! Why, this Spaniard has been most generous with us. And Edward says they are all very decent.'

'Well, they do not suit my palate,' Peregrine said curtly. But in his eyes there was a curious gleam that made Miranda uncomfortable. He was trying too hard to convince everyone of his impatience with Amarillo. What was the impression he was trying to create, and for whose benefit? Again she felt a stab of unease. Peregrine was planning something, but what it was she could only suspect. She had a terrible feeling that the thought of Amarillo's gold had not vanished completely from his mind.

That night, it was impossible to induce sleep. For hours after Aunt Zoe had gone to bed Miranda continued to pace restlessly up and down the garden, the strange aspects of the night lending vividness to her fantasies. Her head whirled and throbbed with thoughts of him, some clear, others diffused, but all painful. In between outlines of his face floated images of Malamma, the woman who was his mistress. Agonising shafts of jealousy pierced her again and again as she saw them entwined in each other's arms, passing the night in making passionate, fevered love . . . Oh, how she hated her at this moment!

Then she shook herself impatiently, appalled at the insanity of her silent wanderings. *I am intoxicated with this man,* she mourned within herself. *I know nothing about him, I do not even know his name. But he has a power over me that is frightening. And within a week or two I shall sail out of his life for ever . . .*

Over breakfast the next morning, Aunt Zoe fixed her with a gimlet eye. 'You did not sleep well,' she said, not as a question but as a statement.

'No,' admitted Miranda. 'It was too . . . hot . . .'

'It was not hot at all,' her aunt retorted. 'I needed two coverlets to keep out the chill.' Miranda remained silent, immersing herself in peeling a tangerine. 'You met him yesterday, didn't you?' The question came so unexpectedly that Miranda's fingers halted in surprise. Aunt Zoe laughed shortly. 'You need not answer. I can see it in your face.'

Miranda resumed her task of peeling the fruit. 'Yes,' she said calmly, 'but not by design. He just . . . happened to pass by where I was sketching.'

'It is not desirable for you to meet him,' her aunt said abruptly.

'Why not?' Miranda forced a laugh. 'He is a gentleman, and has been kind to us.' She gave a brittle laugh. 'You don't need to worry, Aunt Zoe, it is unlikely that we shall meet again. It was a matter of chance that we did so yesterday.'

'Have you told Peregrine?' she asked sharply.

'No . . . It slipped my mind.' She rose quickly. 'I have requested him to lend me a horse. I would like to explore at least some of the island before we leave.'

'Alone?' Aunt Zoe said, aghast.

'No. I doubt if he will trust me to wander about alone. There will probably be an escort of some sort.'

'I do not like the idea,' Aunt Zoe wailed. 'Anything can happen in this place . . .'

'Nothing will happen,' said Miranda impatiently. 'I shall be quite safe, and I need the information to fill all the gaps in my diary.' Without waiting for Aunt Zoe's response, she went inside. In her room, however, she paused and thought. She had mentioned the matter of the horse so impulsively to Aunt Zoe, but it was more than likely that he would not even remember. With a frown she realised that she did not even know where he lived on the island. Was it with Malamma? She clenched her fists in another storm of jealousy, and closed her eyes in despair. *I must stop thinking about him as anything but a benefactor in time of need*, she cried in silent pain. *He is a man from another world, and our lives belong to different planets, different universes altogether. I am gripped by an insanity that I must shake off, or else I shall rot in hell for the rest of my life* . . .

There was a knock on her door. The horse, Lori indicated with a gesture, had arrived. Miranda drew in a long breath. He had not forgotten!

The escort who came with the horse was a young European Miranda had not seen before. He did not carry a musket, but in his belt, she noticed, was tucked the inevitable pistol. He smiled genially, and even bowed.

'El Español has sent for you the horse you had requested. We shall leave whenever you are ready.' He spoke fairly good English, and Miranda learned later that he was, in fact, a Brazilian who had received some education in a missionary school run by Americans. More than that she knew he would not say.

Before they started out, Miranda made a point of introducing him to her aunt. He was such a pleasant-looking young man that even Aunt Zoe seemed reassured.

'Now don't wander too far,' was all she could think to say. 'I do not like to eat alone, so be sure to return before luncheon.'

Miranda was not unused to riding, and her present

mount was a gentle chestnut mare already fitted with a side-saddle. She was wearing a simple dress of pale blue calico which hugged her slender form well, suggesting discreetly her well-formed, firm breasts and emphasising the smallness of her waist. She had left her hair loose and it fell around her shoulders in shining waves of pale gold, but she needed her straw hat to protect her from the sun. It was one that she had bought in Callao, although she had not used it much. Her skin had lost much of its paleness since they had started on their voyage and shone now with a healthy light tan that accentuated the gold of her hair.

She smiled at her escort. 'Where shall we start?'

He looked surprised. 'I do not know,' he said. 'It is for El Español to decide.'

Her heartbeat faltered. 'El Español?'

'Yes. He will escort you personally. I am merely to take you to the crossing.'

Miranda closed her eyes in an unbearable surge of joy. He would be with her again today! What an unpredictable man he was! He had given no hint of his intentions yesterday. She felt a twinge of guilt as she thought of Aunt Zoe, but then dismissed it sharply. Nothing mattered if she was going to see him again, nothing and no one . . .

They waited at the crossing for nearly half an hour before they heard the rapid staccato of horses' hooves approaching from a distance. He came flying round the bend, then reined sharply and stopped alongside.

'I'm sorry if I kept you waiting,' he said brusquely. He turned to the young Brazilian and said something in Spanish. Immediately the lad saluted and, digging his heels into the sides of his horse, turned and rode away.

'What would you like to see?' he asked, his eyes roving her body slowly, but without any particular expression.

I don't care, thought Miranda wildly, overwhelmed by his presence. *I don't care where we go or what we do as long as you are with me* . . . But, aloud, she only said with appropriate demureness, 'Whatever you think is advisable.'

He did not smile, but the hardness of his eyes seemed controlled and his manner was leisured. 'The women on the island are very curious about your golden hair,' he said. 'Perhaps it is only fair that, if you wish to observe them, they should also have a chance to observe you!'

'All right,' she laughed self-consciously. 'It would interest me to see how your islanders live.'

They rode for a few moments in comfortable silence. The path they were taking was not one on which she had been before. It seemed to be climbing towards the mountain. All around were sugarcane fields with people working in them, men and women. They waved, and he waved back with a smile. 'You seem to have an island that is very happy,' she remarked.

'Yes,' he said shortly. 'It is. Because we have kept foreigners well out. Those who are here are as deeply caring of these people as . . .' He paused.

'As you are?'

'Yes.' It was said very quietly.

'But you are a foreigner, too!'

He wavered on the brink of a reply, but then changed his mind and snapped, 'You ask too many questions. Let us restrict ourselves to the present excursion.' He quickened his pace and Miranda was forced to fall silent as he sped on ahead.

On top of the hill she could see a dense forest of trees so high that they towered like giants above the other foliage. Once again the air around them was warm with a strange fragrance. She caught up with him and asked him what it was that was so prevalent on the island.

'Sandalwood. See those trees ahead? That is a sandalwood forest.'

'Sandalwood! But that grows only in Asia, doesn't it?'

'No. It also grows in other places quite well. Indeed, Hawaii is known as "The Fragrant Tree Country" because of it.'

'Oh yes,' she exclaimed, 'I remember now. I have read about it.'

By the sides of the track they followed were fields of plants she could not identify. 'Taro and sweet potatoes,' he explained. 'Both staples of this island, and of many others in the south seas. Over there,' he pointed to the other side, 'pineapples, and a fruit known as passion fruit.'

Miranda looked around in wonder at the variety of the island's produce. Every foot of soil appeared to be covered with something of value. It was obvious that there was no lack of Nature's bounty on Amarillo. Apart from fruit and vegetables, there were poultry and eggs, pigs, and fish of every description in the sea. 'You appear to need nothing from the outside world,' she said slowly.

'No,' he said contemptuously, adding with a slight change of voice, 'Least of all, ships like yours.'

She chilled at the scorn of his tone. 'You really do hate us, don't you?'

'Yes.'

'*Why?*' she cried, incensed. 'We do you no harm.'

'Not yet,' he said grimly. 'But you will. You will bring trouble to Amarillo. I feel it like a fishbone in my gullet.' Then the note of anger vanished and there was just fatigue in his voice. Fatigue and a strange sadness. 'You whalers,' he said, 'have done more harm in the Pacific than anybody else. Have you any idea how many hundred thousand whales have been killed and *wasted* over these past years? Do you know that only one whale out of every three is saved for oil, and that not more than one-third of those killed can be accommodated on board and that only one out of every five killed can be secured? The rest just float away to rot and provide meat for the sharks.' He was getting angrier by the minute. 'Besides, your whaling sailors wreak more devastation on land than on sea, for on whichever island they touch they kill and rape and destroy—did you know that, little innocent-eyed, golden-haired, silver-tongued Miss Chiltern?' He glowered at her with such fury that she quaked before it. 'You will bring trouble to Amarillo—and I shall be unable to stop it. Everything I do for you is against my better judgment!'

Spurring his horse sharply, he disappeared in a cloud of dust towards the top of the hill. Shaken by the intensity of his feeling, Miranda stared after him; then, immersed in thought, she followed.

He had galloped deep into the sandalwood forest, where it was marvellously cool and the fragrance all around was heady. Some of the trees were laced with wild orchids blooming in multi-coloured profusion. At the foot of one tree was an extraordinary flower shaped like a boat in bright blue and red with a cascade of thread-thin stems of purple and gold rising out of its centre. In spite of the agitation in her mind, Miranda stopped and watched it, riveted.

'That is called Bird of Paradise. It was brought to the island from south-east Asia by my father.' He had joined her again, unnoticed, and was again in complete control of himself. He said it very casually, his usual distant self. Miranda was startled. It was the first time he had mentioned his father!

In a clearing, Miranda saw a group of men hewing the sandalwood into log-lengths. 'What is it used for? Do you sell it?'

He looked at her with a touch of scorn. 'Nothing from

Amarillo is sold. The islanders use it in their worship rituals and in their homes for its scent. They also use it to build their temples. It is,' he said softly, 'as valuable as gold.'

She followed him through the forest, observing everything with consuming interest. He had a word for everyone they met. It was obvious that they gave him not only respect but also their trust. She watched and listened in silence, oblivious of the curious stares around. He came from an alien race himself, and yet how much he seemed a part of these people! She became suddenly conscious of the deep understanding that must exist between them.

He had dismounted and was walking through the trees, holding the reins of his jet-black horse while she followed, still mounted. Every now and then he pointed out some strange plant, describing its use in food or in the local system of medicine. His knowledge seemed prodigious, as was the pride with which he spoke. But his manner towards her remained distant and correctly formal. It was as though the shutters had been pulled firmly down, and she was not to be allowed any more glimpses at what lay within.

They cleared the forest and came to the edge of a cliff. The panorama around was spectacular and, on an adjoining hilltop above their own, she noticed a single stone structure. It was a low white house, that hugged the earth with long, spread-out arms. From where it stood, alone and solitary, it commanded a view on three sides of the entire valley. Without even asking, she knew that this must be where he lived. It was a house of such lonely beauty that she felt a small catch in her throat and longed to look inside. Had she wanted to imagine his home, she could not have dreamed of one that seemed so appropriate to his personality—remote and alone. She wondered for a moment if this was where they were headed now, and the thought brought a warmth to her face. But he turned to walk in the direction opposite to it; it was obvious that he had no intention of allowing her any more familiarity.

Half-way down the hill upon which they now were, snuggled a tiny village on a shelf. She could see people outside the grass huts and hear children playing with noisy laughter amidst the trees. They took a path that led towards it.

As they approached, a young woman, smiling, her brilliant white teeth sparkling in the sun, came forward to greet them. Lovingly, she linked her arm through his. For a moment they spoke, and then he turned to Miranda. 'This is my sister. She says she is very pleased that you have come.'

His sister? This was completely unexpected. A question trembled on Miranda's lips, but she could not find the words to ask it. He stretched out his hand and helped her to dismount, his fingers holding hers firmly. It was the first time she had felt his touch, and a wave of excitement charged through her body. He held on to her hand for perhaps just a shade longer than necessary. Then, gently, he released it.

'Her name is Noela,' he said, one arm wound fondly around the girl's shoulders. Miranda said nothing, but continued to stare, perplexed. He smiled and tilted his head to one side. 'Our mother was Polynesian,' he said, and in his eyes gleamed a spark of strange defiance.

Miranda averted her head to hide her surprise. So that explained, at least partly, his obsessive love of Amarillo. But what about his father? Surely he was Spanish? She longed to ask, but dared not. He guarded his privacy fiercely—this much about him she knew only too well.

As though guessing the direction of her thoughts, he laughed. 'You are shocked?' He taunted her, enjoying her discomfiture.

'No,' she replied. 'I am not shocked. Why should I be? I am merely . . . surprised. To the world outside, your ancestry is clouded in secrecy.'

He shrugged. 'I am not concerned with the world outside, and I do not see why the world outside should be concerned with me. They are of no consequence . . . any more.'

They walked to the hut, which was obviously his sister's home. It was quite small and low, and the roof was made of plaited strips of palm. The walls, with no windows, were lengths of matting, and the whole hut was bound together with ropes of sennit, which, he explained, was made from coconut fibres. The front was open and it was immaculately clean. There was no furniture, the family obviously living on the finely woven rush mats spread out on the floor. Outside in the open a wood stove burned brightly, and on it sat an enormous pot.

Noela said something shyly to her brother and glanced at Miranda. 'My sister wants to know if you would like to have some *poi*.'

Miranda pointed to the pot. 'Is that *poi*?' He nodded. 'What is it?' Then, before her kind hostess could think her curiosity impolite, she added, 'But, whatever it is, I would love to sample it. Thank you.'

He conveyed the message to his sister, then explained, '*Poi* is made from taro and it is a starch that is held in high regard by islanders throughout the south seas. It is very nourishing and can be eaten by anyone from infants to the aged.'

While he talked, Noela quickly went round the side of the hut and returned holding a taro plant which she had obviously just plucked, for the earth still clung to it. For a moment or two she spoke volubly to her brother, who then interpreted what she had said. 'Apparently, one has to be careful how to prepare this for *poi*. First the leaves are removed and used as spinach. Then the peeled stalks, this section here, are set aside and eaten like asparagus. Even the flowers are eaten, and they taste like cauliflower. These big corms that are left are then boiled and peeled and pounded to make *poi*. Dr Gómez calls it the perfect food. Try it. In any case it is almost lunch-time.'

Quite a few islanders had by this time gathered round them, all chattering and obviously asking questions, for he looked at her often, and his eyes gleamed with amusement. 'The women want to know if they can touch your hair,' he said with a laugh. 'They feel it must be made of real gold.'

Miranda blushed at suddenly becoming the object of all their attention, but obligingly removed her hat. A hushed murmur of admiration went up from the group, and some of the women stroked her hair with light fingers, taking care not to pull or tug. There was no coarseness or vulgarity in their manner, just a very gentle, unselfconscious curiosity. Nevertheless, Miranda could not help feeling embarrassed and, observing her crimson face, he smiled and said something. Immediately the women retreated.

Inside the hut, places had been laid for them on the mats, with large banana leaves spread out on them to be their plates. The spoons were made of hard coconut shells.

'Are you not eating?' Miranda asked him as he watched her from outside.

'No. I have had enough *poi* to last me a lifetime. It is not one of my favourite dishes.' He sauntered off out of sight.

Cautiously, Miranda dug her scoop into the steaming mass and took a mouthful, almost burning her tongue in the process. But her eyes showed her surprise, for it was delicious, soft and savoury. Noela sat by her, smiling. Suddenly she said something. It was a question that Miranda could obviously not understand. Noela pointed out of the entrance to where El Español had disappeared. She repeated the question and, suddenly, the one word Miranda could understand was—Rafael. It was, quite clearly, his name! She paused in her eating and turned it over several times in her mind. Rafael, Rafael, Rafael . . . It had a sound to it that matched him perfectly. Delighted with her unwitting discovery, Miranda laughed, and Noela looked pleased without knowing what had made her guest so happy.

He was waiting outside for her, holding a small boy in his arms, surrounded by a group of islanders. She thanked Noela as best she could, and stood quietly on the sidelines while he concluded his conversations. It amazed her to see with how much gentleness he talked, his voice slow and quiet. He seemed like another man altogether from the one who had faced her on the wharf with iron in his soul. Yet his authority even now, as he smiled and laughed, was total, and the arrogance of his stance remained the same.

Standing next to her she saw Noela watching her closely, her eyes deeply troubled. '*Yo tengo miedo . . .*' she breathed softly in Spanish, shaking her head from side to side, '*Yo tengo miedo por tí . . .* ' Then she quickly went inside the hut.

Miranda stood stock still. Noela's words had shocked her beyond measure. She knew enough Spanish to be able to make out the meaning of the single phrase—*I have fear for you!* She remained motionless, staring straight ahead but without seeing anything. She was even unaware that El Español had finished his busines with the villagers and was standing next to her observing her curiously.

'Is anything wrong.'

Quickly she shook her head, and forced a smile.

'Nothing. Shall we go?' But all of a sudden she felt depressed again.

They continued down the same path into the valley. The rays of the sun caught a glint of water. 'Is that a river?' she asked in surprise. She had not seen it before.

'Yes. The Amarillo.'

The path was steep but the horses were sure-footed, used to the ways of the island. They stopped at another village surrounded by strange-looking trees bearing even stranger fruit. It was the size of a round, slightly elongated, pineapple with a light green rind. 'Is that what is known as breadfruit?' She was curious.

From his belt, as they passed under the trees, he pulled out his dagger and, reaching upwards, sliced one off and cut it in half. 'Yes, it is breadfruit. This is another favourite in the south seas. It's part fruit and part vegetable, depending on the stage of its ripeness. Would you like to try some?'

She shook her head firmly. 'No, thank you. I have tried it before in the Marquesas, and that will have to last *me* a lifetime!' she said, remembering his remarks about *poi*.

He laughed. 'Well, if you do not like breadfruit,' he said lightly, 'you will have a hard time living on the island!'

'I shall not be living on the island,' she reminded him quietly. 'I leave when the ship sails.'

For a fraction of an instant he seemed to freeze into immobility, but then immediately recovered. 'Of course,' he said with an easy smile. 'For a moment I had forgotten that.'

A hollow developed in the pit of her stomach and her throat went dry. She swallowed and an agonising pain passed through her heart. He too had fallen silent and remained so until they reached the river-bank. At their feet, the Amarillo flowed past swiftly. It was not very wide and was cut into a deep gorge which was cool and wooded. He dismounted and held out his hand, but she pretended not to see it and got down from her horse unaided. He knelt by the water and stared into it for a long while. Then he put his hand into the torrent and scooped up a handful. He rose and, even though the water drained through his fingers in large drops, his hand remained cupped.

'Do you know what this is?' he asked. She shook her head. 'This,' he breathed, 'is the curse of Amarillo!' His eyes narrowed into slits and his face was so intense that she was shocked into silence. He wiped his wet hand on the sleeve of his shirt. 'This is what makes men come here by the hundreds, year after year, bashing their brains out against the reef, consigning their souls to the devil, turning themselves into animals—just to reach this river.' He laughed long and loud, and it was not a pleasant sound. 'Gold,' he said. 'This is the river of gold . . . Does that word not make your heart hammer and your soul sick with desire to possess it?' There was such fierce mockery in his tones that she blenched and stepped back involuntarily.

'No!'

But he hardly seemed to have heard her, so ravaging was the passion that appeared to grip him. His face was mobile with emotion, the indication of some inner storm that seemed to tear him apart. He stood motionless and inflexible, yet writhing within. Then his tall body unknotted itself and his shoulders dropped. 'Wherever there is gold—that most exquisite of all metals . . . there is, ironically, evil,' he sounded suddenly fatigued. 'This is the bane of Amarillo—and this is what your Peregrine wants . . .'

Her head jerked up in horrified surprise. 'Peregrine . . . ?'

'Did you not know?' he taunted, his mouth curved in

a vicious smile. She flushed with guilt and he broke out into derisive laughter. 'Your face tells me that you do! But,' he added very quietly and with controlled menace, 'he will not get it. The gold of Amarillo belongs to the people of Amarillo. You can tell him that from me when you see him.'

He leaped on to his horse and cantered away. For a few sick moments she stared after him with terrified eyes. How had he found out what was within Peregrine's thoughts? Surely he had not been fool enough to relate his wild ambitions to others? Her heart filled with cold dread for her fiancé. He was young and hot-headed and had not yet learned either discretion or wisdom. Was he planning something that would plunge them all into disaster? Slowly, with a leaden heart, she mounted the mare again and followed the track along which he had galloped away.

He was waiting for her at the top of the hill. There was no sign on his face now of the horrible emotions it had borne not more than half an hour earlier. Instead, it was impassive and once again cold and forbidding. They rode side by side and he continued to point out objects of interest to her as they doubled back from the sandalwood forest. She listened now with only half an ear, the agitation in her mind too great to allow complete concentration.

Suddenly she became aware that he had stopped talking. With a frown, she turned to him. He was observing her curiously. His eyes were unusually soft. 'I have upset you,' he said gently. 'That was not my intention.'

Her eyes filled with unexpected tears at the caress in his voice, and she quickly looked in the other direction. 'Then what was your intention?' she asked, with more sharpness than she wanted.

He did not answer her question. Instead, he continued

to look at her reflectively. 'You . . . disturb me very strangely,' he said in a voice so low that she could hardly hear him.

Her breath again knotted in her throat. 'I . . . do not mean to . . .'

'Perhaps. But nevertheless you do . . . and I do not much care for it!' A shadow of a smile flickered over the corners of his mouth, then vanished. 'Why do you stay with that boor?' His eyes glowered with sudden anger.

'Who?' she asked, taken aback by the rapid change of subject.

'Your . . . betrothed.' His lips curled in contempt. 'He is not worth a single strand of your beautiful golden hair.'

She felt hot colour climb up her neck. Was there anything about them that he did not know? 'I do not think that it is any concern of yours!' she threw back, equally angry.

He ignored her comment by merely shrugging his shoulders, but his eyes continued to blaze unaccountably. They rode in awkward silence. Her anger evaporated like a puff of smoke, but his profile remained stern and unbending. He was riding so close to her that she could almost stretch out and touch his hand, but with a monumental effort she refrained from indulging in any such unwise exercise. Yet she felt her heart perform strange acrobatics against her breast, and she bit her lip to control them. Suddenly, his presence was overpowering. She felt she would have laid down her life just at that moment for a mere smile from him.

They arrived back at the crossing at which they had met that morning. The overhead sun had slunk down to the western horizon and the hills and valleys were bathed in a golden light that set everything on fire. He pulled the reins of his horse, and halted.

'You are right,' he said quietly, and there was no trace of anger in his face. 'It is no concern of mine.' The raven-black eyes were shuttered. 'I'm afraid I shall have to leave you here.'

She nodded, but despondent that the parting had come so soon. 'I understand.'

Unexpectedly he leaned forward and reached for her hand, then held it in his without speaking. Miranda closed her eyes, afraid of what he might see in them, and her limbs dissolved with an ache that was magical. She knew she was trembling, but she did not pull away the hand resting in his.

'You could have been killed coming through the passage,' he said, musing almost to himself.

'Yes, but my stars were smiling upon me that day,' she breathed.

'Were they? I wonder . . .' Her hand in his lay forgotten, and his eyes were troubled. Then he said abruptly, 'I'm sorry I tore your sketch yesterday.'

'Then . . . Then why did you?'

Very gently he uncurled the fingers of her clenched hand one by one. 'Because I know you will remember me without it.' He bent his head a little and placed on the palm of her hand a single kiss. Then he closed her hand again and returned it to her. 'I am glad that you will be sailing away very shortly.' The blackness of his eyes was smudged with a strange emotion that she could not fathom. 'More for your sake than mine. I shall not see you again.'

It was a long while before Miranda was even aware that he had gone. Then, with eyes blurred, she opened the palm of her hand and held it against her lips.

She knew that now, from this moment on, he had damned her for ever.

CHAPTER FIVE

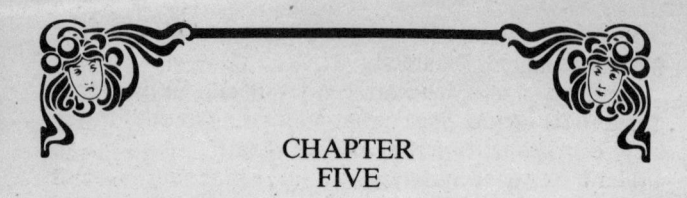

It was not until she walked into the garden and saw Aunt Zoe sitting there, ominously waiting, that Miranda returned to the world of reality with a jolt.

'Where have you been, Miranda?' Her aunt's voice quivered with anger and concern. 'You promised to return by luncheon!' The pale anxious eyes were sharp with censure. Miranda stared back at her dazedly, barely listening. Slowly, she walked to the chair, sank on to the grass and buried her head in her aunt's lap. Alarmed, Miss Chiltern put her hand under her chin and forced her to look up. 'What has happened, child?' she asked, suddenly fearful. 'Are you all right?'

Dully, Miranda shook her head and buried it again in the lap. A vast sigh shuddered through her body. 'No. I am not all right. I think that I am going mad . . .' Then, unable to say any more, she burst into long overdue tears.

'There, there . . .' her aunt stroked her hair soothingly, utterly bewildered by her emotion. 'There, child, there . . . Don't cry . . . Tell me what has happened . . .'

Miranda shook her head in despair. 'I do not know myself what has happened,' she whispered between her sobs 'But I have never felt so confused in all my life . . .'

For a moment Miss Chiltern said nothing. There had always existed a very close bond between her and the niece she had brought up as her own daughter. Instinctively she reached out for the reason for her unhappiness. 'You have seen him again,' she said flatly, and her voice was deeply troubled.

Miranda sighed and raised her head. 'What am I going to do, Aunt Zoe? What am I going to do?' It was a cry of pain. 'He will not see me again.'

Her aunt's face dissolved in a surge of tenderness and compassion. 'He is not for you, my child,' she said gently. 'He does not belong to our world.'

'But I love him so desperately,' she whispered in a voice fragmented with anguish.

'You are infatuated with him,' reprimanded her aunt severely. 'It is not an unknown condition.'

Miranda shook her head angrily. 'What I feel for him is not infatuation! It is as if he has taken over every fibre of my body, every thought in my mind. I cannot seem to think of anyone or anything but him . . .' She sighed tiredly and wiped her eyes, better for the passing of the storm. 'It is not I who wished it to be so . . .'

'You were . . . alone with him today?' her aunt asked grimly.

Miranda rose to her feet and ran a hand distractedly through her hair. 'I am always alone with him,' she said dismally, 'no matter how many people are about . . .' Quickly she ran back into the house. In her room she flung herself on her bed, racked with the memory of his last words to her. *'I shall not see you again . . .!'* It was as if he had written her death-warrant—not to see him again, to go away for ever without any words of love, never again to feel the touch of his hand . . . Oh, it was unbearable! Perhaps he didn't mean it! Perhaps the words were spoken without thought . . . Surely he could not condemn her to so cruel a fate!

Her palm still tingled and burned with the imprint of his lips. She dissolved again and again as she remembered the softness of his eyes and the feel of his cool fingers on hers. Surely he felt something for her, too?

Surely there was a fine, fragile thread that did bind them together for those few magical moments? She could not believe that he had been merely playing with her, teasing her, knowing as he did only too well that she cared. She knew that he could not have looked into her eyes without seeing what lay in them; she had not cared to hide it. Why should she? She felt no sense of shame in loving such a man. No matter what the world outside presumed about him, she knew him for what he really was—a colossus of a man full of kindness for his people. She had today seen a side of him revealed to few others from the outside world. It was a side that fired her imagination and filled her with even more love than before . . .

Miranda had no appetite for food, but her aunt forced her to eat a little. She looked extremely worried. 'We must keep this . . . this business from Edward and Peregrine,' she said with surprising wisdom. 'Peregrine, especially.' Miranda shrugged. Suddenly, it seemed to her not a matter of great importance. Saturated, engulfed with thoughts of him, she felt that nothing could possibly be a matter of great importance any more unless it had to do with him. Her aunt fixed her with a gimlet eye. 'Did you say he will not see you again?'

Miranda nodded, then tossed her hair back defiantly. 'But I shall not accept that verdict,' she said emphatically. 'He could not have meant it . . .' Her eyes filled with tears of despair.

Her aunt surveyed her helplessly. 'You must cast him out of your mind, Miranda,' she insisted earnestly. 'He is a man who must have had countless women in his life. Such men are dangerous—and you have no experience of them. You are fresh and innocent, and he will crush you . . .'

But Miranda hardly listened. '*He is a man who must have had countless women in his life!*' Before her eyes floated a vision of Malamma: beautiful, bewitching and hot with passion. Had he left her this evening to go back to her? Did she live with him in that splendid, solitary house on the hill—and did she love him every night as he would want to be loved . . .? Silently, tormentedly, the knives turned in her heart as she continued to torture herself, not listening to a word that her aunt said. All she wanted at this moment was to be alone . . .

But that was not to be. As soon as they had finished eating, Peregrine walked into the room. Miranda's heart sank, and Aunt Zoe stared at him, struggling to conceal her alarm. But if Peregrine noticed their discomfiture and strange lack of welcome, he did not comment on it. Instead, he appeared to be in extremely high spirits, laughing and joking incessantly. Miranda was immensely grateful for his lack of attention, but, listening to him, she felt a surge of alarm sweep through her. With a start she remembered El Español's warning to him. But . . . how could she convey it to him without giving him the context? It was not Peregrine's reaction that worried her at all. Miranda knew now that, come what may, she could not marry him. Indeed, the thought was abhorrent. What alarmed her was that he might invite trouble through his usual thoughtless choice of action and endanger the entire crew.

'I notice there is a horse tethered outside in the shed,' Peregrine suddenly remarked, 'with a groom in attendance. Whose is that?'

Before Miranda could say anything, Aunt Zoe jumped into the awkward silence. 'Oh, that belongs to Lori, and the groom is one of her . . . her sons . . .'

Miranda breathed a sigh of gratitude and threw a smile in her aunt's direction. Secretly, she hugged herself. He had even sent a groom to look after her horse, she thought in wonder. How could she ever believe that she meant nothing to him?

Aunt Zoe rose suddenly, and yawned. 'I think I shall retire now,' she said with a calculating look in her eyes, 'there must be a great deal you two want to talk about.' She kissed Miranda on the cheek and gave her a warning glance. *Be nice to him,* the glance said, *and don't tell him about this absurd obsession of yours . . .*

They strolled out into the garden under the canopy of enormous stars. The moon was beginning to wane, but even so its light bathed everything in silver, making the world around them shine and sparkle with iridescence. Miranda walked beside Peregrine silently, wondering how she was to broach the subject of the gold. But, as it happened, she did not need to.

'I have made up my mind,' he said suddenly.

'About what?'

He laughed shortly, and she noticed that his body went tight with subdued excitement. 'I think you know what.'

She stared at him in dismay. 'Peregrine, you must not think of the gold any more,' she whispered urgently. 'He will mow you down mercilessly if you try anything . . .'

'Who says so?' he bragged. 'He won't even know about it!' he chuckled.

'Oh, but he does . . .' she began, then choked back the rest of the sentence, biting her lip.

He stopped sharply. 'How do you know?' He scrutinised her face through narrowed eyes.

For a second she wavered, then decided against it. Peregrine was already so bedevilled that any further shock would surely make him insane with rage. She laughed and shrugged her shoulders. 'El Español knows everything that goes on in Amarillo, they say.'

He relaxed. 'No,' he said confidently. 'Not everything! I have got information from someone which is not wrong. And Mr Spaniard has no wind of it at all!' He laughed again, triumphantly.

She looked at him, aghast. 'You have an accomplice from the island?'

'Of course,' he said, surprised. 'There is no other way in which it can be done!'

'In which what can be done?' she asked sharply, her hands cold with alarm.

He looked at her impatiently. 'In which I can get my hands on some of that gold. I know now where it is. It is panned in the Amarillo river at a particular spot which is approachable either by boat—or through a tunnel which starts from the harbour. It is well concealed, but I know now where it is. This . . . This person will help me to reach there.' He laughed at the horror in her eyes. 'Don't worry, Miranda, it will be quite safe. Nobody will know—and God knows they have enough to spare. They won't even miss it!'

Miranda found her voice, and grabbed his arms. 'Peregrine, listen to me, *please*! He . . . He will know about it, I promise you that! He will *kill* you rather than let you get to it . . . It belongs to Amarillo. It has nothing to do with us, nothing at all . . . It is evil, Peregrine. Look how many people have died for it . . .' Her voice rose in panic.

He looked at her coldly. 'For God's sake, keep your voice down. I've got a damned guard standing outside! Don't worry,' he said, his eyes gleaming madly, 'I shall not die for it, neither will anybody else.' He glanced up at the sky. 'The moon is still too bright, my . . . my informant feels. We shall have to wait until it wanes further.'

'Who is your informant?' she asked, sick with fear.

His lips suddenly clamped shut and he smiled tightly. 'That is not something that need concern you,' he said smugly. 'But it is someone,' his eyes glistened with excitement, such as you would never have thought possible. Someone who hates El Español as much as I do

. . .' He recollected himself quickly. 'I must go,' he said brusquely, then subjected her to an intense stare. 'If you mention this to anyone, Miranda . . .' He left the sentence unfinished. 'I am doing it for . . . us.'

Without another word, he turned on his heel and was gone.

The horror that froze Miranda's limbs remained for a long time after he had left. Her mind raged with fear and uncertainty. What should she do? Should she warn her father? She knew Peregrine would not listen to a single word of caution from her, so wrapped was he in his greed for the gold. He had no idea that El Español knew what was in his mind—how, Miranda did not know. Was it possible that the 'informant' had been sent to him deliberately? Who was it? Which of the men who served him—for it could be no other. The islanders were not allowed to speak to the crew and, in any case, knew no English. Miranda knew that only two people on the *Amiable Lady* spoke Spanish, and Peregrine was not one of them. How had he got his information?

Half the night she spent walking up and down in the garden, unable to persuade sleep to relieve her from her misery. It was not until the eastern sky was beginning to lighten from indigo to purple that she finally felt her eyes become heavy. But, when she slept, drained and exhausted, her slumber was filled with terrifying nightmares. And still, looming above all else, was the face of the man to whom her body and soul remained mortgaged . . .

Aunt Zoe was already at luncheon by the time Miranda rose the next day. The long sleep, although violent and disturbed, had helped—if not to comfort— at least to dull the ravaging passions of the day before. Across the table, Aunt Zoe observed her unhappy face and reached out for her hand.

'You must not think, child,' she said gently, 'that I

do not know how you feel. I, too, was young once . . .' Her eyes became distant and dreamy. 'I, too, have been in love and I, too, know the agonies it brings, especially when it is a love that is hopeless . . .'

Miranda looked at her in surprise. She had never before seen her aunt in a mood of such emotion.

'I was in love once,' her aunt continued, 'with a ship's captain. He was the most handsome man I had ever seen in my life, and I loved him with a passion that I thought would tear me from limb to limb.' She sighed. 'But he was married. He had two sons. It was unthinkable that he should abandon them. Apart from his wife, I would not have permitted such cruelty. We decided to part. I never set eyes on him again. But,' a tear glistened in her wrinkled eyes, 'I vowed that no other man would ever claim my love . . .'

Miranda listened in amazement. It was a story she had never heard before, and it shook her. 'Is that why you never married?'

Aunt Zoe nodded. 'Marriage to another man was a thought so obscene that I never even considered it!' She sighed, and wiped her eyes with her handkerchief. 'It was the right decision that I made, but when we parted, I thought that I would die. At the last moment, had he made even the lightest of gestures, I would have thrown everything to the wind and gone off with him.' She laughed but with sadness. 'So, you see, my dear, I do know what you are going through. But I also know,' she paused and her voice became solemn, 'that it can only end in disaster for you. I have never met your Spaniard, but I can sense that he is a man like the wind. He cannot be tied down. Like a bird he will always want to fly; he can only take. He can never give any woman any but a thousandth part of himself . . .'

Abruptly Miranda rose and put her arms around her aunt's shoulder. 'Yes, I know,' she whispered miserably.

'I know. In the cold light of day I know how hopeless my love is. Maybe when we sail away, it too will pass, although I cannot imagine such a thing at the moment. He says he will not see me again, and he is not a man who speaks idly. Perhaps he will not . . .'

Gathering her basket of sketching materials, she fled into the forest, longing only to bury herself in some labour that would erase him, if only for a few moments, from her thoughts.

For the next two days Miranda wandered from morning to dusk, scribbling and sketching furiously. She drew everything within sight, but decided to keep a separate drawing-book for the extraordinary variety of orchids that studded the trees. She filled in the colours with care, spending hours over her labours, trying to shut out the torment that withered her inside. On the one hand was Peregrine and his monstrous scheme and on the other the beloved, nebulous face of El Español, who haunted all her moments, awake or asleep. She roamed every part of the forest, pretending that it was orchids she was seeking, but knowing that what she secretly searched for was perhaps a distant glimpse of him. She found a beautiful orchid that she had not seen before, on the very ledge from which she had sighted him on the hill across the valley. Positioning herself on a boulder, she opened the book on her lap and began to draw. The orchid was indeed exquisite, and before long she was totally immersed in her work. It was a lazy, beautiful afternoon, and gentle breezes from the sea rustled the leaves now and again, and the glade in which she sat was cool.

Suddenly she heard the snap of a twig behind her. With a gasp, she turned, wondering wildly if it were he. But it was not. Leaning against a tree not far from where she sat, was—Malamma!

For a moment they stared at each other, Miranda

in confusion and Malamma in cool disdain. Then she strolled forward, and her hips swayed with the same seductive grace Miranda had noticed before. Silently, she came and sat on the grass before Miranda. For a moment she said nothing, chewing idly on a blade of green. Then she spoke, and her dark eyes slowly filled with contempt.

'I am happy that you will be leaving soon,' she said, almost under her breath.

The sound shook Miranda out of her rigidity. Shakily, she laughed. 'You are the second person who has said that to me,' she said with a tinge of bitterness.

'I shall make it so that you will regret the day you ever came to Amarillo.' Her voice now shook with a sudden passion. She tossed her rich black hair over her shoulder and her eyes blazed. 'He will never love you,' she spat out viciously. 'There have been a hundred, a thousand, such as you in his life. But he returns always to me!' A smile of cruel triumph curved her sensual lips.

'In that case,' said Miranda dully, 'there is no need to hate me. You should rest easy.'

Malamma sprang to her feet. 'Oh, you cannot lull me with all your fancy words like you have lulled *him*! It is not clever words that win the heart of a man—it is the satisfaction that he receives when he lies with you.'

Miranda felt a wave of nausea, but she clenched her fists in an effort not to retaliate. 'I am sure you are right,' she said evenly. 'You know much more about these things than I do.' She returned to her drawing pointedly, unwilling to continue this abhorrent conversation.

But Malamma was far from finished. 'You have caught his fancy for the moment,' she hissed malevolently. 'But when you are gone, he will forget you with ease.'

Miranda looked at her sharply. Beneath all her spite,

Malamma sounded deeply troubled. She wondered why. 'I have no doubt he will,' she said. 'Why, then, are you so agitated?'

'Because it hurts me that he thinks of you even for a moment,' she said, enraged by Miranda's continuing calmness. 'I hate you for every moment that he spends with you!'

'There have not been many,' said Miranda dolefully. 'I can assure you of that!' *And there would not be any more*, she thought grimly, but saw no reason to inform this vicious woman of that.

'Since you have come,' Malamma breathed, and suddenly there was a note of panic in her voice, 'he has not lain with me once . . .'

Miranda snapped her book shut and rose abruptly, her face flooding with colour. 'I don't want to hear any more,' she said angrily. 'I have no interest in your . . . your relationship with . . . him!'

But Malamma, consumed with fury, barely heard her as she paced up and down like a beautiful caged panther, her lovely face contorted and her bosom heaving with emotion. 'No man, not even El Español, spurns Malamma,' she whispered, her eyes ignited like glowing coals. 'No man! I shall teach him a lesson he will never forget in all his life . . .'

Miranda picked up her basket, trembling, wanting to close her ears to the tirade. 'Please don't say any more,' she pleaded. 'I don't want to hear it, I don't . . .'

'El Español will rue the day he turned me away from his bed,' Malamma muttered, now not even aware of Miranda's presence. 'I shall destroy him . . . and Peregrine will . . .' Abruptly, suddenly aware of what she had said, she stopped, her eyes wide and startled at what she had just let slip.

Miranda went stiff with shock, and the basket slipped from her nerveless fingers. *Peregrine!* 'You know . . .

Peregrine?' she whispered incredulously.

Malamma's head came up with slow defiance. 'Yes. I know Peregrine.'

'But . . . but El Español will *kill* you when he finds out . . .'

Her blazing eyes became cold and shrewd. 'He will not find out,' she said triumphantly. 'And he will not believe you if you tell him! In any case you will not—for your precious Peregrine, too, will die if you do!'

Miranda's eyes dilated in horror as another realisation struck her. Peregrine's informant! *Malamma* was Peregrine's informant! Frantically, she grasped the girl's arms and shook her. 'You must not do this thing, Malamma,' she gasped. 'Peregrine is young and immature. He cannot match El Español in this game, and you must not let him. Make him forget about the gold, *make* him! You will not succeed in your scheme . . .'

Angrily, Malamma shook herself free. 'We shall succeed,' she said coldly. 'It is all arranged.'

'But you will never, *never* be able to leave the island . . .'

She ignored the remark. 'Peregrine will stay with me and we shall sail to the next island. I know it well. It will not be difficult.' She subjected Miranda to a look of black hatred. 'Peregrine loves me! And El Español will be the laughing-stock of the islands when it is known that he has lost his woman to an American sailor . . .' She laughed scornfully. Still laughing, she made to walk away, casting a look of contempt at Miranda's appalled expression. 'If you tell him,' she said softly, 'your Peregrine will die before the sun sets—and you know it!' With another toss of her beautiful hair, she turned on her heel and disappeared through the trees. The sound of her laughter rang out again and again before it faded completely in the distance.

Now there was no doubt left in Miranda's mind as to what she should do. Her father had to be immediately informed of this desperate situation. There was no one to whom she could turn who would be of any help now. Aunt Zoe, apart from being unable to solve the problem, would be unnecessarily alarmed. For a wild moment she was even tempted to seek out El Español, and her heart leaped in painful anticipation at the idea. But she knew that that would be disastrous. He would vent his wrath on everyone, including her father and all the other innocent members of the crew, and there was no knowing what his retaliation would consist of. What he did to Malamma she did not care about, but to endanger her father would be criminal.

But the decision was far easier taken than implemented! How was she to inform her father of it unless she met him face to face? Impatiently she waited for evening to come, hoping that it would also bring a visit from him. But she knew that the repairs were now nearing their end—how agonising was that thought!—and that he was being kept inordinately busy. Miranda was grateful that Aunt Zoe had become greatly intrigued by the manner in which islanders wove their lovely cane mats. As a result, she was kept well occupied all day in taking instructions from Lori, and seemed not to have noticed Miranda's increased agitation. If she did, she put it down to her hopeless love for the unattainable Spaniard, and contented herself with occasional solicitous enquiries and discreet silences.

The evening wore on and Captain Chiltern did not come. Miranda knew that Peregrine would not. She spent a bad night, tossing and turning, and waited impatiently for the dawn. With the first light, she was out of bed and, after a quick wash, went outside to look for the groom. She knew that she herself would not be allowed to get anywhere near the harbour but it was possible that she could send a note down with him. She had composed a brief letter with the utmost clarity.

Dear Papa,
There is a matter of some urgency upon which I would like to consult you. Please come as soon as you can.

The note would probably be read en route, but it did not matter. It revealed nothing.

With the help of Lori, she managed to make the groom understand where the letter was to be taken, and sent him off forthwith. She waited impatiently for either a reply or for her father in person, unable to settle down to anything. But when the groom returned, it was with a reply that sent her spirits plummeting.

Dearest Miranda,
Your note alarmed me somewhat, but Peregrine was with you yesterday. He tells me that you are both well. Therefore, I shall *try* to visit you this evening, but I cannot guarantee it. In any case, I have requested that Dr Gómez see you today in case Zoe is again not well. Forgive me, dear, but I am anxious to leave as soon as possible, and at this stage my presence here is necessary.
Your loving Papa.

Her father had not taken the note seriously! Naturally, Peregrine would do all he could to prevent a meeting between them until he had completed his nefarious plot—if indeed he could! Another note sent so soon after the first would arouse suspicions. She had a wild impulse to ride her horse down to the harbour and insist on being allowed to see her father, but even though she might succeed, the entire harbour would be alerted to her presence and they would certainly know that something was afoot. Miserably, she realised that there was nothing to be done but to wait for her father's visit, and hope that it would be that evening—and pray that Peregrine would not plan to do anything disastrous tonight.

Sounds of horses' hooves later in the evening sent Miranda flying to the front terrace, but she was bitterly disappointed to see that it was only Dr Gómez. Forcing a smile, she welcomed the kindly doctor, trying not to show her disappointment. He examined Aunt Zoe carefully, proclaimed her now absolutely fit, and agreed to spend a few minutes on the lawn chatting before he moved on to his next patient.

'Oh, by the way,' he said, as he was rising to leave. 'There is a feast tomorrow evening in one of the villages. I have El Español's permission to ask if you two ladies might be interested in coming as my guests? It promises to be something different from what you might have seen before.'

'Oh, we would love to,' said Miranda immediately, with forced enthusiasm, as she was in no mood for festivity. 'Is it far from here?'

'Not very,' said the doctor. 'I shall come and fetch you at sunset. Does that suit you, Miss Chiltern?' He turned to Aunt Zoe.

'Most definitely,' she said firmly. 'I have heard much about the beauty of this island from my niece, but have seen nothing for myself except what lies around here. Yes, *most* certainly it would suit me!' She sounded quite cross.

Dr Gómez laughed, and Miranda walked with him to the front. 'Will . . . El Español be there?' she asked casually, pretending to remove a speck of dust from her dress.

'He may be,' the doctor said, mounting his horse. 'But with him there is no telling. He is most unpredictable. Good night, Señorita. *Hasta la vista mañana.*'

Mañana! Miranda smiled bitterly to herself. Who knew what terrors tomorrow would bring! She wondered briefly if she should have given the good doctor a further message for her father, but then realised it would not have borne much fruit. The doctor had patients to see and many villages to visit. She could hardly ask him to interrupt his business and make a special trip to the harbour for her. Dejectedly she went inside to wait again for her father.

She waited until very late that night, sitting in the garden, watching the sky, and the moon that had waned further. But he did not come. Obviously, she finally accepted in utter desolation, his work at the harbour had not permitted him to leave. In the meantime she prayed that Peregrine would stick to his word and wait until the moon waned completely before he plunged himself—and all of them—into perdition! If she could talk to her father before then, perhaps all might still not be lost.

CHAPTER SIX

THE BEACH was lit with flaming torches as far as the eye could see. Under the dancing coconut palms were hundreds of islanders, the vibrant colours of their *pareus* and sarongs brilliant even in the half dark. Everywhere was a feeling of excitement, and peals of laughter rang out every now and again interspersed with the shrieks of children involved in some boisterous game. A gigantic barbecue pit glowed red-orange and upon it were being roasted enormous quantities of meat and fish. A pile of vermilion lobsters lay heaped on platters and in calabashes, awaiting their turn on the fire. Somewhere in the background throbbed the seductive rhythm of a drum. There was, in the warm aromatic air of the night, a feeling of joy.

Miranda and her aunt stood and watched in astonished silence while Dr Gómez explained to them the reason for the festivities. A woman who had longed for a child over many years had finally given birth, and everybody on the island wanted to share in their happiness.

'How many people live on Amarillo?' Miranda asked, her eyes scanning the crowd for only one of them.

'Three thousand, seven hundred and thirty-three.'

'You know the numbers so well?'

'Yes; for every one of them is precious, and every new birth is a matter for celebration. Forty years ago,' his voice became dry, 'when El Conde first discovered Amarillo and gave it its name, there were over twenty thousand . . .'

'What happened to the rest?' Miranda asked with widened eyes.

He shrugged. 'Over the years they have been killed off, either by successive waves of butchering sailors or by the diseases that they brought with them.' He laughed bitterly. 'Diseases unknown in these islands until then.'

'Oh, how dreadful!' Aunt Zoe exclaimed, while Miranda paled.

'There would have been not one living soul left on this island if Rafael had not segregated it by force. And yet people come . . .'

'For the gold . . .' Miranda breathed, thinking of Peregrine.

'Yes. Had El Conde not discovered it, he might still have been alive.' An unusual spark of anger showed in the placid eyes.

'Who was . . . El Conde?'

'El Conde?' He looked surprised. 'He was Rafael's father. El Conde Felipe de Quintero. I thought you might have known.'

She shook her head slowly. 'No. I did not know.' So, his name was Rafael de Quintero, perhaps a Spanish Count! 'And . . . and his mother was of this island?'

He looked at her sharply. 'How do you know that?'

She smiled faintly. 'It is . . . rumoured.'

'Come, let us walk ahead,' he said, suddenly noticing that her aunt was beginning to look tired. 'We shall seat ourselves near the drummers and watch the dancing.'

'What a splendid sight!' Aunt Zoe exclaimed, as they set off. 'Your islanders are very handsome people.'

As indeed they were. The men, their chests bare and glistening with oil, were striking specimens of manhood with their full heads of black hair, their perfect teeth and their large, luminous eyes that always seemed to be laughing. The women, equally striking, wore flowers in their flowing hair and round their wrists and ankles.

Some men wore ceremonial capes made of coloured feathers and skirts of rush grass. It was a riveting sight.

But Miranda observed it all with only half her mind, her eyes continuously probing the sea of faces for just a single one. It was not to be seen. The doctor led them to a stretch of sand beneath the palms, where rush mats had been laid on the ground for them. Here the drums were louder and they could see the islanders dancing and swaying to the throbbing rhythms. The liquid grace with which they moved was a joy to watch.

Suddenly, the dancers were joined by another. It was Malamma! Miranda's heart stopped for a moment, but then the relief flowed through her body. If Malamma was here now, this would not be the night Peregrine would choose for his escapade. Perhaps there would still be time to warn her father. As Malamma swayed bewitchingly, the other dancers stood aside, for she was undoubtedly the best of them all. Tonight she was bare-breasted, and her superb figure undulated with a sensuality that must have set every man's pulses racing. No wonder Peregrine had not been able to keep his head—Malamma was exquisite. She danced now with total abandonment, with a passion that shone out of her eyes like a flame. She swayed and swirled and pulsated as if in a trance, hardly aware of the crowds around her. It was the most sensual dance Miranda had ever seen, and even Aunt Zoe sat still, her mouth open and a hand over her heart.

And then the dance was over and a great sigh went up from the crowd. 'Upon my word!' gasped Aunt Zoe, fanning herself vigorously. 'Upon my *word*! Who is this fantastic creature?'

'She is Malamma . . . El Español's woman.' Dr Gómez glanced obliquely at Miranda as he said it, but she averted her head, pretending to be absorbed in watching Malamma as she walked past them, her head held high like a queen.

There was an awkward silence, then Miranda turned calmly to the doctor. 'You were telling us about Amarillo?'

'So I was, so I was,' he said, then stopped and sighed heavily. 'Amarillo has a curse that has made us more unfortunate than most Pacific islands—and I think you know what it is. Gold! From time to time we have been plundered mercilessly. I should know . . .' he smiled bitterly, 'for I was one of those who came to plunder.'

'You?' Miranda started in disbelief.

He nodded. 'Oh yes, that was the intention, but . . . I could not. I was a healer, not a destroyer! And when I saw the actions of my fellow sailors, the sight of the gold made me sick.' His eyes clouded in memory. 'I decided to abandon my ship and stay on. Felipe gave me refuge and befriended me. I have been here ever since.'

'And then?' Miranda felt instinctively that that was not all. There was something else he wanted to tell them, but he seemed to be searching for words.

A vast shudder went through the doctor. 'And then,' he said, speaking very low, 'came the day that changed Amarillo for ever. A shipload of men, more brutal, more diabolic, than any others, found their way through the passage. They swarmed over the island like locusts. They opened fire on the unarmed islanders, killing hundreds. They razed to the ground every hut they could find, carrying away gold by the sackful.' His voice quivered as he re-lived the horror of the day. 'They raped and killed hundreds of women, slicing with their cutlasses all men who intervened. We were helpless, totally helpless . . .' His voice faded for a moment. 'One of the women they ravished and killed was . . . Rafael's mother. They made Felipe watch, and then blew out his brains on the spot. Rafael was only seventeen years old . . .'

Miranda and her aunt stared at him in horror, unable to find words to say what was in their hearts. It was a terrible tale. Dr Gómez wiped his forehead with his handkerchief and struggled for a moment for control. Then he continued in a voice that was calmer. 'Rafael went crazy with grief and a rage that was frightening to watch. And out of the carnage of that day was born this man, the man the world knows as El Español. Perhaps I should not use the word "man". Rafael was no longer a human being; he had become a demon.'

'It would have happened to any man under the same circumstances,' Miranda said, her voice trembling.

The doctor nodded. 'True. But I wish it had not been Rafael . . . Anyway, for four years he was almost out of his senses. He vowed that he would replace every ounce of gold stolen from Amarillo—and he did. He also vowed that he would hunt down every single man who was on that whaler that day—and he has. It was only when the last of them had been destroyed that his thirst for vengeance was finally quenched . . .'

'But where did he hunt them out?'

'All over the Pacific, in Portugal, Spain, England . . . He said he would not rest if even one were left alive. Then, when his terrible crusade was over, El Español finally returned to Amarillo.' He sighed. 'The anger is now spent, but the scars have not healed. Perhaps they never will. There is something inside Rafael that is dead . . .'

The drums had now reached a crescendo and with a final, thunderous roll they faded out completely. For an instant there was a vast silence, then everybody broke out into clamorous cheering. When it, too, had died down, the doctor turned to Aunt Zoe. 'I fear I have depressed you enough for one day, Miss Chiltern, and I am sorry. Now, shall we eat?'

Succulent aromas filled the night air as sizzling hunks of meat and fish turned on the fiery spits. Their plates were piled high with enormous helpings and, with their food, they sipped glasses of *kava* wine. People stared at them, but kindly, pleased to have them in their midst, plying them with more and more food.

'I could eat a horse,' said Aunt Zoe briskly, digging into the mountain on her wooden platter. '*Even* after your terrible story!'

The doctor laughed. 'Horse is one meat, alas, that we will not be able to offer you,' he teased. 'Rafael brought some horses to the island some years ago and they have bred very successfully here. They are far too precious to eat!' His eyes twinkled, and Aunt Zoe laughed.

As they ate, Dr Gómez explained the composition of each dish, and even Aunt Zoe declared herself well satisfied with the purple *poi* that went with the meats. Miranda ate distractedly, suddenly aching to see *him* again. She could not bear the thought of all the torments that he had suffered. She longed to ease his pain, soothe his brow and kiss away the sadness from his eyes . . .

And then she saw him.

They had finished their meal and, in an effort, perhaps, to lighten her mood of introspection, the doctor was in the midst of an anecdote. Even before she saw him she could feel his eyes touching her from somewhere in the distance: She turned round and saw Noela. She smiled, and the smile was returned by a silent laugh. Miranda's eyes moved again, searching frantically, and suddenly her heart lurched and her breath knotted. She found his eyes, and they seemed to impale hers for an eternity. She could not look away. But then, he did. He did not smile.

There was a crowd about him, and it was later, much

later, when Miranda had given up all hope, that he walked towards them. He was a head taller than those around, and the crowds parted respectfully to make a path for him. With him was Alvarez and some of the other Europeans that Miranda had seen on that first day on the wharf. One or two she did not recognise. It was not until he was almost upon them that she saw, walking next to him with supreme arrogance, Malamma, her stride still that of a queen.

He halted before them and bowed imperceptibly to Aunt Zoe. To Miranda he gave only a fleeting glance. Then he smiled at her aunt, and his whole face lit up as the smile warmed his eyes.

'I am glad to see that you are well again, Miss Chiltern,' he said gently. 'I trust Fernando has been looking after you well?'

For a moment even Aunt Zoe was tongue-tied, completely overwhelmed by the easy majesty of his appearance and not at all prepared for the encounter. 'Oh y-yes . . .' she stammered. 'Th-thank you for all the t-trouble you have t-taken . . .'

'It is my pleasure.' He tilted his head to one side and his smile broadened. 'You will be relieved to know that the repairs to your ship are almost completed. You will be able to sail soon.' Even though he smiled as he said it, the import of his words was not lost on Miranda. She knew they were meant for her, and it was really he who was relieved . . .

With another bow, he walked on unhurriedly. As Malamma passed her, Miranda felt her triumphant eyes look her up and down, revelling in her position as El Español's woman. The message in those mocking eyes was an open challenge: *Tell him if you dare and see what happens to your Peregrine!*

Miranda felt sick with misery. However much she wanted to, she could not tear her eyes away from his

tall figure as he walked away. Soon she would be gone
—and he was relieved that it was to be so!

The journey back to the villa in Dr Gómez's delightful
little pony trap was unusually silent, as each sat lost in
private thought. Even Aunt Zoe had little to say. The
feast had been enjoyable, but the unexpected meeting
with El Español had left her, for once, speechless. It
was only after Aunt Zoe had gone inside, with many
expressions of gratitude and pleasure at the outing, that
Miranda had a chance to speak to the doctor.

'Why did you tell us the story?' she asked as he was
getting into his trap. 'Is it not true that El Español does
not like his life to be revealed to strangers?'

The doctor paused and looked at her closely for a
moment. Then he nodded. 'Yes, it is true, but . . .' He
paused again as though searching for words. Then he
continued, ' . . . but you of all people have a right to
know.'

'Why?' Her question was barely audible.

'Because . . .' His voice softened. 'My child, it is
futile to love someone who cannot love. You are entitled
to know why.'

He settled himself in the seat, flicked the whip once
and the trap lumbered away.

Inside her room, Aunt Zoe sat motionless on the bed,
making no effort to remove even her cloak. She looked
up as Miranda came in, and her eyes were deeply
troubled. She sighed heavily.

'He is cold,' she said, 'as cold as a slab of marble.'
She rose from the bed and took off her cloak, then
sighed again. 'But,' she said, and her eyes suddenly
shone, 'he is a *man*—a man such as it is difficult to find
anywhere.' Miranda said nothing, but stood by the
window, gazing out silently. 'Nevertheless,' her aunt
added briskly, 'he is not a man for you—if indeed he is
for any woman! You must forget him, Miranda, you

must cast him out of your mind. He can give you nothing but heartbreak.'

Miranda gave a short, brittle laugh. 'He has cast *me* out,' she said bitterly, 'and I shall cherish the heartbreak, for it will be the only remembrance that I shall take of him . . .' Quickly, before her voice could break, she fled out of the room.

It was very early the next morning, even before they had risen, that Captain Chiltern walked softly into Miranda's room and shook her awake gently. The room was still in half-darkness as Miranda struggled out of slumber. As her eyes discerned her father's features looming above her face, she felt the ice crawl through her veins. A single look at his expression told her all she wanted to know. She clutched her throat with a hand.

'Peregrine . . .?' she whispered.

His expression changed to one of astonishment. 'You *knew*?' he asked incredulously.

Dully she nodded. 'Yes. I knew. It was why I sent you the note . . .'

His face filled with bitter remorse. 'Oh, my God . . .' he breathed, hating himself. 'If only I could have guessed . . . If only I could have guessed . . .' He buried his face in his hands.

Glazed with horror, Miranda watched him, unable to move. And she had been so sure that it was not the night Peregrine would choose! But she had seen Malamma at the feast—surely he would not have ventured forth without her? Setting aside her raging conjectures, she leaped out of bed and put her arms round the heaving shoulders.

'Tell me what happened, Papa?' she asked gently, forcing herself to remain calm.

He raised his anguished face and took her hand in his. The story he related was bare and unfinished, for he was not yet in possession of all the facts. But one fact was incontrovertible. Peregrine had taken advantage of the feast and the resultant absence from the harbour of all but a handful of guards. He had swum through the tunnel that was located in a remote corner of the lagoon and made his way through it to the area where Amarillo's gold was panned along the river. The gold was stored in an underground room, and he had not only found the cavern but had also managed to break in through a window. Unfortunately for him, in spite of the feast, there remained two islanders on guard. Peregrine was apprehended without any trouble at all. To make matters worse, he had managed to secure a pistol from somewhere, which he had fired at the guards. Fortunately he was such a bad shot that he had missed. It was, in Captain Chiltern's words, the most ham-handed operation one could imagine, planned by an impulsive, brainless fool.

His anger, which mounted as he related the story to Miranda, evaporated the minute he had finished. He slumped in a chair, staggered at the enormity of Peregrine's crime. 'We are finished,' he said, shaking his head in despair. 'We are finished on Amarillo!'

Miranda listened to the account in stony silence. Then she asked fearfully, 'And what has happened to Peregrine now?'

'He is in custody awaiting El Español's judgment on what is to be his fate. The harbour is tense, and rife with rumour as to what he will do. My men are all confined on the ship under armed guard. There is much anger. We do not know what will happen, but I fear the worst.' He again buried his head in his hands. 'I fear the worst.'

'Was Peregrine . . . alone . . . ?' she asked.

The Captain shook his head. 'We do not know. There is much that is still to be revealed. It all happened soon after midnight, and I have only just received these details myself. Their men are reluctant to talk, and it was with great difficulty that I was allowed to come here to give you the news.' He wiped his forehead with a tired hand. It was obvious he had not slept that night. 'I am sorry for you, my child . . . It is the ruination of your life . . .' His eyes filled with tears.

Miranda comforted him as best she could, her own heart like a leaden ball against her chest. She could only think of one thing as she sat with her arm round her father's heaving shoulders—El Español would never forgive her for this, never! It was only because of her that he had allowed the ship to enter. It was a betrayal of unforgivable magnitude.

They decided before Captain Chiltern left that, for the moment, the news must be kept from her aunt. There was still much that was not known and, until they learned what was to be their fate, there was no point in either conjecture or panic. He left, promising to try and return later.

To avoid having to face Aunt Zoe with a tell-tale expression, Miranda escaped into the forest before her aunt was up. The sun was just beginning to rise, but the breath-catching beauty of the morning failed today to bring her anything but messages of menace. The lovely valleys, still touched with indigo, seemed to spell cold horror, staring back at her with impassive, accusing faces. She wandered far and wide, visiting familiar and well-loved spots, but they brought her no comfort. Amarillo for them was closed for ever. In his terrible rage, El Español would see to that. They would be lucky to escape with their lives.

But the news, when her father finally returned almost twelve hours later, was far worse than she had expected. Captain Chiltern faced them in the garden with his face ashen and his hands shaking.

'Peregrine is to be shot at dawn tomorrow morning!'

With a cry, Aunt Zoe fell back into her chair in a swoon and Miranda flew to fetch her salts, while her brother fanned her in frantic alarm. Lori rushed about, not knowing the cause but sensing trouble, bringing cool coconut water and wet towels. It was a half-hour of confusion, but when Aunt Zoe had been revived, Edward Chiltern was more in control of himself. They sat in the garden facing each other wretchedly.

'They say El Español has gone berserk with fury. Even his own men tremble to enter his presence. Peregrine has been clapped in chains and is tied to a stake on the beach so that everyone may observe him. He is dumb with shock, too befuddled to recognise even me —not that we are allowed near him. They say . . . he had an accomplice, a girl from the island . . .' He raised his eyes to look at his daughter. 'Did you know about this, too?' Shamefully, she nodded, mortified now at her own silent complicity in the plot.

'Then why did you not tell me?' her father cried, not in anger but in raging sorrow. 'Why did you not give me a hint of what he was plotting?'

She hung down her head, unable to meet his eyes. 'Because I did not believe that he was serious, until . . . until . . .'

'Until it was too late,' he added heavily. 'Do you know . . . who the woman is?'

Miranda hesitated only minimally. 'No,' she said with firmness. 'No, I do not.'

'Well . . . It does not matter any more, I suppose. They say she stole a canoe and rowed away in the confusion. Nobody is quite certain as to who she is, but no doubt they will find out soon enough.'

'You must try to see El Español . . .' Aunt Zoe said agitatedly.

Her brother cut her off with an impatient gesture. 'Do you think that I have not tried to?' he cried. 'Since early this morning I have been begging, *pleading* almost on my knees, for but five minutes with him. But he has refused to see me—or anyone else from the ship. You know that none of us, except Dan, has set eyes on him even once since we arrived. Even so, I have begged for his indulgence for a few minutes only. And he has refused.'

'Then what is to be done?' Aunt Zoe asked, as tears began to trickle down her cheeks. 'We cannot let the poor boy die . . .'

'He deserves to!' Captain Chiltern shouted with rare lack of control. 'He has ruined us all. By Gad, he deserves to be horsewhipped, *horse*whipped!'

'Yes,' Miranda said sadly, 'he does. But instead, he is going to lose his life . . .'

Immediately Edward Chiltern's rage collapsed like a pricked balloon. His face went white. 'What am I saying!' he muttered, stricken. 'What am I saying . . .' He shook his head again and again. 'The poor lad, the poor misguided, foolish lad . . .'

It was very much later, after all the lamps had been extinguished and Aunt Zoe had been finally persuaded to go to bed with a sleeping-draught, that Miranda made her decision. It was quite clear in her mind now what she had to do. No matter what the consequences might be for her, she owed this much to Peregrine. Had she not remained foolishly silent, had she taken his supposedly idle fantasies more seriously, had she not been so involved in her own dilemmas, she would have informed her father of Peregrine's nefarious plottings much earlier. And, perhaps, this horrendous incident could have been averted. Now she had to make reparation, however hateful the prospect might be. She had to try everything within her power to save Peregrine and, possibly, the *Amiable Lady*. According to her father, resentment against them ran high among the islanders. Some were determined that the ship would not be allowed to leave the harbour; that it should be blown up and destroyed—with all the men aboard. Admittedly there was much anger, and words spoken in anger might soon be forgotten, but yet there was considerable danger. What if El Español agreed to the demented demands of the men around him? What if he were not able to contain the terrible fury that they said raged within him, too?

It was a prospect too horrible to consider. There was only one thing left to be done. She had to seek him out —and the devil take the consequences!

She had to wait until Lori and the two girls had also gone to sleep. She wondered if guards had also been placed at their own gate, but when she went outside to check, there was nobody there. The groom, who usually slept in the shed near the horse, was nowhere to be seen. Perhaps, hearing of the excitement in the harbour, he too had rushed off in an effort not to miss anything. It was already past midnight. Peregrine was to die at dawn. There was no time to be lost.

Quickly Miranda saddled the horse and mounted her. The mare neighed once gently, then silently trotted out. The moon—that cursed moon!—that had guided Peregrine on his way only last night, peeped in and out through huge banks of clouds and lit Miranda's path well. She remembered the way to the sandalwood forest and traversed it without meeting a soul. She knew that, even if she did, nobody would stop her for they all knew she had ridden through this very forest side by side with El Español.

At the edge of the cliff she paused and looked ahead. On the distant hill she saw the blurred outlines of the white house. Not a single light showed in its windows. She felt cold at the thought of the reception she would receive from him. It was possible she would not be allowed to pass through the gates, for surely there were guards posted there. She would have to enter by stealth —if she could—and find her way about in the dark.

Slowly, picking out her path with care, she moved towards the house. Soon the sandalwood was left behind and replaced by another, denser, jungle. There was a narrow winding bridle-path through the trees and, oddly enough, the mare seemed to know where she was going. It was possible, Miranda realised thankfully, that the horse had come from her familiar stables and hence was familiar with the way.

Suddenly, out of the darkness ahead, loomed the vague outlines of a white wall. She reined her horse and dismounted. For a while she listened, but all was quiet: not even the owls seemed to be stirring and the only sounds were those of night creatures as they rustled through the undergrowth. She shuddered and moved on, following the outlines of the wall to a far corner. Beyond, the ground fell sharply towards the sea and the sound of the booming surf was louder.

Positioning the horse as close to the wall as she could, she climbed up on the saddle and, leaning on the wall for support, swung herself on to it. In front of her lay a garden, wild and fragrant, and even in the gloom she could pick out great bunches of flowers hanging from the trees and bushes. She closed her eyes and jumped, landing on a heap of dried leaves. A stab of pain shot through her as she felt her hands and arms being scraped by a thorny bush, but she ignored it and stood up. There was no one about. Before her, in the midst of the gardens, stood the white house.

Was he in? Asleep? How would she find him? Perhaps he would refuse to see her. He would gaze upon her with eyes of hate. The thought was agonising. She could not bear to consider that those same eyes that had looked upon her with such tenderness, if only for a few fleeting moments, would now demolish her with their scorn. Yet none of the visions that now rose before her eyes could taint the love that consumed her from within. She loved him just as desperately as before.

As she neared the house, she was suddenly aware of the faint glimmer of a light in a downstairs window. She climbed up the steps to the open terrace, and working out her bearings, proceeded towards it, her heart in her mouth. The doors leading off the terrace were open, and that did not surprise her. She knew there was no crime on Amarillo; there was no need for it. Even the gold was under slack supervision, which accounted for the ease with which Peregrine had reached it. The danger lay only from outsiders . . . She cringed with shame at how despicably they had repayed Amarillo's hospitality.

She was in a large room sufficiently illuminated by pale moonlight to guide her between obstacles. There did not seem to be anyone about. Suddenly her heart throbbed uncontrollably. Ahead, in the dark, she saw a single line of light coming from beneath a door. Even before she opened the door, she knew that he was behind it.

It was another large room, sparsely furnished and austere. Bookshelves lined the walls, and the floors, of finely grained wood, were covered with scattered rugs. More than that she did not notice for, all at once, she saw him. He sat at a table at the far end of the room in front of an open window. Beside him burned a single lamp. There was no sound in the room except that of the scratching of his nib as it moved rapidly across the paper.

She watched him for a moment, filled with love and longing. His thick hair was wild and unruly, as always, and on his face was an expression of deep concentration. A lock of hair fell upon his frowning forehead and he raised a hand impatiently to brush it aside. As he did so, he lifted his eyes and saw her. For an instant his hand stilled in mid-air and his face tautened. But in his eyes, dense and black, there was no surprise. It was as though he knew she would come.

For a seeming eternity they stared at each other across the chasm of their separate worlds. Then he spoke. His voice was without inflection, but the words he said were chilling.

'I know why you have come,' he said, 'and the answer is No. You may leave.'

He continued with his writing and did not look up again.

CHAPTER SEVEN

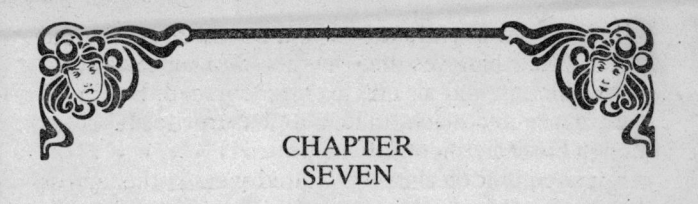

MIRANDA HAD come prepared for disappointment, for scorn and even humiliation. But the cold-blooded indifference with which he dismissed her now had never entered her thoughts. A boy's life hung in the balance for a crime he had not succeeded in committing—and this man had nothing more to say about it? She felt her anger rise. Slowly, but with determination, she walked further into the room up to the desk.

'No, I will *not* leave!' she informed him indignantly. 'You will have to throw me out if you wish to rid yourself of me!'

He still did not raise his head, and continued to write as if she had not spoken at all. She waited, galled by his deliberate lack of concern but not daring to intrude further. At length, he put down his pen and looked up. 'There is nothing more to be said. Peregrine will die at first light.' He could have been hewn out of granite, so unmovable seemed his face. He leaned forward and picked up the pen again.

'A young boy is to lose his life by the stroke of your pen, and it affects you not at all?' she cried.

'No. Life in the Pacific is cheap. One man more or less is of no consequence.'

'How can you be so heartless?' she burst out, outraged by his callousness.

The smile that twisted his lips was cold and ugly. 'Once before you accused me of being so. Surely now you are pleased to see how correct your assessment was?'

'Peregrine is foolish and impulsive,' she urged, determined not to despair yet. 'That is a misfortune, not a crime.'

His eyes ground into her implacably. 'He is also greedy! *That* is the crime he must die for—and as an example to others.'

'But his greed went unsatisfied! He stole nothing.'

'It was not for want of trying. It is the intention that is being punished. The result is immaterial.'

'But he is only a boy, surely . . .'

His head snapped up from the paper. 'And,' he interrupted scathingly, 'your husband to be! I regret that you will now have to look elsewhere for a bed-mate!'

He was intolerably offensive, and the taunt went home. She flushed. He was obviously under the impression that she was pleading for Peregrine's life because she loved him. What a blind fool he was! Yet she felt no compulsion to enlighten him. It would not matter to him one way or the other.

She realised that to be on the defensive would serve no purpose. 'Peregrine could not have conceived of this plot alone, and you know it. He was helped by one of your own islanders—and who knows what temptations were laid in his way?'

'Yes,' he agreed casually, 'Malamma shall also pay for it. But that is my business.'

Miranda was startled to know that he was already aware of the identity of Peregrine's accomplice and that it troubled him so little. Did he have no feeling in him at all? 'So!' she exclaimed contemptuously. 'It would appear that both of us are to be left without bed-mates!'

For the first time a flicker of annoyance crossed his face, and there was a stiffening of the jawline. She watched with perverse pleasure. She was prepared to tolerate his anger and suffer his humiliation, but she found his icy indifference unbearable. That, more than anything else, lacerated her beyond measure.

'We shall both find others,' he said finally, his cavernous eyes hard and flint-like. 'I perhaps sooner than you. And for this . . . *inconvenience* to you, I am truly sorry!' She knew he was mocking her, but she also knew it had to be borne. 'You are wasting your breath, Miranda.' His voice was suddenly a shade less harsh. Without noticing it, he had for the first time used her name and, even in her despair, it brought a glow to her cheeks. 'This time I shall not change my mind.'

Her hands trembled slightly. Encouraged by the softening of his voice, she began, 'I know that you regret having let our ship in . . . '

He cut her off with a sharp gesture. 'I do not regret it,' he snapped. 'On the contrary, I am grateful for it! You have helped to refresh my memory that had been dulled over the years as to what animals men can be. Indeed,' he glared at her angrily, 'I am beholden to your golden tongue for having softened me enough to obscure my judgment. It is a lesson that will stand me in good stead in the future—I shall not be tempted to soften again!'

Now he was really angry. He rose from the table and paced the floor like a caged cat. Quite irrelevantly she noticed again the sensuous grace of his movements.

'Ever since you set foot on this island, you have turned everything within me into incomprehensible chaos! I find myself doing things I have never done, thinking thoughts that have never before crossed my mind. Of all the misbegotten people on your ship I think it is *you* I hate most of all . . . ' He was now wild with fury, his face looming above hers, slit-eyed and vicious. 'Do you realise that half the island is demanding that your ship be blown to perdition—with everyone in it? Do you know what forces of savagery you have let loose in

Amarillo? I have killed men for less—and you now have the gall to face me with this, the most preposterous request of them all?'

His nostrils flared like those of an enraged bull, but in all this he had not raised his voice even by a tone. She felt chilled, suddenly, by the force of his hatred. But she knew that she had to fight it out to the end. This, at least, she owed Peregrine. She did not love him, but they had played together as children, had shared games and toys, and it had been decided that they would now share their lives . . .

Fearlessly, she matched his terrifying, tormented gaze, her head high and defiant and her eyes unwavering. 'And have the years also dulled your memory of what an animal *you* once were?' she cried, heedless of anything except the need to lash out at this brick wall of a man that she faced. *He hates you,* a little demon whispered inside her again and again, but she pushed it aside impatiently. 'Have you forgotten all those years when you terrorised the Pacific with *your* greed? What does it matter what your own greed was for—gold or blood? The ends you achieved were the same, the *means* you used were the same! And now, not satisfied with wreaking vengeance on the entire Pacific, your greed for blood is still unsatisfied, and you turn your hatred towards a brainless boy whose only crime is that he allowed his avarice to get the better of his intellect?' Her cheeks were white with fury and her blazing sapphire eyes as blue as the Pacific under the midday sun.

His face went pallid, but he did not explode further. It was only by the ashen lips and the look in his eyes that she could tell the extent of the venom inside as he towered over her like a volcano on the verge of eruption. But, although quavering, she did not show him that she flinched.

'Yes, I have done vile things,' he breathed, and his

voice was dangerously steady. 'And I have been an animal like everybody else. But the vilest thing that I have ever done . . .' he paused fractionally, 'was to look upon *you*. Any man who allows his senses to be dulled by a piece of skirt is the lowest of the low. And—as for anything else I have in my heart, greed for blood, vengeance . . . That is none of your damned business. It is *mine*!'

She felt suddenly sick at the finality of his rejection. She could no longer bear the terrible sword-edge of his tongue; his cynicism was searing. Every nerve in his body seemed to be revolting against her presence. But even with her crumbling confidence, she stood her ground.

'The deaths of your father and mother have been avenged enough, Rafael . . .'

'That is for me to decide!' His eyes narrowed, glittering furiously. 'Who has been talking to you?'

She ignored the question and turned away from him. 'You gave me something in my hand,' she murmured unhappily, her tones dull and lifeless. 'Was that also . . . vile?'

There was a small silence. He spun on his heel and walked to the window. 'Yes,' he said with his back to her and without expression. 'That especially.'

The cruelty with which he turned the knife revived her and sent a surge of rage through her, cutting across her despondency. She gripped the door with white knuckles. 'If I were an islander,' she spat out at him, flailing him back, 'I would be mortified for the shame you bring on Amarillo!'

'If you were an islander . . .' he turned round slowly with the flicker of a smile ' . . . you would be my woman!'

Her heart flew into her mouth and her throat constricted. With a supreme effort she tore her eyes away from his deeply enigmatic, mocking ones. 'Spare him, Rafael . . .' she whispered.

'*No!*' He was inflexible, but suddenly his shoulders drooped.

Miranda sighed in final despair. She knew that, now, there was no more to be said. They had used up all their words. She had failed—and Peregrine was going to die . . . He suddenly noticed her bruised arm.

'There is blood on your hands!' he exclaimed, as she moved through the door.

'I know,' she replied, her eyes brimming with tears, 'and on yours too!'

She closed the door behind her.

There was no difference in the manner in which the sun rose the next morning. It was the same golden orange rising out of the ocean like Aphrodite, bathing the world in its life-giving luminescence. The ocean was the same, the breezes emanating from it carried the same aromas, even the huge banks of cumulus clouds looked the same as the day before.

But, sitting on her terrace watching the first light of day, Miranda knew that, from now on, nothing would ever be the same again. Oh, how she hated this shameless sun and every one of its golden tentacles for having brought with it Peregrine's death! And how she hated the man who had ordered it to be so!

She had no remembrance of how long she had been sitting on the terrace. Neither could she recall her return from that monstrous house in the dark earlier hours of the morning. She remembered running through the sandalwood trees, gulping in the pervasive perfume as her lungs swallowed air and ached with the exertion in her chest. It was not until she had reached home that she had remembered about the horse that she had left behind. Well, it didn't matter any more. Nothing mattered any more. Peregrine was dead—poor, pathetic little Peregrine and his dreams of gold—and how she longed that she might be too!

For it was her silence that had sent him to his grave, as sure as the sun would shine tomorrow. Had she spoken earlier, his life might have been still pulsating within him. It was a burden she would have to bear always, until the last breath in her body. She tried not to think of the abhorrent assassin who had compounded her torture and made such pitiless mockery of her desperation. He had hurled abuses at her, crippled her with his slicing scorn, and then piled upon her the final humiliation—'*you would be my woman!*' It was unthinkable that even through his hatred he could consider such an abomination. To think that there was a time when she had deceived herself into believing that she loved him! The extent of her miscalculation made her close her eyes and bury her head on her knees in shame.

As the morning progressed, the pall of gloom over the villa thickened. Miranda and Aunt Zoe sat in the garden, numb with grief. Her aunt thumbed listlessly through her Bible. They could think of no conversation; there seemed to be no words left to exchange.

After a long, miserable silence, Aunt Zoe raised her head from the Holy Book. 'Why did you not try to seek him out?' she blurted. 'He might have been merciful.'

'He is an animal,' Miranda replied, and she was surprised at the calmness with which she could speak. 'He does not know the meaning of the word.' Her aunt stared at her, uncomprehending. 'No, I must correct that. He is not an animal, for animals have finer feelings often denied to humans. He is a reincarnation of the devil . . .'

'Yes,' her aunt whispered. 'That he is. For you to love him . . .'

'I do not love him,' she retorted sharply, her voice

trembling with anger. 'You were right. It was an infatuation that has now, mercifully, passed. I loathe El Español. He is truly as cold as a fishmonger's marble slab. I could not bear to see him again!'

She rose and went into her room, lying back on the bed and gazing unseeingly at the ceiling. Outside she could hear Lori and the two girls talking in hushed whispers. Probably they were discussing the grand spectacle of the execution that had taken place at the harbour. Everybody must have been there—a cause for jubilation, an occasion not to be missed! Sick with nausea, Miranda covered her face with her pillow, trying to blot out the horrible images of her fevered imagination. She knew her father would come to give them a description of the event and, suddenly, she could not bear the thought of seeing him, of hearing him speak the words.

Quickly she ran out of the house once again to escape into the blessed anonymity of the woods. It would be comforting to be surrounded only by Nature and not see a human being for some time. How loathsome the human race could be, and how defiled she felt at the thought that once she had felt love for this man, the most repellent of them all!

There was not a soul in the woods, but in the distance she could see men working in the fields and could hear snatches of song. That they could sing on a day like this seemed to her unbelievable. Perhaps they would even hold another feast to celebrate Peregrine's execution—and the destruction of the ship, if they went ahead with it. She knew not where she wandered, but she must have walked for miles, her hair loose and uncared-for, her clothes the same that she had worn the night before. Then, exhausted with her travels, she finally slumped to the ground and leaned against a tree. She closed her eyes and let the tears pour down unheeded. She wept for Peregrine and for herself and for the passing of all her dreams. And then, drained and without energy, she slept.

The forest was cold and darkening when she opened her eyes again. She got up hastily but could not remember which way she had come. For a while she tried to find a path, but there seemed to be none. She walked first in one direction and then in another, attempting to find some familiar landmark, but the area was completely strange to her. Choosing a path at random, she first walked through it, and then began to run. The undergrowth was thick and she had heard that there were snakes on the island, and scorpions and all kinds of strange, horrible spiders . . .

For the first time since she had been on Amarillo, she felt fear creeping through her heart. The woods were dark and smelled of dampness. Who knew what terrors lay hidden among those deceptively beautiful leaves and flowers! Sinewy tendrils brushed her face as she hurried through the foliage, and each time she could barely suppress a scream.

Suddenly, ahead, somewhere in this wall of blackness, she heard the sound of horses' hooves. With a gasp of relief she quickened her pace towards it. Horses meant a track, and once she could find a track she would be able to regain her bearings. The road appeared in front of her quite suddenly. The forest ended, and ahead lay the welcome sight of fields and a flickering light or two. The horses had obviously passed on. Perhaps it was her father carrying his bundle of gory news . . .

She stepped on to the dirt track, looked around, and realised where she might be. She had wandered far from the villa, but this road would take her back there. Keeping a lookout for ditches and potholes, she began to walk along it. Once again there was the sound of muted hooves. It could be some of El Español's monstrous men, full of liquor and high spirits after the successful destruction of their captive. She felt sick at the thought of encountering them, and ran up a low bank and positioned herself behind a tree.

There were four or five horsemen, and as they came nearer she could hear their raucous voices engaged in some heated discussion. She clung more closely to the tree, wanting even less that they should discover her. They passed close by and for a moment she held her breath, but they went ahead without pausing. She waited an instant, then stepped down again on to the track. She could still see, in the pale moonlight at the end of the road, a tangled bunch of men's heads and horses' legs.

The confused jumble of outlines disappeared round the corner, but she noticed with some slight apprehension that one figure still remained. There was a brief pause, and then it started to move back towards her. She halted abruptly in her steps and peered through the gloom. Why was this man returning? She wondered if there was time to conceal herself again but there was not—and before she knew it, he was upon her. It was Alvarez!

He stared down at her from his saddle, and in the light of the moon his eyes seemed to glint. He removed his hat and bowed in a low sweep, laughing hatefully. 'Ah!' he exclaimed. 'The silver-tongued Señorita! What were you doing in the bushes, eh?'

A cold hand gripped her heart but, throwing her head back sharply, she began to walk. Before she could take more than a step or two, he jumped down from his horse and his hand caught her wrist in an iron grip. With a gasp, she tried to wrench her hand free, but he held on like a vice.

'Let me go, you . . . you *brute* . . . !' she screamed, now truly frightened.

He laughed under his breath malevolently, and put his other arm round her waist, drawing her to him. 'You have brought us much trouble, Señorita,' he muttered thickly. 'Perhaps it is time you made us some recompense.' She reeled at the fumes of liquor on his hot, rancid breath.

Terrified, knowing that her strength could not possibly match his, she showered a rain of impotent blows on his chest, then reached out with her hand and dug her nails into his cheek.

With an oath and a roar of pain, he put a hand against her throat. 'Why you little bitch . . .'

She struggled violently in his hold, but his grip only tightened, and she felt the breath squeezed out of her body. When she felt the blackness descend before her eyes and the life being choked out of her, his hold suddenly loosened and he was wrenched away from her with such force that she tumbled to the ground. She was seized by a paroxysm of coughing, and her head reeled, but through the daze she heard the sound of a blow like a gunshot, followed by the sickening crunch of breaking bones. With a resounding crash Alvarez went flying back into the bushes, and lay there writhing in pain. She heard the rasp of an angry breath.

'Now get out before I kill you,' a quiet voice said. 'You're drunk!'

It was El Español!

Dazedly, holding his mouth with shaking hands, Alvarez climbed out of the ditch. Without looking up, he slunk towards his horse. As he removed a hand to pick up his hat from the road, she saw that it was covered in blood, and his jaw hung down loosely. With a last baleful glance at Miranda, still cowering on the ground, he clambered painfully on to his horse and vanished. For a moment she watched the figure disappearing in the dark distance. Then, slowly, she looked up at El

Español. He was standing by his horse, his hands on his hips.

'What the hell are you doing out here alone at night?' he ground out angrily. 'Don't you know there are men about thirsting for your blood?'

She did not hasten to reply, but picked herself up off the ground and stood unsteadily on her feet. Her face composed itself into an expression of supreme scorn. 'Why?' she asked coldly. 'Isn't one execution a day enough to quench their thirst?'

There was a very long silence. Then he said with characteristic quietness, 'Get on the horse. I'll escort you back to the villa.'

She drew herself up defiantly. 'I would as soon entrust myself to the hands of the devil! There is no difference between you and that . . . that barbarian. You're both as evil as a witch's curse!' She took a deep breath, wanting nothing more than to wound him as mortally as he had wounded her. She started to walk away.

With an oath, he leaped on to his horse and, leaning down, put his arm round her waist and lifted her off the ground as easily as if she were a piece of driftwood. 'I don't give a damn what you think of me, but I can do without your blood on my hands!' Roughly, he pinned her down in front of him like a bundle of laundry. She started to struggle, furious at the indignity.

'You have the blood of hundreds on your hands,' she gasped, as the horse galloped away and she felt the saddle bite into her flesh. 'What difference does one more make? And life is cheap in the Pacific . . . ' She gritted her teeth against the pain of his relentless grasp.

'True,' he said grimly. 'But I like to choose my own victims, not have them thrust upon me by others. Now if you move another inch, you'll get a touch of what Alvarez got, so stay *still*!'

It was agonising for her to have to lie so that she had

to rest her head against his shoulder and suffer his arm round her waist. Tears of helpless anger gathered in her eyes, and she bit her lips till they almost bled in an effort to stop them from falling so that he would feel them. Closing her eyes and making her body as rigid as she could, she tolerated the interminable journey. They galloped so fast that every bone in her body seemed shaken out of its natural position, and the pain was constant and biting. Yet she did not make a sound. He seemed to be in a mood of total recklessness as they flew up the track, and the silvery trees whirred past them in a blur. She could feel his breath, burning and savage, in her ear, and she averted her head so that she could obliterate it from her senses.

They arrived back at the crossing in an incredible burst of speed. As the horse slowed down, he released her abruptly, and with a crash she fell to the ground. 'Now,' he said through clenched teeth, '*you can go to hell!*'

She appraised him with a look of cold hate. 'There is a canker in your soul that makes you what you are, Rafael. I am glad I am not an island woman to be defiled by your touch. I *despise* you!' She was astonished at the calmness with which she could speak. Without a backward glance, she walked away, and behind her she heard his horse gallop up the hill. She had exorcised El Español from her heart. She would not need to see him again. For all she cared, he could be dead!

Outside the entrance to the villa, she stopped abruptly in her tracks. There were two men lounging around with muskets, one European and the other Polynesian. Beside them stood three horses. Her father had arrived! Absently she noticed that her own horse, left behind last night, was back in the shed. Her heart almost stopped beating as she thought of all the news her father would have brought. He must have witnessed

Peregrine's execution. After all, it was not like El Español to miss such an opportunity to cause them more pain!

She did not go into the garden, but entered through the front of the house and went into her room. She examined her face in the mirror, and was shocked at what stared back at her. Her hair was tangled and unkempt and her face looked like a white blur with deep sunken eyes ringed with black. Her dress was torn from its many encounters with thorns in the forest. Around her throat were ugly bruises where that brute Alvarez had pressed his diabolical fingers. She shivered as she re-lived for a moment the terrible adventure, then shook it off resolutely. El Español's intervention may have been timely, but it left her untouched now. It lessened in no way the revulsion she felt for him.

She washed, scrubbing her face till it shone, then combed her hair and brushed it out thoroughly, delaying the meeting with her father for as long as she could. She changed into another dress and rubbed her hands and arms with cream. Around her neck she knotted a scarf, so that the bruises would not be visible. Then, as slowly as she could, she stepped out into the garden.

As soon as he saw her, Edward Chiltern jumped out of his chair, his face contorted with worry. 'Where have you been, Miranda?' he cried. 'We have been distraught with fear for you!'

Her aunt immediately took out her bottle of salts and inhaled deeply, turning her eyes heavenwards in silent gratitude that her niece had returned unharmed. At the sight of their faces, Miranda's heart spilled over with agony and a lump rose to her throat that she could not swallow. Without a word, she went towards her father's outstretched arms, laid her head against his well-loved, comfortable chest, and burst into tears.

He hugged her tightly, stroking her hair with gentle

hands. 'You should not have been wandering around by yourself at this time of night, my dear,' he said in a voice shaking with relief. 'There is much anger tonight on the island, and people are in an ugly mood.'

'Why?' she asked dully. 'Are they not yet satisfied with what they have done? Has he ordered that we should all be executed as well?' She raised her eyes and looked at him miserably.

A frown creased his brow and he stared back at her in perplexity. 'Is it possible that you have not yet heard?' he breathed in disbelief. 'Oh my poor child, my poor, poor child . . .' He hugged her again.

She struggled to free herself, and stood back. 'Heard what?' Her voice rang with alarm.

'Peregrine has been spared. He was not executed this morning!'

CHAPTER EIGHT

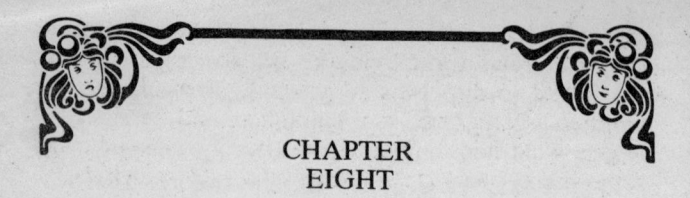

Miranda listened to her father's news in stunned silence, interrupted only by the occasional happy chucklings of her aunt. The execution order had been rescinded minutes before it was carried out. The harbour was thronged with people: there was not one vacant space. The crew of the *Amiable Lady* had been forced to the decks at gunpoint and ordered to watch Peregrine Holmes die. The wretched boy, petrified and babbling incoherently, was released from the stake and allowed to cower on the ground for a while so that the crowd could see the man who was to die for trying to steal their gold. The firing-squad consisted of four men, two Europeans and two islanders. Just as the order to fire was to be given, a rider came cantering down the road and on to the beach. He dismounted in front of the firing-squad and held up his hand. From his pocket he withdrew a kind of document, which he handed to Alvarez. As Alvarez glanced through it quickly, his face distorted with astonished fury. The document was passed from hand to hand and then, finally, read out to the crowd.

What it said was very simple and contained in a single sentence: Peregrine Holmes was not to be executed, by order of El Español!

There were mixed reactions to the startling announcement. Some islanders roared with frustrated anger while others sighed in relief that the boy was to be spared. For a while there was much confusion, and the crew of the *Amiable Lady* were quickly sent below deck in case the crowd turned violent. But the islanders were persuaded to disperse and gradually the harbour had emptied. Peregrine, too befuddled and terrified to realise what had happened, was hastily whisked away somewhere, but was still in custody—very much so!

'The island is rife with rumour, some wild, some believable, but nobody knows what made him change his mind so suddenly.' The Captain still looked bewildered, but very happily so.

'What does it matter?' asked Aunt Zoe querulously. 'All that matters is that he is not dead. Do you know what is to happen to him now? Surely they will not release him unconditionally?'

Her brother shook his head. 'Perhaps not. We have given up trying to fathom the mind of this man. But, whatever his decision, it could not be as horrific as this barbarous execution.' He looked at his silent, impassive daughter. 'You had not heard anything?'

Miranda shook her head. 'No,' she whispered in a daze. 'I had not heard anything . . .'

She sat paralysed by the news, unable to feel even relief that Peregrine was alive. Why had Rafael not told her? Why had he remained silent?

Her father rose to go. He wiped his brow with his hand. 'Thank God this day is over,' he said fervently. 'We have much to be grateful for. Peregrine is still alive by some miracle. I cannot but feel gratitude towards El Español, although I have never set eyes on him. It was the act of a brave man to cancel the execution in the face of such a public clamour for Peregrine's guts.'

Aunt Zoe looked alarmed. 'You said there is anger among some of the islanders?'

'Ay, that there is, and plenty. Some of them are a bloodthirsty lot and feel cheated of their entertainment! It would be best not to wander around too freely. We are confined to the ship and not even allowed on shore, but, thank goodness, the repairs are done. Whatever little remains, we can manage ourselves once we leave here.'

'There is no danger now of sinking?' Aunt Zoe asked very anxiously.

Her brother smiled. 'None. They have done a damned good job of it, I'll give them that. There was far more damage than we had thought at first. But it's all patched up, and we should reach Honolulu safely.'

'And . . . Peregrine?' Miranda asked, coming back to reality.

'We do not know yet,' he said. 'It depends on El Español. They say he will make a decision tomorrow.'

'And the . . . accomplice? Has . . . he been found?'

Captain Chiltern sighed, then looked at Miranda awkwardly and with obvious embarrassment. 'It was not a man,' he said gently. 'It is said to have been a woman. She managed to leave the island in a canoe, but they say El Español has already sent out boatloads of men to the neighbouring islands.' He sighed again. 'It is doubtful if she will be able to escape for long.'

Inadvertently Miranda shivered. Escape from El Español's wrath? Never! For a moment an involuntary pang of compassion shot through her body for the fate that awaited the woman who had belonged so fiercely to El Español. It was not an insult he would take lightly, and his vengeance would be truly fearful.

Captain Chiltern walked towards the house on his way out. There was a lightness in his step that had not been there for many a day. He looked at Miranda, and smiled cheerfully.

'Well lass,' he beamed, 'the day we have all been waiting for has come at last—we sail on the morning tide, day after tomorrow!' He rubbed his hands together joyously. Then his smile vanished and his face became sombre. He put a hand on her shoulder. 'I'm sorry about Peregrine, lass. I hate to see you suffer heartbreak like this . . .'

She forced a valiant smile. 'It's . . . it's all right, Papa.' Nevertheless, a solitary tear squeezed itself out of her eyes and rolled down her cheek. Who was she crying for, she wondered? Peregrine? Herself? Hastily she brushed it away with an impatient hand.

Her father kissed her on the cheek. 'Now, don't you fret, lass. What's happened has happened and cannot be changed. But I promise you one thing . . . I'll find you the best damned husband in all of the United States, you just wait and see!'

Miranda returned to the garden and sat down beside her aunt, staring into the nothingness of the sea. For a moment Aunt Zoe surveyed her through shrewd, half-closed eyes.

'Edward is a fool,' she snapped. '*All* men are! I could have told him what made the man change his mind!' She took in Miranda's impassive profile and her voice changed. 'You went to see him last night, didn't you?'

There was no point in denying it. 'Yes,' she said flatly.

Her aunt's eyes were deeply disquieted. 'I am afraid for you, my child. You will suffer much . . .'

That is what Noela had said too—'*Yo tengo miedo por tí.*' Miranda sighed. 'It is not a situation of my making. One cannot always control the waywardness of one's heart—if one can at all.'

She was on a collision course with disaster, upon a sea that held nothing but catastrophe. But she was helpless to do anything about it now. He had taken over her mind and everything else with it: she had no will of her own. She thought about him all night. There was no other image that appeared before her eyes. How could she have ever deceived herself into believing that she hated him, despised him! It was her pique talking, nothing else. She was still as intoxicated with him as she had ever been. And what a terrible injustice she had done him! How little she had trusted him—and her own judgment! Whatever it was she had seen in his eyes that very first day on the jetty had not been an illusion of her imagination. It was still there—but how easily she had let herself think the worst of him!

She would never see him again, and she would have to carry the burden of her injustice away with her to live under its weight for ever. She knew that her love would remain unrewarded, and it was a love about which he would now never become aware. It was a thought of intolerable pain.

The whole of the next day was occupied in packing their belongings into the trunks. Miranda was grateful that she had work to do, and that there were so many details to consider that she had no time to brood. She felt dead and heavy with lassitude, but forced herself to continue. Her aunt watched her silently, her forehead creased in a permanent frown. Then, unable to control her agitation any longer, she asked, 'You will not go to . . . see him before we leave, will you?'

'No.' Miranda continued with the packing.

'It is just as well,' her aunt sighed in relief. 'You would only break your heart further.'

'Yes.'

Her aunt touched her arm gently. 'I know how you feel, child. I know exactly how you feel.'

'Do you?' asked Miranda dispassionately. 'Did your Captain love you very much?'

Her aunt looked surprised at the sudden question. 'Of course he did! Why, he worshipped me!'

Miranda laughed with immense bitterness. 'Well, then, you cannot know how I feel. Rafael hates me. He considers me vile. He rues the day I first set foot on

Amarillo. And after yesterday, no doubt he will hate me even more.'

'Why, what happened yesterday?' Her aunt's eyes dilated with alarm.

'It doesn't matter now,' Miranda said tiredly. 'It is all over.'

In the evening, Dr Gómez came to bid them farewell. Miranda felt a rush of affection for the kindly man who had done so much for them. 'We shall miss you, Dr Gómez,' she said with sincerity. 'You have been a great support to us.'

He peered at her closely, but made no comment and contented himself with talking to her aunt. Miranda made abortive efforts to concentrate on their chatter, but failed. Like restless night creatures, her thoughts darted back and forth around a single candle. She would never again see that rare, wondrous smile that sometimes illuminated his beloved face. Nor would she ever again watch his coal-black eyes soften or glimpse their tenderness, fleeting and infrequent as it had been. How would she live with such a loss? How could she survive such deprivation?

'Peregrine's punishment has been decided,' Dr Gómez was saying. Her attention jolted back. Astonishingly, the doctor chuckled, and they both stared at him in surprise that he should take such a grim matter so lightly. 'He will not be allowed to leave the island, Rafael has said. Instead, he will suffer a retribution that is truly appropriate.' They both looked at him in alarm, but his eyes continued to twinkle. 'Peregrine will be made to work on panning the gold!'

'The gold?' Miranda cried, utterly astounded.

The doctor laughed again. 'Rafael feels that any man willing to lay down his life for gold must be cured of his greed. He must be made to live with it day and night until he is sick of the very sight of it!'

Aunt Zoe's mouth fell open for a moment and then she burst into roaring laughter. 'Well, bless my soul!' was all she could say over and over again. Even Miranda felt her lips twitching as waves of relief washed over her. Nevertheless, she cringed further. How neatly he had turned the tables on her, and how accurately he was throwing back all the insults she had heaped on him!

'Don't worry about Peregrine,' the doctor said. 'Rafael's wrath is enormous indeed, but so can be his kindness. He has punished the boy enough, and Peregrine will be a better man for it. If nothing else,' he laughed, 'he will hate the sight of that damned metal for the rest of his life—begging your pardon, ma'am.'

'How long will he keep him here?' Miranda asked.

The doctor shrugged. 'Until he has had enough. That is up to Rafael.'

'Is there still ill-feeling among the islanders?' Miranda asked anxiously, not so much for their sake but for Rafael's.

Dr Gómez looked thoughtful. 'Yes, there is. Some of them believe that Rafael was . . . prevailed upon to reverse his decision, and they don't care much for the idea of their leader being influenced by . . . anyone.' He coughed and glanced meaningfully at Miranda.

She crimsoned and looked away. 'Will the reversal . . . damage his standing on the island?'

'Only for a while, perhaps,' he said comfortingly. 'Rafael is well loved by the people. He is, after all, one of them. He has shared much of their sorrow, just as they have shared his. They will not disobey him. He has done too much for Amarillo already. No, the anger will pass. It always does. These are beautiful, gentle people and incapable of bearing resentment, especially against Rafael.'

Miranda breathed again. How much trouble they had

made for him! Perhaps his hatred of them was justified after all. Her agitation, silent and secret, kept mounting with the ticking away of each moment. It was as if her life itself was ebbing away. She sat numb and withdrawn, swallowed up by her remembrances and regrets . . .

Dr Gómez rose to leave with many expressions of good wishes and warm sentiments for a safe journey home. Miranda saw him out to his pony trap. As he was about to climb up, he turned to her suddenly.

'Do not go to see him, Miranda. It would not be wise.'

She was startled that he had so accurately read her innermost thoughts. She began to deny that she intended to, then her shoulders sagged and she could not lie.

'I cannot leave without seeing him once more. There are . . . things to be said . . .'

'You will be hurt,' he said gently.

'Nothing could hurt more than to leave him without a single word of farewell.'

He sighed. 'Rafael . . .' he searched for words. 'Rafael is too deeply scarred to be able to give love. Surely you must know that by now?'

'Malamma . . .' she began, but he cut her off immediately.

'What he gave to Malamma was not . . . love. That, too, you must know. It would not be enough for someone like you.'

It would be enough, her heart screamed, it would be more than enough! But she could not voice her feelings. Instead, she said, 'It is not love that I ask of him. It is . . . forgiveness. I have wronged him terribly. The wrong must be reversed.'

He shook his head. 'Let it lie, Miranda; let it be forgotten. He has been wronged by many. It does not worry him.' He laid a paternal hand on her arm. 'I have known Rafael since he was a boy. For someone as fresh and innocent as you, he can only mean . . . disaster.'

A small silence hung between them. Then she swallowed back the heartache that his cruel words had unleashed, knowing that he meant only kindness. 'I shall . . . think about it, I promise you.' But she knew that it was a hollow promise, for she would not be able to keep it. There was a diabolical force inside her that would push her to him, regardless of the consequences. It was a force she did not have the strength to repel. She had to see him once again, if only for the last time.

She made no attempt to conceal her intentions from her aunt. Miranda knew how fearful, how apprehensive, she was, but she hardly heard her pleadings, so powerful was the stimulus within her. This last glimpse of Rafael would have to endure a lifetime; indeed it was the only thing that *would* sustain her through a lifetime! There was no power on earth that could now stop her from going. Her aunt relapsed into helpless silence, knowing that her wilful niece was now possessed by the devil himself.

'May God be with you,' she wailed tearfully. 'You will need his guidance.'

But Miranda only laughed, her eyes radiant and her heart soaring on magic wings. 'I am long past caring about tomorrow, Aunt Zoe, for there is nothing beyond tonight!'

She saddled her horse, thankful that the groom was probably in the kitchen eating his meal. Her fingers trembled as she tightened the girth and she felt impatient at every moment wasted. Then, springing lightly into the saddle, she sped into the night, unmindful of the dark, knowing that the horse would lead her to her destination safely and unerringly. What if he refused to see her? The unwelcome thought produced a moment of panic; then she cast it aside disdainfully. He would not refuse to see her! Something inside her told her that he was waiting for her, that he knew she would come —and the reassurance made her quiver with impatience.

She left her horse at the same spot from where she had climbed over the wall the other night. She avoided the thorny bush that had scratched her then and landed this time on a patch of soft grass. Her heightened senses this time noticed every corner of the garden, even though it was nearly night. Through the darkness she saw the huge clusters of magnolia, the red hibiscus, the overhead bunches of fragrant frangipani and a thousand other blossoms spreading away before her. She inhaled the many perfumes of the night, knowing that she might never do so again. Her eyes misted at the thought, but she brushed the pain aside. She would not cry tonight. There would be enough time for tears later on.

Even before she had reached the terrace, she saw him. He was sitting on the balustrade and looking straight at her! Her heart leaped into her mouth, and she stopped. For a moment he remained motionless, then rose and slowly walked down the steps. She watched him without moving, her eyes caressing in turn every feature of his face. A moonbeam caught the black of his eyes as they glistened in the dark.

He walked up to her and paused. He leaned against a tree and crossed his arms against his chest. He laughed, and it was like a gentle rustle in the trees. 'I wondered if you would come.'

'You knew that I would,' she said, breathless with the hammering of her heart. She swallowed to wet her throat. 'We sail with the first tide tomorrow . . .'

'Yes, I know.'

'I came to ask your forgiveness . . .' She stopped and pushed aside a wayward tendril of hair from her forehead. 'I did not know that you had . . .' He said nothing. Struggling for words, she carried on, stumbling and stammering, ' . . . that you had reversed your decision. I . . . I was unspeakable . . .' She paused, but still he remained silent. the silence unnerved her. 'Say something, Rafael,' she pleaded. 'Make it easier for me . . .'

He shifted the weight of his leonine body from one foot to another. 'Why?'

It was not said harshly, but she was startled. 'Because . . . I spoke yesterday in anger. I meant nothing that I said.'

'What makes you think it would have mattered even if you had?'

But she was not put off, for there was no sting in the words. In the dark, she smiled. 'It would have mattered. I saw it in your eyes.'

'You see in my eyes things that do not exist!' Then he sighed as if with an immense tiredness. 'You should not have come tonight, Miranda. I can only hurt you.'

'So everyone has already told me.'

'Then why have you come?'

'Because I have another request!'

'Another . . . preposterous request?'

'Yes—more preposterous than all the others!'

She could hear the breath that he held in abeyance. 'Oh?'

'Will you grant me this one last request?'

'No!'

'You refuse it without even knowing what it is?' she cried.

His voice was suddenly very quiet. 'I know what it is.' He turned and strolled away a short distance. He walked slowly with the grace of a gazelle and, even without touching him, she felt the irresistible attraction of his body. He seemed to summon her to him so forcefully that she held on to a tree, fearful of being swept away. He came and stood close by. 'Don't ask me, Miranda . . .'

'Why not?'

'Because,' he said softly, 'I might not be able to refuse!'

'Do you want to refuse?' she challenged him, emboldened because she could no longer think clearly and her head whirled with his nearness.

'No. But I must.' —

Her eyes filled with tears. 'Rafael, let me stay . . .'

'*No!*' He ran a hand distractedly through his hair, his agitation visible in his tormented eyes.

'I will not be able to leave tomorrow . . . I will not be able to leave you . . .' He heard the despair in her voice and, with a supreme effort, he again controlled himself.

'Miranda, you do not know what you say!'

'I do, Rafael, I know perfectly well what I say.' Her tones were quiet, but she trembled as if with a fever.

'You would give up your home . . . for me?'

'Yes.'

'You would hurt your family and damage your reputation beyond repair, for me?'

'*Yes!*' She threw all caution to the winds.

'You would never then be able to go back to your world . . .'

'*You* have become my world,' she said simply. 'There is no other.'

But still he did not relent. 'You have built in your mind the image of a man who does not exist! I am a brutal man, Miranda. I am savage, and in my heart there is a wildness that cannot be tamed.' He was determined not to spare himself. 'I shall hurt you beyond measure.'

'You will not do so willingly,' she said miserably.

'And what if I . . . tire of you? What then?'

'I shall make another preposterous request, and ask you to kill me before you do.' Her vision blurred and she felt her knees would not be able to support her any longer.

Suddenly his eyes dissolved in a sea of liquid black. He lifted a hand and, with infinite tenderness, touched the side of her cheek. With a sob, she went into his arms, opened wide to receive her. He drew her, gently, against his chest and with a single sigh of defeat, buried his mouth in her hair. 'My foolish, brave, innocent Miranda . . .' he murmured. 'You don't know what you ask . . .'

'I love you, Rafael,' she whispered against his lips. 'I would die without you . . .' The warmth of his body caressed her through the thin layers of cotton that clothed them, and she felt his heartbeat against hers. Her knees trembled and he held her even closer so that she would not fall. His lips searched out every corner of her face, lingering agonisingly, and the touch of his hands on her neck, on her shoulder, on her breast plunged her inextricably into the vortex of the whirlpool that sucked her in without pity.

'Don't love me, Miranda,' he breathed, even as he stroked her body into rapture. 'Because I can give you nothing in return, nothing.'

'You have given without even knowing that you give.' Her voice was fragmented against the heat of his breath.

His hands stilled, then he raised them and cupped her face in his palms. He kissed her very gently on the lips, and his black, boundless eyes were smudged with pain. 'You are young and fresh and untouched—'

'Only for you . . .'

A spark of anger shone in the black depths. '. . . and I am only human! However much you may think so, I am not made of stone!'

'Then prove it to me, Rafael,' she gasped in challenge,

no longer hearing her own voice. '*Prove it* . . . I *love* you, Rafael . . .'

His hands slid down and caressingly encircled her neck. His eyes narrowed dangerously, and the violence packed in his body seemed ready to explode. The hands round her neck tightened. 'Don't challenge me idly,' he ground out through clenched teeth. 'Don't you know how much I want you?'

She put her hands over his, still about her throat, and loosened them gently. She kissed each in turn. Her eyes were brilliant. 'I love you, Rafael—' her smile did not falter '—you are the only man I can ever want . . .'

His mouth came down on hers with such violence that, had he not been clasping her, she would have fallen. All the latent passion of his body seemed to pour into his lips as they forced hers open. Inside her mouth, his tongue darted and lashed, probing every corner, seeking, demanding, until she felt limp with rapture. She raised her arms with an effort and wound them round his neck, her flesh dissolving like torrid wax above a flame.

'My lovely Miranda . . .' he whispered huskily while he covered her face with a thousand kisses. 'Don't ever regret this, my darling . . .'

As lightly as if she were a feather, he picked her up and, with her face buried in his shoulder, carried her inside. She had no idea where he was taking her, nor did she care. All that mattered was that she was with him and that his skin was warm against her lips and his heart beat as frantically as hers underneath her hand on his chest. He laid her down in the dark and with fevered fingers tore at the buttons of her dress. With a gasp he buried his face in the hollow between her breasts as his hands roved her body mercilessly.

A gasp rose to her own lips but he strangled the sound with his mouth, hot and hungry and unwilling to wait a moment more. She felt his flesh, warm and taut, against her and she strained towards him in an agony of ecstasy, whimpering with the pain that flooded her body. His hands, rough and wild, fanned her young, sleeping flesh into flaming life, plunging her into an inferno such as she had never known. Breathlessly, choking with love, she matched him kiss for kiss, caress for caress, while her senses fled and the world was blotted out. In her tumultuous daze she thought she heard the sound of surf thundering against the coral, but it was only her own blood pounding remorselessly at her temples. She felt herself being carried away, far away, above all the mountains of the world, wafted high among alien clouds that seemed aimed at the stars.

There was no time and no thought, only the violence of his wild love-making. And when the universe exploded around her ears, she was blinded by flashes of brilliant light that dazzled her and sent her spinning back to earth like a slowly fading meteor. She felt washed with a delicious, devouring pain and bathed in a sweet, sweet languor that dulled her senses and left her drained and exhausted. In a haze of pain and bliss, she clung to him as he cradled her in his arms and enveloped her in his love.

She must have slept, for when she opened her eyes, her head lay cushioned on his shoulder and he was very still. As she stirred, he turned his head and kissed her. He caressed her face with his fingertips, as soft as silk. His tenderness brought tears to her eyes, and they fell on his shoulder.

'Why are you crying?' he whispered as he kissed her eyes. His expression was tight with anxiety. 'I am a brute . . .'

She stopped him with a kiss. 'I love you, Rafael . . . It is just my love overflowing . . .'

He lay back with his eyes open and stared up at the

ceiling. 'It is not a love that will bring you happiness.' His voice ached with a terrible regret.

'It already has,' she said softly, dropping a kiss on his shoulder. 'If life brings nothing else, there will always be this . . .' She ran her fingers through his thick, tousled hair and smoothed it off his forehead. 'Tell me that you love me, Rafael?'

He smiled, that rare, slow, wondrous smile that, even in the darkness, filled the room with light. He turned and took her again in his arms. Very gently, he placed a kiss on her forehead. 'Yes, I love you. Perhaps in more ways than you will ever know.'

'Tell me . . .'

But he shook his head, the smile lingering. 'There are some things that cannot be put into words, but since you read my eyes with so much accuracy, you will see it there every time I look at you.'

She ached for him again, engulfed and enthralled by his tenderness, by the liquid emotion in his eyes and the silken touch of his hand.

'Why did you change your mind about Peregrine?' she asked, sitting up so that she leaned above him across his chest.

He did not answer for a moment, gazing silently up at the ceiling. Then he took a deep breath. 'Because,' he said surprisingly, 'my initial decision was unjust.'

'Then why did you make it in the first place?'

'Why is it,' he asked with a laugh, 'that you must have the answer to everything?'

'Because I love you, and I want to know everything that you think. That is the greed that *I* have!'

He laughed with genuine amusement. He raised his head and kissed her lightly on the lips. 'You have a curiosity that is alarming, even in a woman.'

'Then *satisfy* it!'

A sardonic smile played about his lips. 'I could not

tolerate the thought that he would one day be your husband.' She noticed that his face darkened even now with latent anger.

'You were *jealous* of Peregrine?' she cried in disbelief. 'You—the great Español?'

'Even the great Español is human,' he said drily, 'although sometimes you may find it difficult to believe!' The black, mercurial eyes clouded again. 'I would have killed Alvarez for laying his filthy hands on you,' he muttered between his teeth. With his fingers he caressed the bruises on her neck. 'I still might!'

She looked down on his thundery face with faint alarm. 'Nobody exists for me but you—and never shall,' she said softly. A thought flitted through her mind. 'What will you do with . . . Malamma . . . ?'

Immediately the veils descended upon his eyes and his lips tightened. 'That is still my business!'

'Did you ever love her?' She was unable to suppress the question that had tormented her for so long.

His face softened. 'No.'

'But she was your woman . . .' she persisted in a small voice, still racked with jealousy.

His expression softened further into a faint smile. 'I have had many women . . . Surely you must know that? But they were of no consequence.'

'Not even Malamma?'

He laughed, and pushed her down suddenly on to her back. 'No, no, *no,* not even Malamma. How many times do you want me to say it?'

'Until I can believe it!'

'I don't give a damn whether you believe it or not,' he said grimly, holding her in a fierce grip. 'And don't mention her name again to me, or I'll slap your behind!'

'Do you usually thrash your women?' she asked, teasing, so happy that she didn't care what she said, knowing that he loved her.

'Yes. Every wretched one of them!' But she knew he teased back.

She laughed under her breath and twisted her fingers lovingly in his hair. Then her face became suddenly sober. 'You will be kind to Peregrine . . .'

'*Damn* Peregrine!' he snapped. 'Don't mention him to me again either, or I'll change my mind again and put a bullet through his yellow belly!'

She sighed and slipped her arms round his neck, pulling his head down over hers until their lips met and kept meeting until he groaned in an agony of desire. 'I hate you for doing this to me!' he muttered thickly against her ear, kissing it again and again. 'Before you came, Amarillo had one curse, that damned gold, and now it has two!'

He looked at her so furiously that she froze. 'I can't bear it when you say that,' she whispered tremulously. 'Tell me that you jest . . .'

He groaned again, then sighed as the breath in his lungs collapsed. 'I've never met a woman like you before,' he said, still angry. 'You affect me like a fever and I can no longer think with reason. I should have killed you when I had the chance.'

'Then kill me now,' she said softly, 'but do it with love!'

He made love to her again and this time there was no wildness, only a tenderness that left her shaken and weak in his embrace. He stroked her hair with a hand full of love, and she lay in his arms content and with such soaring happiness that she thought she would burst with it. Then his hand stilled and a strange tension seemed to take over his body. Curiously, she looked up and saw him staring at the window. The colour of the sky was beginning to change from black to indigo with touches of shell pink towards the east. The blood in her veins seemed to still and turn slowly into ice. Dawn!

Anxiously, she looked at his face and at his eyes, motionless and impassive. A terrible fear filled her heart. 'Rafael, tell me again that you love me . . .'

For a moment it was as if he had not heard. Then he turned to her and enfolded her in his arms so tightly that she could barely breathe. 'Yes, I love you . . . You must know that by now.' He loosened her abruptly and again stared out of the window, one arm still about her. Then he whispered very softly under his breath, '"I'll say yon grey is not the morning's eye, 'tis but the pale reflex of Cynthia's brow . . ."'

Her heart leaped with hope as she recognised the quotation from *Romeo and Juliet*. 'Then you'll let me stay with you . . .?'

He turned, and his lips slowly, lingeringly moved down her face and sought hers. He kissed her with infinite gentleness. And against her lips he murmured, 'No.'

She went rigid with shock, revolting against the harshness of his judgment. But before she could say anything, he put a finger against her lips. 'Hush, my darling, and listen to me . . . I love you as I have never thought it possible to love a woman. But . . . it is not enough. For *you*, it is not enough.'

Dr Gómez's words! 'It *is* enough,' she cried fiercely. 'It is enough, Rafael, I want no more . . .'

'But you will, Miranda,' he said, gentling her. 'And I cannot give it—yet. There are things that I have to do . . .' He kissed the corners of her frozen mouth. 'I need time, my darling one, I need time.'

'Time for what?' She was overwhelmed with despair.

'Time to become a human being again. You yourself said . . .'

'No!' she cried, panic-stricken with remorse. '*No*! I meant not a single word, Rafael, I promise you . . .'

He sighed and lay back with his hands crossed beneath

his head. 'I cannot forget, Miranda.' His voice was low and still very tender, 'I am haunted by spectres from the past. I am a defiled man . . . and I am still crazed with hate . . .'

'But the past cannot be changed, Rafael, by destroying the future! Your wounds will heal, Rafael, I will *make* them heal!'

'Sometimes,' he said musingly, 'I am still an animal . . . It is not easy to live with me. And there are things that I must do . . .'

Her eyes swam in helpless tears. 'Whatever you are, I love you. I shall wipe away your memories, Rafael; they will die and wither away with the sheer force of my love!'

'They will *destroy* your love! But yes, they will die and wither. That is why I need time.' He took her hand and kissed it lightly.

But, ravaged with despair, she snatched her hand away from his and faced him with wild eyes. 'Then why did you let me love you? Only to send me away again?'

'I let you love me because . . . in your love I feel a human being again and because you have made me feel love.' He struggled a moment for words. 'And because, if I have a son, I would want him to be yours . . .'

She clung to him and buried her face on his chest. 'I shall not be able to live without you, Rafael, I cannot . . . Especially now, especially now . . . Don't you see that?'

'And you regret it already?'

'No,' she whispered, 'I shall never regret it, never!'

'Then you will have to learn to live without me, at least for a while, just as I shall have to suffer being without you, my beautiful, precious Miranda of the golden hair . . .'

'I cannot go,' she said, terror-stricken.

'I shall find you, wherever you are,' he promised, his

eyes wretched and tormented, unable to bear her tears.
'I shall come for you, I promise . . .'

But she hardly listened to his words, staring at him with demented eyes. 'Kill me if you like, Rafael,' she pleaded wildly, 'but don't send me away from you, *please* . . .'

He looked at her for a moment, his eyes tortured pools of blackness. Then, abruptly, he rose from the bed. 'All right,' he said suddenly. 'All right.' She stared at him disbelievingly, then collapsed on the bed almost fainting with relief. He would not send her away! She could stay with him, and love, and be loved by, him! Oh, what joy—what unspeakable joy!

In the brightening room he stood by the window, gazing out. She could see the outlines of his tall figure.

'Are you thirsty?' he asked suddenly.

She tried to swallow, but her throat was as dry as sand. 'Yes.'

A moment later he handed her a glass. 'Drink it.'

She drained it in a gulp, then lay back suffused with happiness. He came and reclined beside her, then opened his arms and held her close to him.

'Will you truly let me stay, Rafael?' she asked again, still bathed in an incredulous joy, cradled safely in his arms.

'Yes.'

Delirious relief swept over her. 'I love you with all my heart, Rafael,' she murmured sleepily against his warm, wonderful golden skin.

'I love you too, my darling one. Don't ever forget that, not for a moment.' He put a finger under her chin and raised her face to his. For a long, long moment he kissed her and she filled with sweetness. She gazed up at him through sleep-filled eyes, and smiled. Through a haze she saw with dreamy surprise that there were tears in his eyes.

She nestled against him and closed her eyes. Just before she slipped into an ethereal oblivion, he murmured against her ear, 'Forgive me, Miranda, forgive me . . .'

But she was already asleep.

CHAPTER NINE

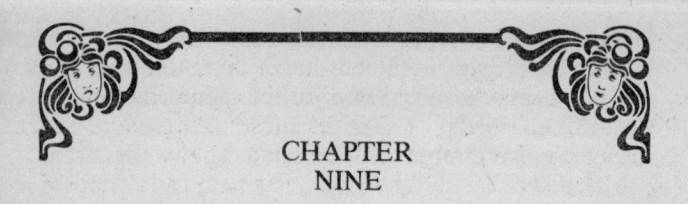

THERE WAS light and yet there was not light; there was sound but still all was silent. Brilliance and gloom, thunder and quiet chased each other interminably in her head. It took a long time to come awake, and when she did it was like still being asleep. Her hand reached out and touched the pillow next to hers. 'Rafael . . .?'

There was no reply. Then a hand, cool and comforting and full of love, soothed her forehead and stroked her hair. She smiled. 'Rafael . . . is that you?'

There was a pause, then someone said, 'It is I, dearest child. Thank the Lord that you are awake!'

It was the voice of Aunt Zoe!

Miranda's eyes shot open, but for a frozen instant she lay still. 'Aunt Zoe . . .?' she frowned dazedly. 'How did you reach here?'

Her aunt's face, white and drawn, loomed above hers in the half gloom. 'I have been with you, child, since . . . since . . .' She relapsed into silence.

With an effort that made her head whirl, Miranda struggled to sit up, but she couldn't, and fell back with a groan. Her tongue felt thick and swollen and nausea flooded her. 'Where is Rafael?' she asked in rising panic. 'Where is he—and how did you reach here?'

Her aunt made no response and she saw with astonishment that her eyes were filled with tears. Clamorous alarm bells began inside Miranda's head and, with a determined effort, she heaved herself up on her elbow and looked around. Her eyes dilated with cold horror.

She was in her cabin on the *Amiable Lady*!

With a cry, she stumbled out of bed, clutching the wall for support, and looked out of the porthole. The sky and sea were pink with the sunset. All around was the ever-moving carpet of the Pacific. They were at sea!

Miranda moaned like an animal in pain and crumpled on to the bed with her head buried in her hands. 'No,' she whispered. 'No, no, oh *no* . . .! Why did you bring me back, *why?*' Her voice rose to a scream.

Her aunt struggled to control her, trying to put an arm round the heaving shoulders, but Miranda shook her off angrily. 'Go *away!*' she screamed in agony, her eyes wild and staring. 'Oh, go away . . .' she moaned again and again.

'Miranda, darling, it is for the best . . .' her aunt began desperately, but she did not hear a word, shaking her head and rocking back and forth in torment.

She felt a glass slipped between her lips with such force that, before she knew it, she had gulped and the liquid sailed down her throat. She hit out at the glass, sending it clattering into a corner, then dissolved into a storm of tears, repeating his name over and over again. 'Rafael, Rafael . . . Oh, my darling Rafael . . .'

As the sleeping-draught began to take effect, her eyelids became heavy and she could no longer keep them open. It was dark when she woke again, and a small night-light burned in a corner. For a while she lay still, numb with the fear that blocked her mind. At the table her aunt sat reading her Bible under the tiny lamp. As her memory again came jerking back, Miranda moaned, and her face crumpled.

'Why did you bring me back?' she whispered brokenly.

Her aunt was by her side in an instant. She bent down and kissed her on the forehead. 'I didn't.'

'Then how did I get here?' Miranda cried angrily.

With a sudden shock she realised she had no memory of anything beyond falling asleep in Rafael's arms. Her eyes became frightened. 'Wh-what happened?'

'He . . . brought you back to the villa.'

'Rafael?' she laughed in agonised disbelief. 'You are lying, Aunt Zoe! How can you tell me such an untruth?'

Her aunt's eyes misted and her lips trembled. 'It is the truth, child. Rafael carried you back.'

'*Carried* me back?'

'Yes. You were . . . unconscious.'

Miranda let her head fall back on the pillow and her eyes were stunned. It did not take her long to put two and two together. The drink he had given her was drugged. After she had drifted into unconsciousness, he had taken her back to the villa. Rafael had tricked her—he had lied to her and made false promises! He never had any intention of letting her stay. The enormity of his deception plunged her into a state of such shock that she could not even cry. The cruelty of his judgment deprived her of all sensation, and her mind was devoid of all thoughts save one. Rafael had deceived her!

At some time during the night she felt the fever rise and her body became hot and prickly. For four days Miranda lay burning and sunk in delirium. She floated in and out of consciousness, only very vaguely aware of faces and voices filled with anxiety and love. But she heard nothing and her staring eyes saw nothing—save the face of the man who had cast her out without a thought.

The fever finally broke. She woke up one morning, damp with sweat, limp and exhausted. Mentally she felt as if she were hollow. And in her breast she could not even hear the beating of her heart.

She breathed deeply, then asked in a voice that was very quiet, 'Tell me what he said, Aunt Zoe?'

Her aunt sat on her bed and hugged her, greatly

relieved that the fever had passed. 'He . . . told me to look after you well.'

'That was all?'

'Yes. That was all. But his face was that of a man suffering the tortures of hell.'

There was silence in the cabin. All that could be heard was the ticking of the clock on the wall. There were tormented questions in Aunt Zoe's eyes, but she could not ask them. The child was in a state of shock. Whatever her experience, it had been terrible—terrible!

Miranda began to cry with her face to the wall. All day long she cried, not noisily but with an intensity that was frightening. It was as though, through her tears, she was trying to wash away her pain; but the more she shed them, the more pain there seemed to be. It was unending.

Captain Chiltern peeped in every now and again, his face scored with lines of worry. He had been petrified with fear when Miranda had been carried on to the ship on a litter and deeply unconscious. Aunt Zoe had reassured him that it was only a sudden fever and that his daughter would be perfectly well within a day or two. He had wanted to summon Dr Gómez immediately, but his sister had managed to dissuade him. Being unaware of everything that had happened while they were at the villa, he had accepted his sister's explanations, as had all the members of the crew. Many of them looked at each other knowingly. The poor lass had suffered a terrible shock over young Peregrine. It was only natural that she should now capitulate under her dreadful sorrows.

In the meantime the *Amiable Lady*, shining and fit again, forged ahead towards Samoa. The whaling was excellent and the stoves bubbled incessantly with precious oil. The holds were now bulging with brimming barrels and the men were again happy and smiling.

Of course, Peregrine Holmes was being sorely missed on board, but then, everyone agreed, it was his own fault. He was lucky to have got away with such light punishment. Indeed, he deserved worse! Nevertheless, the feeling of relief at leaving the accursed island of Amarillo was great and universal. Even though the crew had not been harmed, the spectre of the faceless man who governed their every move had been unnerving, and everyone vowed fervently never to return.

The first day that Miranda was fit enough to venture on deck, the crew welcomed her with heartfelt smiles. Everyone knew that it was because of the Captain's lass that they had lived to see this day.

'It's good to see you up and about again, Miss Miranda,' Bert Paulton beamed, 'and that's a fact. We owe our blasted lives to you, Miss Miranda, and that's a fact too!' He stood back triumphantly, pleased with his little speech. Several of the others nodded in serious agreement.

Miranda managed a faint smile, then looked away. Bert leaned forward and his expression was sombre. 'We're all sorry about Mr Holmes,' he said in funereal tones. 'But at least his life was spared, and we should be grateful.'

Aunt Zoe came flying on the deck and shooed them all away like flies. 'Now come on,' she said severely, 'off with you lot! You're a lazy bunch of rascals with nothing to do except loll around and gossip all day, and *that's* a fact, for sure!' Hastily they went back to their jobs, for there was not a single man on board who did not have a healthy respect for the Captain's sister's tongue.

Without a word, Miranda went below again and locked the door behind her in the cabin. It was much later, when she could no longer bear her aunt's incessant rattling of the doorknob, that she got up from her bunk and unlocked the door. Her aunt burst into the cabin in a flurry of panic. 'What were you up to, child?' she gasped, distraught.

For the first time in days Miranda smiled, but without warmth. 'It's all right, Aunt Zoe, I am not about to kill myself. I don't think he is worth dying for.'

'Thank the Lord you're beginning to see sense, Miranda,' she exclaimed with overwhelming relief. 'Men like Rafael should be hanged and quartered!'

'Perhaps.' Her face was blank. 'But I would be obliged if you would not mention his name to me again. I never want to hear it as long as I live.'

The journey towards Honolulu proceeded smoothly, and the whaling remained good. They called at Samoa, the Ellice Islands and many others, but Miranda did not step ashore. Her strange somnolence worried her aunt and father considerably, but they kept their peace, allowing her to heal in her own time and at her own pace. Edward Chiltern still believed that it was for Peregrine that she mourned, but her lack of visible emotion was unnatural, and they both feared that if she remained bottled up, she would permanently lose her mental equilibrium.

The only member of the crew who had not spoken to her, except in passing, was Dan. Silently, from a distance, his canny eyes saw much that the others did not. He knew that it was not for Peregrine that her heart was breaking. Miranda had got into the habit of keeping to her cabin during the day when the crew were about, and creeping up to the deck at night to pace for hours under the welcome, merciful cloak of darkness.

One night she went up on the bridge, where Dan was on watch. Quietly she seated herself on the same coil of rope that she had sat on many, many nights ago, where she had spoken to him of her plan to tackle Amarillo. He watched her in silence without disturbing her reverie, and she sat as if carved out of a block of granite, her hands unmoving and her eyes fixed sightlessly in the distance. Finally, Dan could contain himself no longer. He had known her since she was a child; she had played on his lap and often sobbed on his shoulder when troubled by some childish problem.

'It was an evil day we sailed into Amarillo,' he said sorrowfully, 'even though we had no choice.'

For a while she still said nothing, then she shuddered. 'We had a choice,' she said bitterly. 'It might have been better to let the ship sink.'

He was appalled at the misery in her face. He came and sat beside her and laid a crabbed hand on her shoulder. 'He is controlled by demons, Miss Miranda. He cannot be tied down.'

'Yes,' she said absently, her thoughts once again floating away into the distance. 'Yes.'

'But he did treat us well,' Dan went on doggedly, determined to defend his hero. 'And he will not harm Mr Holmes. The young scamp deserves his punishment, light as it was under the circumstances.'

She rose. 'We all deserve our punishments, Dan,' she said wearily, 'light or heavy.' She turned and went down again.

That night Miranda cried again, her soft moans like those of an animal racked with pain. She knew she had nobody to blame but herself, not even him. '*I can only hurt you,*' he had said. But dulled by love—or infatuation!—she had been blind to everything, dazzled by the radiance of the man. She had believed, foolishly, that she could make him love, change his heart back into flesh and blood. And she had been wrong. She remembered his whispered words of love, his smooth promises, the tenderness of his eyes and hands . . . How hollow they all seemed now! Yet she could hardly blame him for having taken what was so freely offered. She had thrown herself at him, forced him to love her, heedless of all the warning bells. '*I have had many women*,' he had told her. Well, she had become yet another. Waves of shame swept over her, one after another. How low she had sunk—and how easily he had triumphed!

Listening to her quiet sobs, her aunt thanked the Lord in silent relief. The child is getting over it, she thought to herself in deep gratitude. The tears will sweep away the heartbreak. It is only a matter of time.

The next morning Miranda systematically went through her diary. She tore out every page that she had written on Amarillo and, shredding them into fragments, flung them out of the porthole. From her sketchbook she removed all the drawings she had made on the island, and with them did the same. She paused as she came upon the impromptu sketch she had made of him astride his horse on that distant hill. It was still faceless, but its lines were so faithful that for a moment her heart wrenched with agony. Then, seized by fury, she pulled it out of the book with such force that all the other pages fell apart and drifted to the floor. '*I know you will remember me without it.*' No, she vowed to herself as she destroyed it viciously, I will *not* remember you, you unspeakable limb of Satan! I will tear out every remembrance of you from my soul even if I have to cut it out with a knife!

But it was a promise to herself that Miranda was destined not to keep, although she did not know it then. Three days before the *Amiable Lady* was due to sail into Honolulu harbour, she realised that the last laugh, after all, would belong to El Español.

She was going to have his child. It was six weeks since they had left Amarillo.

* * *

Edward Chiltern sat slumped in the chair with his head held in his hands. His face was like white chalk and he was having tremendous difficulty in speaking. Sitting opposite him, her mouth set defiantly and ready to give him her best argument yet, was his sister. Miranda lay on the bunk, staring up at the ceiling with her usual impassive expression. There was no way of knowing what was passing through her mind.

Her father groaned and raised his head. His eyes were wretched. Then he rose and walked to the bunk. He sat down and enfolded Miranda in his arms. 'My poor child,' he whispered, distraught. 'My poor, wronged child . . .'

Miranda lay quite motionless in his arms, then, suddenly, smiled. 'It's all right, Papa,' she said gently, 'I shall survive it . . .'

His face contorted with rage. 'If I could,' he muttered grimly, 'I would kill him!'

'It was not his fault alone,' Miranda said quickly and for no reason. 'It was mine, perhaps wholly mine, for loving him . . .' She turned her face away.

'What are we going to do?' Her father was pacing up and down the tiny confines of the cabin.

His sister rose and took command of the situation firmly. '*I* know what we shall do,' she said with a determined set of the mouth. 'These are matters that men know nothing about. You just leave it to me, Edward. Miranda and I will manage.'

A look of pathetic hope sparked in his eyes. 'What do you plan?'

'Never you mind,' she said severely. 'Never you mind. This is between me and Miranda. Now, off you go! We have matters to discuss.'

Shaking his head, mumbling to himself, he opened the door. He gave Miranda a worried look. 'Are you . . . all right, child?'

Miranda nodded. 'Perfectly, Papa. I have never been better in all my life!' Her aunt looked at her in surprise, for she sounded astonishingly cheerful!

'And not a word, Edward, to anyone. Mind your tongue! I know what you're like after a couple of glasses of ale.'

'Do you think I'm mad?' he asked irritably. 'Of course I shall mind my tongue!' Slamming the door behind him to emphasise his annoyance, he stumped away.

Aunt Zoe turned to her niece and positioned herself on the bed with fierce determination. 'Now,' she said with forthright practicality, 'it is six weeks since we left Amarillo, therefore it is still not too late.'

'Not too late for what?' Miranda asked vaguely, still smiling strangely and lost in her thoughts.

Her aunt clucked in impatience and lowered her voice. 'Not too late to get rid of it, of course; what else? I know that these island women have all kinds of herbs and remedies that will do the job. It won't be painful and it won't take long. By the time we are ready to sail from Honolulu, you'll be as right as rain again, you'll see!' She sat back and looked at Miranda triumphantly.

With an effort, Miranda pulled herself out of her reveries. 'What are you talking about, Aunt Zoe?'

Her aunt threw up her hands as if driven to the limit of her forbearance. 'About the *child*, Miranda, what else? You'll have to get rid of it, of course! I know it's a sin, but God will forgive us.'

'But I don't want to get rid of it, Aunt Zoe,' she said softly. 'I want to have the baby!'

For a moment her aunt wondered if she had heard correctly. Then she gasped. '*What?* Do you know what you are saying, child?'

Miranda smiled, and it was not a smile that was pleasant. 'Yes, I know what I'm saying, Aunt Zoe. I want to have the baby.' She sat up abruptly and grabbed her aunt's arms in a fierce grip. Her eyes shone as if demented. 'Don't you see that I must?' she asked angrily. 'It is the only way in which I can pay him back for his deceit! He said he had nothing to give me!' she laughed crazily. 'Well, he has given me something— and that he can never take back! I have to have his child, don't you see Aunt Zoe? *I have to* . . .' She burst into tears and sobbed hysterically.

Horrified, her aunt cradled her and stroked her hair absently, murmuring words of meaningless comfort. Why, the poor child was losing her mind! What she suggested was unthinkable! The whole world would laugh at her, mock her and treat her like dirt. How could they ever return to Nantucket—or even face the men on the ship? Unhappily, Aunt Zoe recognised that what she herself was suggesting was a sin in the eyes of man and God. But where her niece was concerned, she held nothing more sacred than her well-being. God had so many sinners on his hands already, that one more would make very little difference to him . . .

Miranda had been stunned and horribly frightened when it had dawned on her that she was with child— Rafael's child. But, after the first shock had worn off, strange new ideas had begun to form in her mind. That he did not love her she now knew to be a fact that she had been too blind to recognise earlier. The pain of that realisation was unbearable, but she was determined that she would eradicate it in time. At least for that one night he had loved her, and that was something not even he could take away from her. The child that was growing in her womb was something even more tangible. '*If I have a son, I would want him to be yours* . . .' Not for a moment did she now believe those smooth, hollow words he had whispered in her ear. But she had seen the yearning in his eyes, for every man wanted a son as an extension of his own image.

And now Rafael would have a son, and he would be hers. And he would be hers alone! Within her now she had a part of him, flesh of his flesh, blood of his blood, but Rafael would never see him. He would long for him and yearn to hold him in his arms, but he would do so over her dead body. The thought flushed her with triumph and filled her with a jubilation that was intolerably sweet, for it promised her revenge!

Aunt Zoe was certain that, once she calmed down and reasoned the matter sensibly, Miranda would undoubtedly change her mind about the child. But, to her astonishment and horror, Miranda remained adamant. Never, she informed her aunt firmly, would she agree to destroy the child and, as far as she was concerned, the matter was settled. Only the means remained to be decided.

When informed about her appalling decision, Edward Chiltern was struck dumb with shock. He could hardly believe that any daughter of his could be so utterly perverse. But he balked from confronting Miranda himself, leaving all the talking, gratefully, to his sister. Finally, when they realised that nothing was likely to change Miranda's mind, they gave in, but with fearful apprehensions. What was to be done now? Obviously, some other plan of action had to be evolved, but what? And *where*?

Miranda herself, oddly enough, seemed to be the person least concerned with the arrangements to resolve the problem. She was perfectly content to leave all the decisions to her aunt and her father, making it clear that she would accept whatever they decided—provided she would be allowed to have her baby. Indeed, her attitude seemed incomprehensibly strange. She had got into the habit of smiling secretly to herself with a dazzling light shining from her eyes, and spending hours on deck staring fixedly at the dolphins and the flying fish. It was an extremely disquieting phenomenon, and her father and his sister had decided that, as soon as they reached Honolulu, Miranda would be taken to the best European doctor on the island and examined thoroughly.

Finally, after a great deal of hushed discussion and argument, brother and sister agreed upon a plan of action. It would involve a complete change in their lives, but it could not be helped. Drastic problems required drastic remedies. After their sojourn in Honolulu, Captain Chiltern would continue on his voyage with the *Amiable Lady* and eventually return to New England. Miranda and her aunt would stay on in Honolulu, where Miranda would be introduced as Mrs A or B or C—it mattered not what—a young widow who had recently lost her sailor husband at sea. They would rent a house, make themselves as comfortable as possible and await the birth of the baby under the watchful eye of a good physician. Edward Chiltern would bring their remaining belongings from Nantucket on his next voyage to the Pacific. It would take at least a year, if not more, but that could not be helped. To return to their home now would be unthinkable for Miranda.

Honolulu was an increasingly prosperous port with a large American colony that was growing steadily. It was just possible that, in the course of her stay there, Miranda might find a respectable, comfortably off gentleman who would be willing to offer her marriage and a home for her and her baby. Since it was inadvisable for the two women to live on their own in an atmosphere as strange as the island of Hawaii, Dan would remain with them. Of course, Dan would have to be taken into their confidence, but about that the Captain had no qualms. They had known each other for many years, and had sailed together often enough to trust each other completely. Dan could certainly be depended upon to keep his mouth shut.

Miranda agreed to the proposition so readily, but with such little interest, that her aunt wondered if she had understood it at all.

'Yes, I have understood it, Aunt Zoe,' she said dispiritedly, 'and it is acceptable to me.' Then, noticing how unhappy and aged her father had begun to look, and how cheerless was her aunt's expression, she was flooded with remorse. Putting her arms round her father's shoulders and placing a tender kiss on her aunt's cheek, she said, 'I have given both of you endless trouble.' Her eyes filled with tears. 'I am sorry, Papa, indeed I am . . .'

He kissed her fondly and tried to make a valiant jest of it. 'Well, what are children for if not to give their parents trouble, eh? Don't worry, lass, we have broad shoulders. And no more tears! It is something we have to make the best of. After all, we are only human.'

'All except one,' she murmured to herself bitterly. 'All except one!

CHAPTER TEN

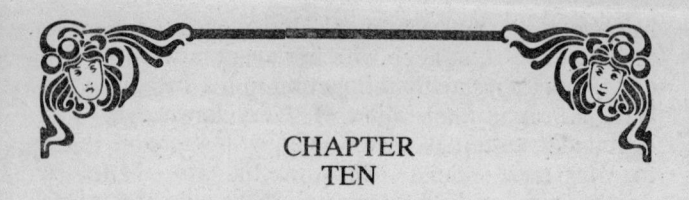

SINCE A SHIP from Nantucket had first discovered Honolulu harbour in 1819, the Hawaiian Islands had become favourite ports of call for all sailing vessels in the Pacific. The shipyard, which had been opened not so many years earlier by two survivors of a wreck, was well stocked to replace essentials and carry out repairs, and there was no shortage of provisions to replenish diminishing stores. There were hogs, wild beef, poultry and eggs, goats, sugar, molasses and coffee, all kinds of luscious fruit and fresh vegetables, in abundance. In addition, shipping offices willingly acted as mailboxes for itinerant sailors to receive letters from home. And, of course, there was good wine and beautiful women—wild, willing women in plenty.

As the *Amiable Lady* approached the peaceful harbour nestling at the foot of emerald-green hills, hundreds of brightly-clad Hawaiians welcomed it with shouts of '*Aloha, Aloha,*' and waved joyously. The ship's crew were massed along the decks, shouting and waving in return, hardly able to contain themselves before they reached the shore. A few lovely girls, bare from the waist up and wearing garlands, laughed, and jumped into the water, swimming out to meet the ship. The crew cheered wildly, and one man, driven mad with excitement, jumped over the side.

Aunt Zoe watched through a porthole, sniffing. 'Dis*gus*ting,' she muttered. 'Dis*gus*ting!'

Miranda observed the scene, shot with pain. How

like Amarillo this island was! How would she be able to bear it? He would be with her every moment of the day, his hateful memory lingering in the turn of every leaf, the opalescent shine of every dawn. She was engulfed in bitterness again, filled with a terrible thirst for vengeance—and on her tongue the taste of a future revenge became even sweeter. Rafael would pay for his trickery, and the payment would be heavier than even his broad shoulders could take!

The matter of finding suitable accommodation in Honolulu proved easier than they had thought. A small white frame-house belonging to an American draper from San Francisco was available, and for an absurdly reasonable price.

'I have to tell you in all fairness, Captain Chiltern,' explained the draper, Frank Partridge, 'that the house is said to have a voodoo on it, hence the low price.' He was a florid, earnest and rather pompous young man in his thirties, God-fearing but somewhat full of his own importance.

'Voodoo?' Aunt Zoe bristled. 'Stuff and nonsense! I'd like to meet the voodoo that can stand up to me!'

'So would I,' said her brother mildly. 'For I would surely like to shake him by the hand!'

And so the deal was struck. As far as the Chilterns were concerned, it was an ideal house for their purposes, not too large to maintain and with a pretty garden surrounding it. Miranda gave her approval without any appreciable enthusiasm. It mattered little to her where they stayed. The only feature that produced any show of animation in her was that the house faced south-west across the Pacific in the direction of the damnable island of Amarillo.

They moved into the house without delay, helped by many willing hands among the crew. There were some curious questions asked as to why Miss Chiltern, Miss

Miranda and Dan Haggerty were to stay on in Honolulu, but it was explained to them that the ladies needed a holiday after so long at sea and Dan's arthritis called for him to be beached for a while—and what better place to rest than in Honolulu?

Dan himself had taken the matter in his stride, for the truth could not be kept from him. He passed no judgments, and made no comments except to pledge himself to their welfare to the best of his ability. Fortunately a harpooner from Sydney was willing to replace Dan on the *Amiable Lady* in exchange for a berth to Nantucket, and an English doctor, also wanting passage to America, was available.

The house was partly furnished, and Frank Partridge was kind enough to rent them some more furniture at a reasonable price and also to offer them furnishing materials at cost price from his shop near the harbour. It was obvious that he was much touched by the sad, sad story of Miranda's recent 'widowhood', and lost no time in offering his services to the family in case of need. The name 'Romero' had been chosen as that of Miranda's late 'husband', for reasons that were evident. If the child looked like his father, with dark colouring, a Spanish name would be more apt.

In the meantime, Aunt Zoe appraised Frank Partridge through seasoned eyes. Yes, she thought to herself, yes. A very definite possibility for the future, especially in view of his already waxing interest in Miranda.

Then came the time for the *Amiable Lady* to sail. The parting with Edward Chiltern was painful for them all, but especially for Miranda. She clung to him, weeping copiously, knowing just how much she would miss his warm, comfortable presence during the difficult days ahead.

'There, there lass,' he said gruffly, holding back his

own tears. 'Time will fly past on wings, you'll see. I'll be back before you have a chance to turn round. After all, there's not much that will keep me from my first grandchild.'

Nevertheless, after he had gone, Miranda wept for hours, feeling dull and desolate without him. That evening, drying her tears, she strolled down to the beach as soon as it was dark. The vast expanse of the Pacific sea and sky seemed to free her spirit and give her strength. For a long time she stood staring out in the direction of the south-west.

'He will come for you, lass, he will come.' It was Dan, observing her with disquieted eyes, not missing the direction in which she gazed.

She was startled, for they had not talked of Rafael since that night on the bridge of the *Amiable Lady*. Oddly enough, Miranda did not mind Dan's comments, knowing how well he understood everything in his quiet, taciturn way. She smiled and then broke into laughter.

'You still have faith in him, Dan? You still make excuses for him?'

He nodded stubbornly. 'Ay, I do. He will come, but in his own time.'

Would he? '*I shall find you, wherever you are . . .*' That was what he had said, too. As if she were now fool enough to believe in any of his empty promises! If he could deceive her with such callous unconcern once, what worth could she put on his words now? None! But, still smiling, she said, 'I hope so, Dan, I hope so. This time I shall be prepared for him—and he will wish that he had not!'

Dan looked very agitated. 'Cast your bitterness aside, Miss Miranda,' he implored earnestly, 'or it will destroy you.'

'On the contrary, Dan,' she said, her smile vicious, 'it is the only thing that sustains me! And, Dan,' she added with a light laugh, 'perhaps you had better stop calling me "Miss" Miranda now or you will invite Aunt Zoe's wrath.'

Gradually their lives in Honolulu fell into an acceptable, pleasant routine. The house was beginning to look cosy and well-lived-in and, under Dan's expert fingers, the overgrown garden had been tamed into pretty docility. Dan had managed to find part-time employment at the shipyard down at the harbour, and enjoyed his work. Oahu, the island upon which Honolulu was situated, was a cheerful, cosmopolitan place with many races living in harmony. From a near-by village they found a young Chinese girl, Mary Ling, to come and help in the house in exchange for English lessons from Miranda. Aunt Zoe had taken to conducting Sunday School classes at the local mission school run by an American missionary couple, and through the school Miranda got other pupils for her English lessons. Mrs Harmon, the missionary's wife, was a trained midwife who took to keeping a kindly eye on Miranda, promising attendance whenever required. The doctor they had found was Portuguese and highly recommended; he had pronounced Miranda in excellent health with no cause for concern.

The days melted into weeks and then months and Miranda's time came closer. She had thrown herself into her daily activities with such fervour that, it appeared to Aunt Zoe, she had almost forgotten about That Man. And, certainly, she appeared to be content enough, somewhat nervous about the impending birth, but nevertheless composed. They had received a letter from Edward Chiltern to say he would be returning to Honolulu in no more than six or eight months' time.

One evening, after all her work was done, Miranda walked up and down the beach watching some tall, handsome Hawaiian lads indulge in their favourite sport —riding the surf. They stood on narrow wooden boards and, with marvellous balance, crossed to and fro over the crests of the gigantic rollers that crashed down on the beach. She laughed as one of the boys fell into the water and then came up spluttering, but smiling broadly. Then she sat down on a rock and, as always, stared out towards the south-west.

Dan came and joined her, fresh from his work at the shipyard. Sitting on an adjacent rock, he shuffled his feet restlessly.

'You look worried, Dan,' she said curiously. 'All is well down at the shipyard?'

'Oh, ay . . .'

The silence thickened and Miranda looked at him with a frown. 'Is anything the matter?'

He gave a final chew to his wad of tobacco, spat it out vociferously, and then said with abruptness, 'He has left Amarillo.'

If Aunt Zoe was under the impression that Miranda had forgotten Rafael, Dan certainly knew better. He was aware that there was not a moment of the day when he was not in Miranda's thoughts. She felt a chill hand round her heart. 'Where . . . where has he gone?'

Dan shrugged. 'Who knows? There is an English man o'war in the harbour that crossed the *Condor* near the Galapagos, but they could not tell where she was headed.'

Miranda felt a spasm in her stomach and closed her eyes at the sudden pain. 'Has he . . . has he taken to piracy again?'

'There's no telling with him, lass. You know that.'

'But if he is caught, he will . . . hang?'

'It is a possibility.'

She was torn with anguish, but she struggled to control it. Making her expression into one of hardness, she said lightly, 'It is no more than he deserves.' She rose and walked away.

That night Miranda started her labour pains.

Aunt Zoe was dreadfully worried, for there were still six weeks remaining until the delivery date. She sent Dan hurrying for the doctor, but he had gone to Lahaina on the island of Maui, and was not expected back for at least a week. Another doctor, a Chilean, was involved with an emergency but promised to come as soon as he was free. Aunt Zoe then despatched Dan to fetch Mrs Harmon, the missionary's wife. Within an hour the kind lady was by Miranda's bedside.

'Yes,' she confirmed, 'it is the baby. Since it is six weeks too early, she will have a hard time, poor child, but we shall place ourselves in the hands of the Lord and do our best.'

For the whole of that night and the following day, Miranda lay contorted with racking pains. But, late the following night, the Chilean doctor arrived and took charge confidently, much to everyone's relief. He fed Miranda, thrashing wildly and delirious, with herbal concoctions and large white tablets, and they all sat down to wait. Finally, at midnight, when Miranda was limp with exhaustion and alarmingly still, the baby was born. She did not hear its birth-cry.

For the next twenty-four hours she lay weak and unmoving from fatigue and loss of blood, unaware even that she had given birth. But by dusk the next evening she regained consciousness and opened her eyes.

'Is the baby . . . all right?' she whispered with difficulty through parched lips.

Aunt Zoe beamed. 'Oh yes,' she chortled happily. 'Perfectly all right. Here, see for yourself, child.' She placed an incredibly tiny bundle next to Miranda. 'It's a boy,' she breathed. 'A beautiful little boy.'

With a monumental effort, Miranda turned on her side, ignoring the crushing pain, and gazed for the first time upon the face of her son. It was very small and very crumpled, like a balloon that had lost its air. But to Miranda it was the most beautiful sight she had ever seen. With a gentle finger, she felt his skin. It was as soft as a wisp of silk. At the touch of her finger, his eyes opened with a start. They were as black as night and as liquid as the sea, and they stared back at her as if in anger at being disturbed. His skin was the colour of wheat ripening in the sun, and the hair on his head, shining black and glossy, fell around his ears in wild, unruly curls. He opened his mouth, and the sounds of his furious cries filled the little frame-house. With a sharp stab of pain, Miranda hugged him very closely, filled with wonder. He was the image of Rafael!

Very gently she guided his open mouth towards her aching, heavy breast and the feel of him suckling was the sweetest sensation she had ever experienced. She smiled down at him, and tears trembled in her eyes as she pressed his tiny body close to hers. Wave upon wave of a strange overpowering emotion flowed through her and she bent and placed a kiss upon his high forehead. She had never felt so happy or so weak with love as she did now.

'Was her husband's name Rafael?' Mrs Harmon whispered to Aunt Zoe. It was the name Miranda had called out incessantly and unknowingly through her labour. Aunt Zoe looked away and pretended not to have heard. Instead, she sat down on the bed and asked Miranda briskly, 'Well, what are you going to call your son?'

Miranda stroked the silken curls away from his eyes, and smiled softly. 'We shall call him Felipe.'

Nobody looking at Felipe when he was a year old could have guessed how weak and puny he had been at his premature birth. He had grown rapidly, unusually tall for his age, and was strong and healthy, with a temper to match. When denied his way, he had a habit of flashing his black eyes ferociously, clenching his tiny fists and screaming through clenched gums. *He is his father's son, all right,* said Aunt Zoe and Dan to each other privately, but neither dared to suggest such a thing to Miranda.

But it was hardly something that could escape her notice. In every part of her son she saw Rafael—the shape and expression of the fiery black eyes, the hair that curved around his head defying all attempts at taming, the contours of his long, tapering legs, the promise of broad shoulders. And she loved him with a passion that filled her every waking moment. She would sit and watch him for hours, reluctant to drag her eyes away. It was as though Rafael had been returned to her . . .

But she knew now that Rafael would not return. The tiny spark of hope hidden away in the furthermost recesses of her heart had finally flickered and died. For all she knew, Rafael was dead—hanged by the neck somewhere, accompanied by the tumultuous cheering of a bloodthirsty multitude. But even that thought, torturing her for so long, had ceased to agonise. Lost in the joys of motherhood, she lavished everything she had inside her heart on her son, wanting to hold him, to touch him all the time—for it was as though she were holding and touching Rafael. She no longer went down to the beach only to gaze towards the south-west, for he was no longer there. Indeed, Rafael was no longer anywhere, for he was dead. El Español existed no more, and soon even his memory would vanish.

In the meantime, many things had happened in their lives. Frank Partridge, pompous, but kind and principled, had proposed marriage to her for the fourth time —and Miranda had accepted. They were to be married soon after Felipe was a year old in another two weeks' time. She did not love him, but then she had done with love for ever! It was nothing but a meaningless fantasy that had no worth in a hard, practical world. It was time that Felipe had a father, and Frank was a solid, stable and God-fearing man who would accept the child as his own and bring him up accordingly.

Edward Chiltern had returned to Honolulu when Felipe was eight months old and was also happily engaged at the shipyard with no hankering to return to Nantucket. He adored his grandson, as did Aunt Zoe, and the white frame-house was filled with laughter and love. Dan had moved out into his own lodgings near the harbour, but he came every day for the evening meal. Life was running, at long last, on an even keel, for it appeared now that God was finally in his heaven and all was right with the world.

Miranda was in the habit of going down to the harbour every once in a while to look at the shops and to meet Frank for luncheon in his rooms above the shop on the sea-front. One morning, when she went down as usual, she was astonished to see that the streets were thronged with people and there seemed to be more crowds about than usual.

'What is the fuss about?' she asked Frank, as she caught his eye for a moment amid a demanding cluster of customers.

'New ship in the harbour,' he said hurriedly, taking her into the back room. 'They say she's something rare!'

'Oh?' Ships in the harbour came and went every day. There was no particular interest in her voice as she hunted through sample-books to find a suitable cotton print for a new smock for Felipe. It was astonishing, she thought, how quickly he could get through his clothes.

'Yes,' said Frank, hunting round frantically for a particular bolt of material that a customer wanted. 'They say she belongs to that diabolical Spanish pirate.

Thought he had been hanged—deserves to be anyway.'
He exclaimed triumphantly as he found the bolt he was
looking for. He cast a quick smile in her direction as he
rushed out again. 'But then you've probably never heard
of him. It was before your time. They call him El
Español.'

Miranda remained sitting in the back room for a long
while after Frank had gone back into the shop. There
were no particular thoughts in her mind. It was as if her
body was encased in ice, unmoving and numb to all sensation. Then, slowly, she thawed back into life and dazedly started to walk out of the shop and back up the hill.

When she reached the brow of the hill, beyond which
stood their home, she paused and looked down on the
harbour. It was, as always, crammed full of ships and
there were at least forty or fifty masts rising into the
sky. But, for Miranda, the harbour held only one vessel.
She stood proudly on the water to one side, apart from
the others. Her hull was shining black and her prow
rose above the Pacific, bearing the golden eagle. Her
lines were sleek, and the three masts soared above all
the others. From the centre mast floated the personal
emblem of the Queen of Spain. This was *El Condor*.
About that there was no doubt.

There was a moment of panic, a feeling of sinking,
but she rallied almost immediately. Her face became
set, the blood in her body ice-cold. There was much to
be done.

Back at the house, a first glance at the faces of Dan
and her father told her that they also knew. Indeed,
they had hurried back from the shipyard to tell her.
Edward Chiltern looked as black as thunder. Dan
showed no expression at all, but his small, wrinkled
eyes shone like glass pebbles. Aunt Zoe sat in a corner,
a picture of dismal uncertainty. Felipe lay sleeping on
the bed.

For a while, no one spoke. Then Aunt Zoe said breathlessly, 'He cannot know that we are here . . .'

Dan smiled tightly. 'He knows!'

'If he dares to set foot in this house,' Edward Chiltern exploded, 'I shall put a bullet through his heart, so help me God!'

Aunt Zoe interrupted sharply. 'Why don't you ask Miranda what she feels? After all, she should decide—not that he *will* come!'

Everybody looked at Miranda and, to their astonishment, she smiled, perfectly calm and unperturbed. 'He'll come,' she said quietly. Then she laughed, and it was a humourless sound. 'The good Lord will forgive me today if, for once, vengeance is mine.'

Unhurriedly she set about collecting all Felipe's clothes from the house, while they all watched in mystification.

'He shall not come into this house, Miranda,' her father began angrily.

'You will not deny me this moment, Papa,' she said patiently, 'for I have waited long for it. Aunt Zoe, please take Felipe, with all his things, up the hill to Mary Ling's village and stay there. Papa,' she turned to her father and her voice softened, 'please go with them. It will be better. Dan will stay with me.'

Her father made to protest but, realising the mood of implacability Miranda was in, Aunt Zoe hushed him quickly and shooed him out of the house. 'I do not know what Miranda intends to do,' she said with her voice lowered, 'but it is her decision. We must do as she asks us.' She whisked Felipe up in her arms and strode out of the door after her brother.

For a moment or two Miranda looked around to see if there was any article of Felipe's that she had overlooked. A toy lay on the ground and she pushed it under the bed. There was a small pair of trousers lying on a chair. She went to remove them, but then, smiling slowly, changed her mind and left them where they were. Dan observed her in silence, but not even he dared intrude into her mind. She seemed like another person altogether!

Miranda went up to her room, loosened her hair and brushed it with slow, languid strokes. Then, leaving her hair unbound, she changed into a printed cotton skirt and starched white muslin blouse. She washed her face and examined herself carefully in the mirror. Her skin was a golden brown from the sun, and her hair looked more bleached than ever. Through her dark brown glossy lashes, her cerulean eyes appeared more brilliant than they had done for many a month. She smiled slightly and added a touch of pink to her cheeks. And all the while she hummed to herself, for today was the day for which she had lived for over two long years.

Then she went back to the front room downstairs. Through the window she saw Dan standing at the top of the hill looking down on the long road that led to the harbour. He paced around in circles, his eyes returning again and again to the road. Miranda picked up a half-embroidered cushion she had been working on. *I should feel something,* she told herself in mild surprise. *There should be some agitation in my mind!* But there was nothing. Only a feeling of dullness as if all her nerve-ends had gone to sleep. She started to work on her embroidery with concentration.

She worked silently for some time, waiting, waiting for Dan to come and give her some news. But Dan did not come. The rays of the sun pouring into the room began to slant and colour. She rose and lit the lamp. Gradually the day died and the stars came out one by one. Still Dan did not come. Into her mind began to creep a doubt. Was she wrong in her intuition? Perhaps he would not come at all. But just as she was beginning to give up hope, Dan walked in quickly. His face was pale and his hands shook.

'He is coming up the hill.'

Her heart lurched precariously, but only for a moment. Quickly she silenced it and, running her tongue over her dry lips, sat down again with her embroidery. Dan turned and made to go out again.

'He loves you, Miranda,' he said softly over his shoulder as he paused in the doorway. 'Don't be harsh with him—or he may not return.'

But she hardly heard him, immersed once again in her sewing. For a long time there was no sound. Then, even without looking up, she knew that he was standing in the doorway filling the frame. He stood and watched silently, but she did not raise her head.

Then she spoke, but without even looking at him. 'You may come in and sit down,' she said, and marvelled at how casual her voice was. She glanced up, but was prepared for the shock of seeing him again. Everything inside her heaved agonisingly for a split second, but the gaze that met his was as cool as an Arctic sea. She had forgotten how tall he was, and he had to stoop to pass through the doorway. His hair was still wild and tousled, and he wore his customary black trousers and white shirt that she remembered so well. His face was thinner than before, almost gaunt, but as a result his eyes seemed to shine with an even greater opalescence.

He sat down on the chair opposite and stretched out his long legs. He seemed strangely out of place in such a small room, and it pleased her with tremendous perversity to see how uncomfortable he appeared out of his own milieu.

'It is an honour,' she said lightly, 'to welcome the great Español to this humble house.'

'The great Español,' he said sharply, 'is dead!'

'Oh? Well, now that you mention it,' she said smiling

pleasantly, 'I thought that El Conde Rafael de Quintero was also!'

How well she remembered the angry tautening of the jaw! 'I was in Spain.'

She managed to suppress her surprise. 'Oh?' she remarked, holding her embroidery at an arm's length and examining it critically. 'I hear it is a pleasant country.'

He ignored the fatuous comment and leaned forward. 'Why is your name "Romero"?'

She raised an eyebrow. 'It is the normal custom to change one's name when one gets married.'

He sat back slowly and rubbed his chin with his forefinger. 'Yes. I had heard something to that effect.' His narrowed eyes appraised her face closely, but she remained cool.

'I *was* married. Alas, poor Juan died soon after.' She dabbed her eyes daintily with the corner of her handkerchief. 'It was a most awful shock to us, since it had been love at first sight.'

'Where were you married?' he asked curiously, tilting his head to a side. 'In Honolulu?'

She evaded the trap neatly. 'No. In Samoa. It was soon . . . soon after we left Amarillo.'

He sprang to his feet and his face was suddenly contorted with fury. 'Don't lie to me, Miranda,' he breathed through clamped teeth. 'You would never have allowed another man to touch you after . . . after . . .' He seemed to choke on his own words.

She looked up at him in feigned surprise. Then she laid her embroidery down and folded her hands demurely in her lap. She sighed. 'That was nothing more than a . . . a pleasant interlude, Rafael. Surely . . .' she gave a short laugh, 'surely you did not take it seriously? But then, I'm sure you did not! It was really so sensible of you to drug me and take me back to the villa. I was such a silly girl that night—and I am so glad you kept your head, even though I didn't.'

The expression on his face was balm to her soul—Oh how long she had waited to see it! She picked up her embroidery frame again and began to stitch. He moved rapidly and towered over her, his face as dark as thunder. 'Put that damned thing away, or I shall put a light to it!'

With a tolerant sigh, as if humouring a difficult child, she put aside the embroidery and again sat with hands folded in her lap, waiting. He ran a hand distractedly through his hair and her heart recoiled at the familiar, once-loved, gesture. But her expression remained quite placid.

'I told you I would find you, wherever you were,' he said softly, calming down again, pacing the floor restlessly.

She heard the pain in his voice, and filled with triumph. Oh how sweet were going to be the fruits of revenge! 'Did you?' she asked casually. 'I don't remember. We both said such foolish things that night, didn't we?' She rose and asked brightly, 'Would you like a cup of coffee or a glass of ginger beer? Aunt Zoe made some last week, and Papa says it's . . .'

He grasped her by the arm and pushed her back into the chair. 'Sit down!' he roared. 'I haven't finished yet!'

'Oh, haven't you? I am sorry, Rafael, I thought that you had—because I have. What else is there to say?'

She was now in complete control of the situation and her sense of victory was complete. Almost. There was still the most difficult part to be handled but, come what may, she would see it through. He paced up and down for a moment then went and stood by the window with his back towards her.

'Where is my son?'

So, he had heard about that too! She swallowed and

prepared to play her trump card. '*Your* son, Rafael? Oh, I don't think so. I married Juan so soon after that night,' she laughed brazenly, 'that I never could be sure to whom he belonged!'

He swung round, and his face was ashen. 'He is mine —and we both know it! Where is he? I want to see him.'

'Really, Rafael!' she rose and faced him squarely. 'I do think you are being very unreasonable! I am almost certain that he is Juan's child. After all, women do have a way of knowing these things.' She smiled coyly, turning the knife as much as she could.

'*Where is he?*' He spoke quietly, but there was such menace in his tone that, for a brief moment, her courage almost failed her. But then she thought of that night when he had loved her and left her—and her heart hardened again.

'He is not here. Aunt Zoe and Papa have taken Felipe to . . .'

Her interrupted her as quick as a whip. 'Felipe?'

'Yes. We named him after Juan's father.'

His breathing became harsh and ragged. 'Felipe was my father's name,' he ground out.

'*Was* it?' she asked brightly. 'Well, what a coincidence!'

He was by her in two strides. His face was fearful, and he pierced her with eyes that flashed and blazed like lightning. Before she knew what was happening, his hands were round her throat. 'You lie, Miranda,' he breathed viciously. '*You lie!*'

She stood absolutely still, unnerved by the touch of his hands, waiting for his fingers to tighten. But they didn't. Instead they loosened and began to caress the back of her neck. She closed her eyes, ravaged by his touch, wanting to cry out. His fingers tangled in her hair and then, holding her face between his palms, he bent down and kissed her on the lips.

'I said I would come for you . . .' he whispered. 'Why didn't you believe me? I want you, and I want my son.'

She felt her strength drain out of her as all her defences prepared to crumble. She had a wild, deranged impulse to lay her head against his chest and let him love her again. But then, behind her closed eyes, passed the vision of that night and of all her misery and despair at his callous rejection of her, of all the empty words that had led to the monstrous deception. He wanted his son, yes, but only his son!

Slowly the fire died out from her body. She put her hands against his chest and pushed him away. 'He is not your son.' Amazingly, her voice was as steady as a rock. She could have been carved out of marble.

He stood back. 'Then let me see him.'

'No.'

'Why not?' he laughed sardonically. 'If he is not my son, then why do you hesitate?'

'Because I do not trust you. I did once, and . . .' She felt the moisture collect in her eyes and shook her head angrily. 'You do not believe in any law, either man's or God's. Once a pirate, always a pirate!'

He ignored the tirade. 'I do not trust you either, Miranda, and I know that you lie through your teeth. Show me the boy, and let me decide.'

'*No!*'

'Then I will see him by force!'

'If you do, Rafael, it will be over my dead body!' She felt her despair mounting. Would he never go? *Leave now, Rafael,* she pleaded silently. *I cannot hold out much longer!*

But he showed no signs of leaving. Instead, he took a step towards her. 'Don't!' she cried sharply. 'Don't . . . touch me again! In two weeks' time I marry another man.'

He stopped dead in his tracks and his face went white. He recovered slowly, and flushed. 'You seem to be doing a lot of marrying since you left Amarillo!' he exclaimed sarcastically, but she could see that he was badly shaken.

'Felipe needs a father,' she said with venomous sweetness. 'I cannot bring him up on his own.'

'Felipe *has* a father,' he flung back at her angrily. 'Spare me more of your lies!'

She laughed in his face. 'You? A father for Felipe? I want him to grow up a human being,' she said, whipping him further, longing to pay him back for every tear that she had shed. 'Not a devil like *you*!'

For a moment she thought he was going to strike her, but with a tremendous effort he controlled himself. His shoulders seemed to droop and his face became tired and unhappy. 'I had to do what I did, Miranda, there was no other way . . .'

She cut him off with an impatient gesture. 'It is a little late for explanations.'

'I do not intend to give you any,' he said sharply. 'I don't give a damn what you do! Marry and rot in hell, for all I care!' He was now livid with rage again. 'But you cannot keep me from my son. Neither you nor God! I will have him, Miranda, and I give you fair warning.'

'You will have to kill me first, Rafael.'

The look he gave her was full of hate. 'Don't tempt me, Miranda! You know only too well that I do not take challenges lightly.'

He turned on his heel and was about to walk out of the door when his eyes fell upon the tiny pair of trousers she had left deliberately on the chair. He froze, his eyes riveted, and slowly bent down. He held them for a moment and his face looked tortured. Then he looked at her with such venom that she stepped back involuntarily. He replaced the garment on the chair.

'You think you are paying me back for what has happened, Miranda,' he said in hushed tones. 'But you will never be able to punish me enough for what is about to happen.'

She faced him squarely, remembering only the loneliness, the yearning, the lovelessness of the past two years. 'He has not a drop of your blood in him, Rafael, not one. If he had . . .' she smiled a slow, terible smile, 'I assure you that I would have killed him in my womb.'

She watched him stride away with fury and pain, like a wounded animal disappearing back into the jungle. But the smile never left her lips. It was only when he had been swallowed up by the darkness that she sank into the chair and buried her face in her hands. This was the moment of triumph she had dreamed of every moment since that horrible morning when she had woken up on the *Amiable Lady*, cut adrift from him brutally while his lips were still warm on hers. She sat and savoured the moment again and again, trying to find in it the sweetness that she had promised herself. But there was none. All that she felt was a taste so bitter that she wanted to spit it out before it choked her. The sight of his ravaged face should have brought her joy, but instead it filled her only with horror. She had wrought her rever.ge, and he had been demolished. But —who was it that had been punished, Rafael or she?

Sunk in despair, she did not notice Dan come into the room. When he spoke, she started. 'You did wrong, Miranda,' he said levelly.

She raised her eyes and squared her shoulders proudly. 'Only as much as he deserved.'

'He may have had reasons for doing what he did,' Dan persisted. 'At least you should have listened to them.'

'How do you know that I didn't?' she asked sharply, annoyed at his uncalled-for interference.

'By his face,' he said simply. 'It was that of a man plunged into hell.'

'We all get our just rewards sooner or later, Dan,' she said lightly, 'and this is his.' Before he could argue further, she said hurriedly, 'Please go to Mary Ling's village, Dan, and warn Papa and Aunt Zoe not to bring Felipe down, come what may. I shall pack some clothes for them. I shall make arrangements for them to go to Lahaina tomorrow. Mr Harmon's sister lives there and would be happy to put them up for a while until his ship leaves.'

'He will not leave, Miranda,' Dan said. 'He will stay here until he has seen his son. It is not right to keep a man from his son. It is not right.' He shook his head in great agitation, visibly deeply troubled.

She lost her temper. 'How do *you* know what is right, Dan? Felipe is the only thing I have left in life. He is the only one who makes up for the loneliness and wretchedness of the past two years.' Her eyes brimmed with hot tears.

'And do you know what loneliness and wretchedness he may have suffered also?'

The question caught her by surprise, for it was not one that she had ever considered. Nevertheless, with a defiant toss of her head, she dismissed it. 'No,' she snapped. 'But I hope they were not a whit less than mine.'

Dan sighed. He knew that, in her present state of mind, Miranda would not listen to any one. 'Very well,' he said with unhappy resignation. 'Give me their clothes. I shall take them your message.'

'And please prevail upon Papa not to go down to the harbour. He is angry, and may do something foolish.'

'Ay,' said Dan. 'Just as you have.'

CHAPTER ELEVEN

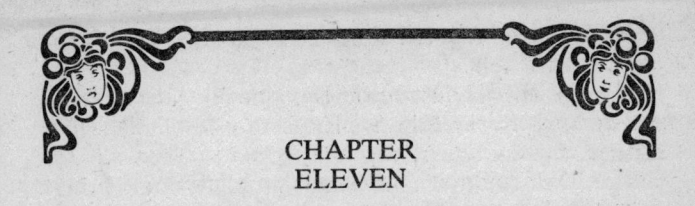

THERE WAS no question of eating dinner. All Miranda wanted was to fall into bed and still the ravings of her mind. She grilled a pork chop for Dan, boiled some vegetables and sliced a fresh pineapple, then left everything under wire-mesh covers on the kitchen table. As she was about to extinguish the lamps and lock the front door, Frank Partridge arrived.

'Sorry to be so late,' he said, flopping down on a chair, 'but I couldn't get away earlier. Phew, what a day! I thought they would buy up the entire shop!' He looked very pleased with himself.

Miranda stared at him in dismay. The last person she wanted to see tonight was Frank! He was sitting in the very chair Rafael had sat in not so long ago and, suddenly, she could not bear the sight.

'I'm very tired, Frank . . .' she began, but he interrupted her immediately.

'I know, I know, but we have to make plans for the wedding. After all, it is only two weeks away.'

Her heart became leaden. Two weeks only! Nevertheless, she smiled. 'Perhaps we should talk about it another time, Frank, since we are both so tired . . .'

'Miranda,' he said sternly, 'I am a man of some standing in the community,' his chest expanded self-consciously, 'and I would like the wedding to be commensurate with my . . . er . . . social position.'

Miranda sighed imperceptibly. Once Frank got on to

the subject of his social position, there was no stopping him.

'I know, Frank,' she said diplomatically. 'That is why we should not discuss such an important issue in a hurry.'

'Well . . . all right,' he conceded ungraciously. 'But we shall talk about it tomorrow. It cannot be put off any longer. I have decided that we shall honeymoon in San Francisco,' a pleased glint appeared in his eye, 'where you can meet my family.' He rose all of a sudden from the chair, put an arm round her shoulders and made an effort to kiss her. She recoiled at his touch and deftly slipped out of his reach, running towards the stairs.

'Excuse me a moment, won't you Frank? I've . . . I've just remembered something . . .' She fled into her room, shaking, and sank down on the bed. Honeymoon with Frank? She shuddered. To let Frank make love to her after she had been loved by Rafael . . .? The prospect filled her with horror. *What am I doing? Why am I destroying myself like this?* Was it hatred for Rafael that was consuming her so inexorably—or was it love? Just the touch of his fingers on her neck, his single kiss, had been enough to make her demented again . . . Was it possible that she could still love such a man—or was it just another delusion?

Pleading a headache to Frank, she despatched him home, promising him whatever he wanted for the morrow. As she allowed him a peck on her cheek, she felt bitterly remorseful. He was a good man, for all his pomposity. He had been kind to them. Why was she using him like this to further her own revenge? He did not deserve it.

Miranda slept badly that night, ravaged with thoughts of Rafael and worry about his fearful parting threat. What did he plan to do? She had to make arrangements as soon as possible to remove Felipe from Oahu. She did not trust Rafael, and she knew he was not a man to give idle warnings. And by morning, when the light of day filtered through the curtains of her room, she had decided on two things. First she would reveal the entire truth to Frank about her life and beg him to release her from the betrothal. And second, she would see Rafael in hell before she let him have a single glance at her son. She had weakened yesterday, overwhelmed by his presence. But she would not soften again. Rafael would continue to suffer for as long as she wished.

During the next two days, however, there was no sign of Rafael or, indeed, any word about what he was doing. According to Dan, he had boarded the *Condor* that night after leaving her and had not emerged again. Miranda was greatly relieved and began to breathe a little more freely, but she went ahead with arrangements to remove Felipe to Lahaina. Mrs Harmon was away from Honolulu on one of the other islands, but was due back that evening. Miranda decided to see her early the following morning to request sanctuary with her sister for Felipe.

Carrying out her resolution, Miranda related the entire story of Amarillo to Frank when he called on the day following Rafael's visit. She did not spare herself. White-faced, Frank listened in silence. From his eyes, she could tell that he was shaken to his core.

'You and that . . . renegade?' he asked finally in shocked incredulity.

'Yes,' she said dully. 'Me and that renegade!'

He struggled for words. 'I . . . I can hardly b-believe it . . .'

'I know,' she said sadly. 'Sometimes I can hardly believe it myself. But I feel you have a right to know, Frank, and make your decision accordingly. Naturally,

I do not hold you to the engagement. I release you unconditionally.'

'B-but what will people say . . . ?' he asked, wringing his hands. 'I . . . I think we should avoid any . . . precipitate action. After all, I do have my social position to consider . . .'

They left it at that. Frank walked out of the house stiffly and Miranda could see how terribly hurt he was. He would inform her of his decision after he had recovered from the terrible shock.

The morning on which she was due to see Mrs Harmon about the removal of Felipe to Lahaina, even before the sun had risen, Miranda was shaken out of her sleep by the most infernal noises. The door of her bedroom suddenly flew open. Her aunt burst in and flung herself on the bed, sobbing hysterically. Behind her walked her father, his face as grey as slate, staring fixedly at the floor.

Miranda's blood chilled as she shook herself out of her sleepy daze. 'Where is Felipe?' she asked with deathly calm. But there was no reply from either of them, and her aunt only sobbed louder while her father opened and shut his mouth without a sound emerging. Miranda fixed her father with a gimlet eye and repeated the question. 'Felipe. *Where is he?*'

Her father suddenly found his voice again and, in a confused torrent, the story poured out. They did not know where Felipe was. When Aunt Zoe got up in the morning in her hut in Mary Ling's village, his crib was empty. They hunted frantically everywhere and asked everyone, but nobody had seen anything. Felipe had disappeared!

Miranda closed her eyes in agony. She knew where Felipe would be—and she also knew how he had got there. Dan! Nobody but Dan could have dared do such a thing. She was suddenly consumed with fury, not only at Dan's duplicity, but at Rafael's ruthlessness. After all that she had already been through, how could he subject her to this additional torture? Felipe was on the *Condor*—and it was possible that the ship had already sailed!

Without saying a word to her still sobbing aunt and her ashen-faced father, Miranda rapidly washed and dressed, her hands and feet frozen with fear. Then she turned towards her aunt, put a gentle hand on her shoulder, and said soothingly with forced confidence, 'Don't cry, Aunt Zoe, dear. I know where Felipe is. I shall fetch him back.'

With a gasp, her aunt sat up on the bed, and her father stared. 'You *know* where he is?'

She nodded. 'He is on the *Condor* with Rafael.' They knew, of course, that Rafael had been to see her, but they had no idea of what exactly had transpired between them. They looked at her questioningly, but she did not enlighten them about what Rafael might intend to do with the boy. 'Don't worry,' she said. 'He is safe. I am going now to bring him back . . .' She fled out of the room before they could ask any further questions. She did not have the heart to tell them that, for all she knew, the *Condor* might no longer be there . . .

Once out of the house, all her pretended confidence vanished and her face crumpled with anguish. *Oh God, oh God—don't let him have sailed away, please, please* . . . On the brow of the hill she paused and searched the harbour below with frantic eyes. There was no sign of the ship!

Panic lent wings to her feet as she flew down the hill, her hair loose behind her, tears pouring down her face like a woman crazed. As she ran, people stopped to stare open-mouthed, but she didn't see them, nor did she care what they thought. He had stolen her darling baby from her; she had to stop him somehow, she *had* to . . .

Gasping with shortage of breath, Miranda arrived at the wharf—and nearly collapsed. The *Condor* was moored alongside. Indeed, the gangway was still down. With a sob of relief, and giving herself only a bare moment to refill her bursting lungs, she flung herself on to the gangway and ran up. A man, suddenly appearing from the deck, tried to stop her.

'Get out of my way, you fool!' she cried, lashing out at his musket that tried to bar her way. The man stepped back in alarm as the musket went flying into the sea. Without a backward glance at him, she rushed on deck and stopped, looking around frantically. It was a big ship—and she had no idea where she would find Felipe. A group of men stood near by, staring at her open-mouthed, their conversation cut off in mid-sentence. Among them she recognised the young boy who had brought her the horse on Amarillo.

'El Español . . .!' she gasped, her eyes beseeching and her voice cracked. 'Where is he?'

The boy's eyes widened in recognition, then, without speaking, he pointed towards the stairs leading up. Lifting her skirts, she ran up and plunged through the nearest doorway. It led to a passage that ran towards the prow of the ship. At the end was another door that was closed. Without pausing, she grabbed the knob and flung it open, almost falling into the room.

He was lying on the floor on his stomach. Next to him, playing with a ship's compass, was her son!

With a strangled cry she swooped down on the child and picked him up, hugging him close to her and covering his face with kisses. 'You . . . You unscrupulous, unfeeling devil . . .' she sobbed in hysterics, clasping her son even tighter. 'How could you do such a thing to me . . .!'

Rafael did not seem at all surprised to see her. Very slowly, without any sign of hurry, he rose to his feet. 'I haven't harmed the boy,' he said mildly. 'I was only playing with him.' He stretched his arms above his head lazily. 'He's a fine lad.'

'Well, fine or not,' she snapped, still panting, 'you leave my son alone! He has nothing to do with you, do you hear, *nothing*!' Tears of relief washed down her cheeks as she sank weakly into a chair. Startled at being so rudely separated from his toy, Felipe now recovered sufficiently to let out an angry howl and wriggled strongly to be put down again. Miranda clung to him even more tightly, fearful that Rafael would try to take the child away from her. But he did not make a move, seating himself languidly in a chair, smiling with charming affability. 'I'm . . . I'm taking him back . . .' she said shakily.

His smile widened. 'Certainly. After all, a child's place is with his mother.'

Her mouth dropped open in astonishment and, taking advantage of the momentary slackening of her arms, Felipe slipped through and crawled back happily to the compass. He looked up at Rafael and gurgled. 'You mean . . . you are not going to stop me?'

He looked shocked. 'Why should I? It is quite obvious that the boy is not mine. I apologise for having doubted your word.'

Miranda swallowed in continuing astonishment. Her mind worked furiously as she wondered whether to be relieved or not. Was it possible that he had failed to see the resemblance? Or could it be that it existed only in her imagination? From beneath lowered lashes, she stole a glance at her son, now totally absorbed in trying to take the compass apart. Surely he could not be blind enough to miss the glaring similarities? Riddled with suspicions, she stared defiantly at Rafael. He sat with his arms crossed, his face serious, but his coal-black eyes alive with faintly mocking amusement.

Miranda pulled in a long breath and ran the back of her hand across her forehead beaded with perspiration. 'You got Dan to abduct him this morning, didn't you?' Her eyes filled with anger.

'Yes. I told you I wanted to see him.'

'And . . . And you are . . . satisfied that he is not your son?'

'Absolutely.'

'And you promise you will not stop me from leaving the ship with him?' She realised what a pointless question that was, for she could not trust him an inch, no matter what he promised. How well she knew that already!

'Why should I? I have no desire to kidnap another man's child. Or, for that matter, another man's fiancée!' His lip curled with contempt. He spoke with such indifference that she winced. Slowly, she rose and made a move to pick up the child. 'Felipe seems quite happy for the moment,' he said suddenly. 'Why don't you let him play a while? Perhaps we could talk for a moment or two.'

'There is nothing to talk about,' she said curtly, but nevertheless perched herself again gingerly on the edge of the chair.

'True,' he agreed blandly, 'but since we are to part, is it not better to part friends?'

She shuddered—he wanted nothing more to do with her! 'You are . . . leaving?' she asked breathlessly.

'Certainly. There is nothing now to keep me here. We sail with the tide.' She was surprised at how low her heart plummeted. 'I am sorry about the other day,' he said quietly. 'I apologise for my undue aggressiveness and I . . . agree with everything you said.' She stared at him. 'On reflection, it appears that we were both carried away by feelings that were . . . momentary. I cannot, of course, condone my own behaviour at the time. It was unforgivable, and I regret it bitterly.'

She did not return his friendly smile, and her face froze. With an effort, she said with as much coldness as she could, 'Well . . . it is all in the past, now. I have not thought about it in months.'

His smile was equally cold. 'I am relieved to hear that. I offer you my best wishes for your impending marriage to Frank Partridge. After so much suffering, you deserve a highly principled man like him. You will indeed help him to further his . . . er . . . social position quite considerably.'

Her eyes dilated. 'You . . . know Frank?'

'He did me the honour of calling on me last night.' The sarcasm in his voice was biting.

Miranda fell silent, unable to think of anything further to say, and staring fixedly at her son. Felipe had now abandoned the compass and was making his way with great determination towards a plate of biscuits that lay on a low table. Rafael rose.

'May I offer him a biscuit?' he asked with cold politeness. 'He seems to be hungry. And you, too?'

Dumbly, she nodded. So, this was now truly the end. He was to sail away for ever in a few hours. Once again he had dismissed her as a casual interlude of no great significance. He had accepted that Felipe was not his son. That was his only reason for visiting her. There was now nothing more that could bind them to each other. He was out of her life for ever and, in any case, he had never loved her . . .

She should have been relieved that everything had gone so satisfactorily according to plan. She had achieved everything that she had set out to do. She should be filled with tranquillity that this despicable episode in her life was now over, that Felipe was still hers and Rafael had conceded defeat.

But, perversely, she was none of these things. Instead,

she was suffused in sick despair. Devastated by the implacable finality of his words, she could barely keep the dull horror out of her face. He, on the other hand, seemed unaffected by this ultimate severance of their two lives. Unfathomable, cold and remote, he could now stand before her and actually offer her a *biscuit*? When her own world was coming crashing down about her ears? Absently, miserably, she took one, loath to show him the extent to which he had wounded her. Felipe was already in the process of crumbling his biscuit with both hands and patting the crumbs gleefully into the carpet. The silence was engulfing.

She swallowed the last crumb, then asked, more to break the silence than out of interest, 'You can now sail out of Amarillo with impunity? I thought there was a price on your head?'

'My head is tough,' he said lightly. 'It has amazing powers of survival.'

'So . . . You are taking to piracy again?' she asked sharply.

'Well, as you yourself said, "Once a pirate, always a pirate!"' He smiled disarmingly.

There was no reason now to prolong the painful conversation. It was time to leave. She sat up straight and squared her shoulders. Her head felt dizzy with despondency. Everything inside her wanted to cry out to him in protest. She longed to throw herself in his arms, assure him that Felipe was indeed his son and abandon themselves into his care, telling him about the overwhelming love she still felt for him . . . But she could not, *would* not! She had done so once with bitter, bitter consequences, for which she was still paying. And in any case, he did not care a hoot for her.

Swallowing hard, she rose unsteadily. 'I am glad,' she said caustically, as a parting shot, 'that your heart survives as well as your head. It is an enviable combination to have.' Swaying slightly, she bent down and lifted her son.

'I wish you happiness in your marriage, Miranda,' he said with every show of sincerity. 'I do not think that he is worthy of your devotion, but then, that is neither here nor there.'

Disdaining a reply, she went towards the door. Courteously, he opened it for her and she stepped through. On the stairway, she faltered. This, then, was the final parting of the ways. She would never see him again, for there was now no reason to. All she would have left were her memories, and even those were like ashes now, for she had meant nothing to him . . .

Valiantly she fought off her tears but could not prevent her vision from blurring. She stumbled. Without a word, he removed Felipe from her arms. She stumbled again and she felt him steady her. All of a sudden waves of blackness came up to meet her and she felt her head spin. She fell again, and this time she kept falling and falling and falling . . . The last thing she remembered was calling out to him in panic, and then the world blotted out completely.

Her return to consciousness was slow. For a while she swam around in the dark, unable to find her moorings. Then, as her senses returned one by one, she appeared to be lying flat on her back on something soft, and her head whirled in interminable circles. Everything seemed to be swaying from side to side and she could not focus her eyes on anything discernible. For a few moments she had no recollection at all, but then, as her memory returned, she sat up with a jolt. She looked around, peering through the gloom. She appeared to be in a large room, but there was something strange about it. She frowned. A room? This was not a room—it was a cabin! All her recollections came thundering back, and she gave a sharp cry.

'*Felipe* . . . !' She struggled to stand, but could not.

Someone appeared by her side immediately and strong arms held her down. 'Lie still.' It was Rafael!

She looked at him in panic and pushed him away. 'Where is Felipe?'

Silently, he pointed to the bed. The boy was lying beside her, fast asleep. She fell back, limp with relief, and wiped her damp forehead with her hand. 'Wh-what happened?' she asked blankly.

'You fainted on the stairs.'

'Oh!' Slowly she got off the bed and stood up. 'I am sorry to have troubled you,' she said unsteadily. 'I feel much better now.' She picked up her sleeping son and, stiffly, made her way towards the door. It was open. She stepped through—then stopped. There was no sign below either of the harbour or, indeed, of Honolulu. All she could see was the heaving black expanse of the Pacific at night. The ship was on the move and they were at sea!

For a horror-filled moment she stared, unable to believe the evidence of her eyes. She went cold with dread and, almost unnoticed, Felipe began to slip out of her arms on to the floor. Rafael bent down wordlessly, picked him up and, tossing him once playfully into the air, put him down on the carpet near the compass. Miranda turned to him, aghast, struggling to speak.

'Felipe is my son,' Rafael said quietly. 'I want him.'

'You've . . . You've kidnapped him,' she gasped, choking.

He smiled very faintly. 'I've kidnapped you, too,' he reminded her. 'After all, a child's place *is* with his mother.'

She snapped out of her shock and, in a blinding rage,

flew at him. 'You . . . lying monster! . . . You . . . You *despicable* villain . . .'

He parried her attack effortlessly, pinning her arms against her sides. 'Now, you listen to me, Miranda . . .'

'No, I shall *not* listen to you, you miserable wretch! You *promised* you would let me take him back . . . You *promised* . . . !' She was sobbing with frustrated rage, her arms held down helplessly.

'You should not have believed me,' he said, unruffled. 'After all, you know how hollow my promises are!' He had the gall to laugh!

'I hate you, Rafael, do you hear me? I *despise* you! You tricked me again, you . . .' Her eyes narrowed. 'What did you put in that biscuit?'

'I should have thought you had learned that lesson by now,' he countered coolly. She managed to release an arm with super-human effort, and lunged at his face. He caught her wrist before her hand was even half-way to its target. His expression darkened. 'Now, will you sit down and *listen* to me or not?'

'*No!* I . . .'

He bundled her under one arm as easily as a piece of driftwood, ignoring the furious flailing of her legs. '*Yes, you will*!' he said grimly. 'If it's the last thing you do, you'll hear me out this time.'

He threw her down on the bed, and lay on top of her crossways so that she could move neither her legs nor her arms. She glared at him balefully. 'Turn this ship round, Rafael,' she ground out, 'or I'll . . .'

'All right,' he said suddenly, 'I will. But, first, you have to hear me out. Is that agreed?'

She realised that it was futile to struggle. Never could she match his strength. 'Do you promise?' It slipped out before she could stop it, and she turned her face away, chewing her lip and glowering at the wall.

He laughed. 'Yes, for what it's worth, I promise.'

Cautiously, he removed his weight from her legs and let go of her arms. He sat up. There was a loud crash, and Felipe's howls filled the room. Before him lay the smashed compass. With an oath, Rafael sprang to his feet and scooped the child into his arms. He laughed and put him down on the bed beside Miranda. Then, from the drawer of a table, he took out a handful of odds and ends and placed them in front of the boy. With a whoop of joy, Felipe leaped on to his new playthings, chortling happily.

'That should keep the rascal busy,' he muttered, re-settling himself on the bed. Miranda watched him in silence, disdaining any reply. 'Did you really think I would let you walk off this ship with my son?' Rafael asked sarcastically. She opened her mouth to speak, but he stopped her with an abrupt gesture. 'Don't trouble to deny it any more. Any fool can see from his face that he is mine! I may be many kinds of a scoundrel, but I certainly am no fool—at least you should have granted me that!'

'Since Felipe is all you wanted, why didn't you kill me first?' she asked bitterly, regretting too late the ease with which she had fallen into his trap again.

'It is possible that I shall,' he said grimly. 'But not until you have heard every word I have to say.' He paused, and then his voice softened momentarily. 'At least I deserve a hearing, Miranda.'

'Why?' she retorted acidly. 'You cast me out without even a backward glance—why should I listen to you now?'

'Mainly,' he said coolly, 'because you don't seem to have much choice at the moment!' He looked at her with sudden exasperation and raked his hair with restless fingers. 'I was in Spain,' he said, and she quickly suppressed a gasp of surprise. 'It would have been impossible to take you with me.' He began to pace up and down the cabin. 'I had not been out of Amarillo for ten years. There was a price on my head everywhere.'

'You *could* have taken me with you,' she cried involuntarily, 'instead of abandoning me the way you did!' Tears trembled in her eyes as she propped herself up on an elbow.

He sat down on the bed and suddenly cupped her face in his hands, his eyes black with anger. 'Don't cry,' he whispered fiercely. 'Whatever you do, for God's sake don't cry!' For a wild moment she thought he was going to kiss her, but he fought off his emotion and let his hands fall again. 'They could have hanged me. Where would you have been then?'

'Where I am now,' she said dully, still not willing to believe a word of what he said. 'Where I have been for two years. Alone and without you.'

'You have never been alone, Miranda,' he said huskily, 'that I do promise you. You have never been without me. By heaven, I've shared with you every tear that you have shed, every ache in your heart . . .' His voice was suddenly ragged. 'I knew when Felipe was born. I felt it in my gut, and I shared with you every one of those pains . . .' He stopped abruptly and stood gazing out of the porthole, while he struggled to control himself. When he spoke again, his voice was calm. 'I was tired of having a price on my head, tired of living on the fringes of the world, tired of feeling hatred instead of love . . . I have a grandmother still alive in Spain. And cousins and aunts and uncles. I had not been to Spain since I was fifteen. I had lived there through my childhood. I felt it was time to renew ties. Besides, there were estates to be seen to. It was not right to let my father's heritage be destroyed through default.'

He walked to the bed and, very gently, removed a pointed object from Felipe's mouth and replaced it inside the drawer. Miranda watched him in silence, her heart seething with emotion and too full for words. She swallowed to remove the lump in her throat and finally ventured a comment. 'They might have hanged you . . .'

Her smiled dryly. 'Indeed! But I had banked heavily on exploiting the greatest of human failings to my advantage. Greed! I made a bargain with the Queen of Spain. In exchange for some of Amarillo's gold, I asked for an unconditional pardon.'

'And she agreed?'

'Naturally! Even Queens are human after all! Besides,' he added with a sceptical laugh, 'my father happened to be a cousin of Her Majesty. I wonder what was her guiding motive: greed or familial devotion! Anyhow, I got what I wanted.'

Her breath caught in her throat. 'And are you a free man now?'

He shrugged. 'Freer than I was.'

'And you have changed your opinion of the outside world?'

'No. I was curious to see whether it was any less hateful than when I had left it. It wasn't. But it was time I came to terms with it. If the world wasn't prepared to change—and it wasn't—then, obviously, I would have to.'

'And have you?' she asked quietly.

He looked at her for a moment. 'Would you want me to?'

She could not meet his eyes. '*Whatever you are, I love you* . . .' she had told him once. She knew now that it was true. She turned her face to the wall. 'No.'

He laughed softly. 'But I have,' he said. 'I must. Hate cannot bring back my mother and my father or erase what has happened. Besides, I don't want my son to grow up thinking of me as a monster, like his mother does!'

A denial trembled on her lips, but she bit it back.

'You were in Spain for the entire period?'

'No. A year. The journey there and back to Amarillo took care of the second year. The Queen needed a great deal of persuasion—and a great deal of gold! I had to return to Amarillo to inform the people about her decision. After all, it is their gold, not mine.' He came and sat on the bed again and, taking her hand, placed a single kiss on the palm, then he folded her fingers over it and returned her hand to her. 'I loved you then, Miranda, and I love you now. More than you can ever know. Certainly more than you deserve.' His voice was so soft that it sounded like the soughing of the wind through the trees of Amarillo. She lay very still. 'Perhaps I should have sent you away that night . . . Perhaps I should not have made love to you . . .'

'Then why did you?' she whispered, trembling like a leaf.

'Because I was never more human than I was that night, and because I love you so very much . . .' Without a word, she slipped into his arms and he held her close. 'Do you still want me to turn the ship round?' he murmured gently against her ear. Imperceptibly she shook her head, letting his love wash over her, cleanse her, sweep away the sorrow and the suffering. 'You belong to me, Miranda. You always have. I told you I would come for you wherever you were . . . Why did you not trust me? Did you really think I would, I *could*, ever abandon you and my son?' She could think of nothing to say, too ashamed at how easily she had hated him, wounded him.

For a long while they were silent, lost in an overwhelming sea of contentment, loving each other silently, all their demons laid to rest. Then he laughed under his breath and kissed the hollow of her neck. 'I think I would like to call my next son—Dan!' He laughed again.

Dan! She suddenly snapped back into reality. 'Dan!' she exclaimed, 'and Papa and Aunt Zoe . . . Why, they will be frantic with worry . . . !' She tried to struggle out of his arms, but he would not release her.

'I hardly think so,' his eyes twinkled briefly. 'Dan knew what I intended to do.'

'And where are we headed?' she asked, not really caring, too choked with happiness for it to make any difference at all.

'Home. To Amarillo, where else?'

It sounded like music in her ears. Home! With Rafael . . . ! She stiffened as another name leaped into her mind. Frank! What about poor, innocent Frank?

'Why did Frank Partridge come to see you?' she asked, pushing him away for a moment.

'Because he wanted me to take you away from Honolulu,' he said drily. 'He said he had his social position to think of.'

'Oh!' Humiliated and aghast at Frank's perfidy, she smarted inwardly. 'And . . . And what did you have to say to that?'

'Oh, I agreed with him entirely. His social position is now, of course, quite secure, but I wouldn't say the same about his dental position. I knocked out two of his teeth.'

She struggled for a moment, not knowing whether to laugh or not. Then, trying to sound severe, she said, 'You should not have done that. He has been good to us.'

'I made misguided reparation for it against my better sense, by buying up half of his damned shop. After all, you and your son will need clothes on the journey and when we reach home. For the amount of money I spent in his shop, I can assure you he would have gladly given me all his teeth!' She had to laugh. He had thought of everything! Rafael's face became stern. 'This . . . This

Juan Romero—he doesn't exist, does he?'

She sighed. 'No.'

He laughed under his breath, visibly relieved. 'You seem to have told me a fair number of lies, all said and done.'

'No more than the number of empty promises you made!' she said sharply.

'Every one of them will be honoured,' he protested. 'You know that you can ask me for anything it is within my power to give you.'

She thought for a moment. 'Even another preposterous request?'

He feigned a groan. 'Yes, damn you, even that!'

'When we are settled on Amarillo, will you send the *Condor* back to Hawaii for Papa and Aunt Zoe and that devious, lovable rascal, Dan?'

'Do I have a choice?'

'No!' she said firmly. None at all.'

'Would you like me to turn the ship round, as you wanted, so that we can go back and fetch them now?' He sounded innocent.

Her eyes widened in alarm. 'No, I don't think so,' she said hastily. 'Later will do just as well.'

He laughed. 'Your Aunt Zoe,' he mused. 'Now *there* is someone I would hesitate to cross swords with . . .'

She laughed and hugged him. 'As long as you treat me well—not as you have done so far—Aunt Zoe will love you as I do.'

'And your father?'

'Papa will love anyone who loves me,' she said simply. She smiled, her cup of happiness overflowing at last. 'And what about Peregrine? How is he? Have you been kind to him?'

'No,' he snapped. 'I have not been kind to him—nor do I intend to be. He refuses to leave the island now, and wants to marry one of our girls.'

Her eyes widened fractionally. 'Malamma . . . ?'

'No,' he said testily, '*not* Malamma!'

'And are you going to allow him to?' She fixed him with a rapier eye, her mouth tight.

His lips lifted slightly in the hint of a smile. '*Do* I have any option?'

'No. Not if *I* have anything to do with it!'

'One of these days, Miranda,' he said irascibly, 'I shall have to learn how to say No to you!' Then, accepting defeat, he sighed. 'Very well, then, your Peregrine can have his island bride. You know,' he added, his smile widening, 'you do seem to have had singularly bad luck with your affianced!'

'*Neither* of them,' she retorted promptly, 'has given me as many sleepless nights as *you* have—and you are not even an affianced!'

'But I am the only one who *is* going to marry you . . .' he teased gently.

She sighed, and ran her fingers through his impossible hair in a vain effort to tame it. 'Yes,' she breathed, 'for my sins . . .' His lips sought hers, but she turned her face away, still not quite done.

'And what about . . . Malamma?'

He kissed her anyway. 'What about Malamma?'

'Did you ever find her?' Her voice was small and worried.

He did not reply immediately, while his lips wandered over her face. 'Malamma,' he said finally, kissing her nose, 'is still *my* business.'

She felt the warmth rise in her limbs as his mouth played havoc with hers and his soft as silk fingers traced the smooth contours of her breast. With a deep, contented sigh of threatened rapture, she lay back, loving him, wanting him, overflowing with a delicious tenderness.

'And what,' she murmured languidly, 'is mine, pray?'

Before he could answer, there was an angry yell from Felipe as he tumbled over the far side of the bed and fell to the floor with a gentle thump. Like lightning, Rafael was on his feet and had his son up in his arms. He grimaced.

'Your business,' he shouted above the din of Felipe's furious howls, 'is to learn how to talk a little less so that I can at least, occasionally, have the last word in some conversations . . .'

She opened her mouth to give him a suitable retort, but he stopped her with a stern gesture. 'And,' he interrupted with exasperation, 'your son has a backside like a dripping deck-mop. Your *immediate* business is to show me how to tie these infernal napkins—pointed side up or down?'

A romance of searing passion set amid the barbaric splendour of Richard the Lionheart's Crusade. Intrigue turns to love across the battlefield... a longer historical novel from Mills and Boon, for only £2.25.

Published on 12th of July.

Mills & Boon

The Rose of Romance